Other works by S.M. Sykes:

Eyes of Blue (book 1 of the Blue series)

A Dim Blue (book 2 of the Blue series)

It's my body, I'll haunt if I want to

Life of a Lycanthrope

Message on the Wind

Every review helps immensely. If you enjoy this book or not, please take the time to leave a review @ Amazon or Goodreads. See the Qr above for links.

Loss of

Blue

(Book 3 of the Blue series)

S.M. Sykes

Printed in the United States of America

First Printing, 2024

Ingram Spark:

ISBN 979-8-8693-3214-1(paperback)

     979-8-8693-3215-8 (ebook)

Amazon:

ISBN 979-8320-68627-1 (paperback)

     979-8323-59230-2 (widespace)

ASIN- B0D29VQB2B (kindle)

S. M. Sykes Books

27196 Indian Meadows Cir

Millsboro, DE. 19966

Table of Contents

Running

Running, always with the running. I had peered off into the void for longer than I thought. While I was contemplating destiny, the caravan moved off without me. We took off running to catch up. Andromeda outpaced me and caught up with the others without any issues. I was winded quickly. Grief and my backpack seemed to be holding me back. My backpack that no longer held a dead cell phone from a dead age. My decision to keep going with this group, to stay with my family is the right choice, I just can't get my heart to believe it yet. It wasn't an hour ago, I was sleeping curled up next to my best friend, my sister. Now, she's gone. All of this is because some bastards decided that their fear was enough to allow them to try and take things from others.

Fear is debilitating to intelligence. They decided that trying to bluff a trained military unit into giving them equipment and food was a good idea. This started a huge gun battle in a very small enclosed space. I wouldn't be surprised if eight of the fifteen bandits that were killed or injured were from friendly fire. When people cannot find their way they typically shut down or lash out. I wish that a few more would've shut down when they were told that they were being left behind. One less person on their side may have swayed the whole situation in our favor. If so, Jordan would be walking next to me on this trip to South Dakota.

Speaking of South Dakota, I can't believe that we are walking halfway across the country to see if a few missiles are still there and useful. We're completely running on faith at this point. Faith that this chemical the scientists are making on the road will work. Faith that they'll be able to make enough to do what they think it will do. Then if the missiles are there and there are enough chemicals we have to have faith that someone here knows how to launch these Cold War-era missiles. Will there be power? Will the missile need some kind of confirmation code to fire off? The President is dead or off-grid.

There won't be any way to phone a friend.

All of this has to go right if we even make it there. Then we have to wait around, for who knows how long, before we even know if it's working. If it does start to work how long before we see any results? What will it do to the environment? This alien spore seems to have caused a lot of changes to the flora and fauna of our world. It's all so much that my mind feels like it's going to explode. I need to try and talk to Matthew about these things, maybe they know more than I think they do. I wasn't with these people long in the Christiana Hospital, so maybe they didn't share everything with me. I mean why would they? Just because I'm Matt's sister? That couldn't be that big of a deal, he isn't even in charge of his squad, let alone the entire unit.

Although, that one guy did say that Matt started something that helped save all of them. How is that even possible? Did he remember it from some Dungeons and Dragons game? Was it some plot to a video game? Or did he learn that much about something in his one year of aeronautics college?

Actually, that may be it.

He may know something about the missiles or how to launch them from his time at Embry Riddle. But the guy said that Matt and this project, not the plan, the project. The project had some poor guy strapped into a chair that may cause buzzing, floating, or hurting. Nothing is coming together correctly here. I really need to get some time to talk to Matt about all of this before my head explodes.

As I think about all of this, I catch up to the last bit of the group. As I reach the rear guard, I slow down to a walk. I need to be able to keep up for the rest of the night until we reach camp. The walking isn't hard and I don't have to think much since we are following a major roadway out of Delaware. I start thinking about the last time I left the state. It was, obviously, before the Fall. Maybe three months before, when Mom, Dad and I headed up to

Philadelphia to watch the Red Sox play the Phillies. Unfortunately, the Sox lost when we were there. Even with that, it was a great day. Any day at the ball field was always a good day.

We stopped at the Christiana Mall to go to the Cheesecake Factory for an early dinner on the way north. The evening games got over so late we needed to eat before we got there. I remember thinking that there was only one thing missing that day, Andromeda.

You thought I was going to say Matt didn't you? Well no.

Back then we were always at each other's throats. It wasn't until we lost him for a while that I realized that I missed him. But, Andromeda had been to a game at Petco Park in San Diego before and she loved watching the players on the field. She used to watch baseball with me all the time. She used to like it so much that my parents would bring her to the ball field to watch me play softball too. Or was that the other way around? Either way, I missed those days. Would we even see an old ball field on our trek across the country? I hope we can see something cool from before the Fall on our way.

"Ma'am. Ma'am!" These words broke my revelry. It was a soldier. I look and see Sergei on his name tag.

"Yes, sorry what can I help you with? Wait!" I suddenly realize what he had said. "Ma'am? Really?"

The guy hung his head a bit before talking, "Your brother wants you near the front of the line with Andromeda. I hope you know who that is."

"Yes, I know who she is. She is the one sniffing your crotch right now," I say as I bat her nose. She knew better. She listened for a second but then started sniffing him again. "Where's Matt?"

"Umm." He said trying to get Andromeda to leave him alone. "He is at the front of the column. I can show you."

"That's fine, I'll find him. Andromeda! Leave it. Come on. Find Matt."

Andromeda stops sniffing and looks up at me. I nod and she takes off towards the front of the line. I have to run again to try to keep up. After a couple of minutes, I slow and figure I will find them both, eventually.

Matt

When I finally caught up with Matt, Andromeda was walking by his side. She had never really walked with him before, but she missed him over the last year too. Otherwise, she wouldn't have left me to go find him. At least she didn't leave me until I told her to. I sidled up next to him and matched his pace. He just looked at me and then back forward.

"Ok, what the hell. This is the second time I could swear your eyes glowed like a Deader's. Why?" I yelled at him after catching the glow in his eyes again. Matt ignored me and continued to walk away, I ran up and grabbed his arm, making him stop and face me.

"Well, we have about two hours before we get where we are going, so let me tell you the cliff notes version," for the next two hours he told me about how they found him dead, revived him and then lost him a couple of more times before stabilizing him on the ride north. He told me about training with the military and how they found out about his ability to walk around Deaders without being seen by them as he did in the hallway the other day.

Wow, was that only a day or two ago? It seemed like years.

His squad was called the Unseen, for obvious reasons. Over the last two years, they found out that each of the soldiers who underwent the procedure to stop their heart for three minutes and then be brought back had this special ability to walk near Deaders and not attract their attention. Some of them also had other abilities that dealt with seeing the spores directly, but he didn't go into much detail about that.

"That is what they were doing in the lab that night before we left. They were turning someone else into an Unseen?" I asked him

"Yes"

"And you were the first one? That is why that guy said it was all because of you, that you helped save lives."

"Most likely. But there are some downsides."

"Oh really?" I chided as we walked. "You can walk around the Deaders without them bothering you. You can read your other squadmates' feelings and intentions so you act as a better unit and you can see better at night. What could be detrimental?"

"I never said I could see better at night," he argued as he cleanly stepped over a piece of rock in the road without really looking at it.

"Then how are you walking out here without a flashlight?" I ask him, as I trip over the stupid thing.

"I can. I just didn't tell you that I could," he says as he smiles. I guess it was a smile. "But the spores take over a bit. I won't bore you with everything tonight, I know this was all a lot to take in. What I am saying I guess, is don't look for this as a cure. The scientists thought that at first. But they're wrong. It's a necessity, but hopefully not for long. Don't look to become one of us," he was now dead serious.

"Ok. I won't but promise me you will write all of this down at some point. Please?" I plead with him. I would love to hear all of the stories or read them anyway.

"Maybe. We'll see."

We came up to the camp as the conversation ended, it wasn't much of a camp but it was only temporary. It actually kind of reminded me of the old wagon trains heading west. There were a couple of the trucks circled up with separate camps in the center. There were also a few tents set up outside of the circles, I think these were going to be for the military personnel so they could keep watch.

We hadn't made it too far today, we hadn't even made it out of Delaware. In the days ahead we would cover more ground. We had six vehicles with two of them being troop transports. Then we had two suburbans, one truck and one Humvee. The plan was for one of the transports to leave in the morning with the truck and the Humvee as an escort. The two suburbans and the other transport would hang back and tear down the rest of camp. Half of the teams would walk from camp and the other half would ride in the transports. The front transport and truck would go about halfway for the day, stop and wait. This would allow the scientists to work on some of the chemicals when the vehicles weren't moving. When the walking members and the other vehicles caught up, the people walking would switch. That way you would walk half a day and ride half. This way we could make better time because people wouldn't be so tired.

That was the plan anyway.

We all know what happens to those as soon as you start to implement them, they fall apart. It fell apart the very first morning. We all got up and ate a small breakfast. Those walking were given some protein bars and water to help with the trip. The problem is that the Humvee wouldn't start. They decided to leave it behind and send a team with the suburban to run security. The other suburban was taking off early to take a group of the Unseen to run point ahead of the convoy. We would not see them again for the trip if everything went right, they would only stop and report back if there was a problem.

Matt told me that the mechanics figured on getting the Humvee up and running in a couple of hours. Once they did they would catch up. Mom loaded up in one of the transports while Matt's squad, Andromeda and I started walking. As we walk everything stays pretty quiet. I don't really know anyone besides Matt and he was keeping up with his squad running security. I just started putting one foot in front of the other until I got where we were going.

I have already decided that I would only ride every once and a while. Andromeda and I were good at walking for long distances, some of the others didn't look like they had been outside much. With the doctors, scientists, mechanics, military and what I thought of as outside specialists, like yours truly, we seem to number about 60 people. Only about 20 of us would walk at a time.

There were scientists, like Testerman, who would always ride so they could work more. It doesn't seem fair, but I guess we need their expertise when we get where we are going.

The first half of the day goes smoothly. The area of Pennsylvania that we are traveling through is called Lancaster County. It was known for being a heavily Amish area. There are still farms around, but no one shows themselves if they still live here. At the halfway point for the day, we swapped riders and walkers, I declined to ride and have Mom take my seat. She starts to protest but knows that she can't walk that far. The argument didn't take long. After a short rest Andromeda and I take off walking for another couple of hours.

The first thing I notice is Susie walking at the edge of the group. At least for this part of the trip, I will have someone to talk to, or torment. Either way, it would be a little more fun.

Susie

I take my time and watch her for a bit before I approach her, I haven't spoken to her since the affair at the Home of the Brave. The one thing that I notice first is that she doesn't carry herself the same. I guess losing that many people under your watch can change just about anyone.

Even someone way too full of themselves.

I start to make my way over to her. Andromeda sees her and takes off running. I start to call her back but figure she would either pounce on her because she missed her or attack her because she didn't like her.

I kind of wanted the second.

Andromeda in her true form stops directly in front of Susie and sits down looking for love. As soon as Susie sees Andromeda she looks around for me. As she looks in my direction I wave and pick up my pace a bit.

"Hello," I say as I get within a few feet.

"I thought you were walking the first shift" Susie states with a frown.

"I did. I took my mom's shift too. I can handle it."

"Well, I hope so. I'm not carrying you. Did you see that the Humvee never met us at the halfway point? I wonder if we lost that thing already. That wouldn't be a good omen." She says as I fall into step next to her.

"I wasn't paying attention. I figure I'll walk most of the way anyway."

"Yeah, but we could use that one specifically for some protection. How's your Mom?" She asks not looking at me. Andromeda has fallen into step on Susie's right. I guess she likes her.

"Good and we found my brother. I wasn't sure if you had heard."

"Yeah, he found you, he also helped find us. Guess your parents did ok with one of you," I look over and see her laugh just a bit.

After that, we fall into a rhythm. We talk a little more, mostly about the Bravers. Susie was the only one who joined us. Between all the people lost during the attack and others not wanting to cross the country, she ended up being the only one who came along. That may be why she stayed talking to me, I was probably the only person she knew, besides my mom.

The day passes easily, but I start to hurt about halfway through the second session. I don't think that I can do this each and every day, 14 hours of walking is more than I thought. But, sitting in a truck and riding doesn't seem right either. It will only give me time to think about Jordan, I miss her enough while walking. So much so I turned four different times today to point out something or just to ask her something. I'm not sure what I am going to do without her.

As we approach the camp I see my brother waiting for me. I walk up, he hugs me but then pushes past me and waves down Susie. I'm not sure what that's about. I don't stop to hear what they talk about, I just want to find my mother and sit down for a while. I tell Andromeda to find her and watch her trot off to do just that. A little while later, I find her in the camp kitchen. She is helping to prepare dinner for everyone. Of course, Andromeda is already lying at her feet eating something. That dog knows how to manipulate everyone.

After dinner, I go to lie down on an open cot and try to get some sleep. My brother stops by to check on me and tells me that he approached Susie to work one of the watch rotations. With the loss of the scouts ahead of us they need a few more people to keep the watch. They want people who are riding in the morning so they could catch up on sleep if they need it. I tell him that I can keep watch too if they need it. He shakes his head and tells me to just get some rest, that tomorrow would be another long day.

He was right.

The next morning I don't want to get up or move. I know that I need to so I force myself to get up, eat and stretch for the day. Andromeda is raring to go as soon as she eats. I always wished that I had her energy. I lose the following days in repetition. I'm glad I have Andromeda and the military guards because I can just lose myself in thought. I'm missing the people I've lost. I keep wondering if all of this is even worth the effort that we're all putting in.

At some point later in the week we enter a state park. I've missed the signs saying what the name was, but you can tell it's a state park because of the trail and campground signs. As we make our way through, the column of people suddenly comes to a stop. I can see the trucks that are supposed to be setting up tonight's camp-up ahead. I'm curious so I find Susie and we walk to the front.

The scene is not promising.

I had heard rumors that we lost contact with the scout group. I blew it off because we shouldn't hear back from them unless there's a problem. Well, I was wrong in a big way. We lost contact with them because they were all dead.

The suburban is a burned-out husk sitting in the middle of the road. It looks like the soldiers took cover on our side of the truck while taking fire from an enemy. It wasn't Deaders. All of the team members were dead and burnt along with the truck. No one seems to be sure how long ago this happened, but the smell was still hanging around and it was horrific. The really bad thing was that the bodies were all burned separately. They all seemed to be where they fell, then set on fire.

Was this to stop them from rising again?

The military circled everyone up and set watch until the rear trucks could catch up. We were switching up the plan, I hope they will explain it to all of us at some point. Staying here wasn't the right one. There are a lot of people who are getting sick from the sight and the smells, not everyone has seen this type of carnage before. A lot of the scientists and doctors hadn't seen any parts of this new world after the Fall, they weren't built for this. I decided to find the people in charge and tell them my two cents on waiting here for the other vehicles.

Who knows maybe they might listen.

Enlisted

As I walk through camp with my ever-present shadow, I run into Matt.

"Who's in charge of this shitshow?" I demand as I see him.

"What? No! You aren't going to charge off and tell people what to do. You're coming with me. You're being drafted into the military, along with Susie. We need to replace our scouts," he tells me this as he grabs my arm and turns me around.

Matt drags me to one of the transport trucks. I get in along with five other soldiers and Susie. From what I can remember it is Matt's squad. Ragsdill, Smith, Reid, Oakley and his sergeant. As soon as we walk up I hear his sergeant talking.

"Ok now that everyone is here let me lay this out for you. The draft is in effect and for the first time in history, women are being drafted. I don't want to hear any shit, this is the reason you were asked to come along. We don't need people just hanging around. Most of the others have their purpose, either cooks, medics or scientists. I hoped we wouldn't need you to step up quite so quickly, yet here we are. Any pertinent questions?"

Susie raises her hand the sergeant nods to her.

"I have heard rumors that your team is different. You aren't doing anything to us to make us different are you?" she asks sheepishly. I think she knows she can't refuse to help unless she wants to walk away completely.

"No. You will not be made an Unseen unless you volunteer for it. If you think it is something you want, think again and then rethink. It has its advantages and has come in handy but as you can tell from the smoking bodies in the street it doesn't make you invincible. We feel that regular humans will be our biggest obstacle on this trip." Sergeant Hayes, that's her name, tells us.

"OK. Gear up and get a vest that fits you pretty close. We need to check the area and make sure whoever did this moved on."

After that, we set to work, once geared up we got together and were set up in pairs. Sgt Hayes wanted to work with me and Matt would work with Susie. That left Smith and Reid and Oakley and Ragsdill to work together.

We set off, each pair in a different direction. The first thing we had to do was make sure the group was safe. It felt odd to walk around with a loaded weapon in my hands, sitting on a watch with one there was ok but walking through the woods with it made me think of hunting with my dad. I hadn't thought about that in a while. I berated myself for letting my mind wander, not only was this important and dangerous, I had to prove to the sergeant that bringing me along was worth it.

I guess that was why she paired up with me.

Thirty minutes later Andromeda let out a low growl, I tap Sgt. Hayes and motion for her to slow. I watch Andromeda trying to read her expression. She has sensed something but I can't tell what it is. Hayes moves to her right creating some separation between us. Suddenly, a man comes crashing through the bushes, he runs right past Hayes and slams hard into my side.

Andromeda jumps on him before I even know what's happening. As I spin to my back I can see his glowing eyes and his hands reaching for my face. I struggle and feel him go limp, the blue disappears from his eyes. I push him hard again and scramble to my feet. Sgt. Hayes is standing behind him, she bends to wipe her knife off on his shirt.

"Looks like one of the men that attacked our guys judging from the double tap hole in his chest. I guess they only burned our people's bodies, not their own. Odd. No matter who it was, once they rise they are still a risk to everyone around," she says, mostly to herself I think.

"How do you kill them? I have never seen one die like that," I asked still looking around for others.

"You separate the brain stem," she put her finger at the base of my skull. "Feel that soft spot. You have to hit them right there.

You probably won't be able to do it too easily because they sense you and turn. He never knew I was here."

"That would be nice."

"Pluses and minuses. But hey, you have your watchdog. She sensed them before even I could. She is a good warning system," Hayes taps my arm and motions for me to start walking again.

"Yeah, I just should've figured out what she sensed earlier. I am too distracted," I explain.

"Well, get your head in the game. Your life and my life are at risk if you don't."

I hang my head a little, she's right. I have to get my head in the game, now more than ever.

We finish the area check and meet the others back at the trucks.

"Alright, the rest of the teams didn't find anything. Our guys must have been ambushed. It seems they only got one of theirs. But it also seems like they moved on. Now get the bags and get ready to walk. We need to head out to scout the forward area. We can't take a truck so we are huffing it. Food, weapons and bags. That's it. Say your goodbyes if you need to we will be out for about a week before we get relief."

We all break off and head off to get our gear. I stop by with Matt to tell Mom what we are doing. She nods but I can see tears in her eyes. She bends down to pet Andromeda on her head and then shoos us off to finish getting our gear. Matt shows me what I need. It seems odd that I was just enlisted and am being put out as a scout. Matt tells me that it's this specific reason I was asked to come, Andromeda and I were looked at as great scouts. We had been on our own for so long that we knew the dangers.

I didn't mention that we stayed in a bunker for a year of that time.

As we get ready to head out Mr. Silver, I don't know his rank, stops us. "Hey, Sgt. Hayes! I need your team to take the truck.

You should be able to carry everyone until you can get far enough out to set a perimeter."

"I thought we weren't getting a truck, Sergeant Major?" Sgt. Hayes asks.

"Well, there has been a change. Just like every day around this camp," Silver grumbles. "We need you to look for supplies while you are out also. You can use the truck to bring them back faster. We need food and fuel. Like usual," he grumbles again.

"Yessir. We will handle it, like usual," Hayes says with a smile. "Washington! Go get the keys and bring the truck up."

"I got it, Sarge!" Matt yells.

"Crap. I forgot there were two of you. I meant your sister."

"I can't drive. I never learned," I explain.

"Well, go with your brother and he will teach you."

"In five minutes?" I ask confused.

"Well, once we are on the road there isn't much to hit and no cops to pull you over for driving without a license," Susie says from the peanut gallery.

While she isn't wrong I hate that *she* had to say it. I am glad she isn't part of the forward group so I won't have to listen to her mouth. I seem to be taking the place of Sgt. Ragsdill. Sgt. Hayes told me that he is being reassigned as a ranking position so they needed the help.

I hope I'm not breaking up the team.

Driving

Matt walks with me to the truck along with my ever-present shadow. We load our stuff in the back and I get into the driver's seat. Now, I will admit that my dad had taught me the basics before. He'd even let me drive around the community, so I wasn't a complete novice. I start it up and set my mirrors as Matt watches and rolls his eyes.

"You know we aren't going to be pulling into traffic right?"

I initially ignore him but then stick my tongue out at him. It just felt like the right thing to do to break the tension. I put my hands on the wheel then reach down and put it in gear.

"OK, now this truck is a bit sluggish at times so just ease the gas until it starts to move then back off just a bit."

It's my turn to roll my eyes at him. "OK, Dad!" I tease but do what he said.

I would like to say that everything went smoothly and I got it right on the first try. But if you know anything about me by now you should know that didn't happen.

First of all, I had it in neutral, not drive. When I figured that out I slam it into drive while the engine was still revved up so the tires spin, throwing dirt everywhere. There are cries from people behind us, the truck kicks forward so hard that I slam my foot on the brake almost throwing Matt through the windshield. Luckily, he had ahold of Andromeda too. Once the truck came to a stop Matt found his voice.

I figured he would yell but he just said. "OK now try it my way. Ease into it please."

I take a second to look at him and then do what he asked. The second attempt wasn't perfect but it was a lot better. I pull through camp and stop behind Sgt. Hayes.

"Any problems Rook?" She asks me as Susie laughs.

"Just a small gearing issue. We should have the mechanics look at that when we get back," I retort. I hear Susie say something but I didn't hear enough so I just ignore it.

Everyone loads up in the truck and we hit the road. A couple of minutes down the line our world is reduced to the engine noise and the six of us, well seven with Andromeda. She suddenly got the urge to sit in the bed of the truck with the other four.

Everyone's a critic.

The plan is for us to stay about a day ahead of the transport, which won't be hard even with finding supplies and running them back. Matt tells me that we are using a combination of old hobo markings and old trail markings to tell the transports where to go and what to avoid, should we find anything. He started to show me the pamphlet he had for the markings, but I swerved to the edge of the road while looking so he figured we should wait.

Probably not a bad idea.

It's not long before Hayes has me stop and the others get out to walk the perimeter line. She wants me to go with Matt about a mile up and stop. If we see anything that should be looked at on the way we either check it out or mark it to be checked, Matt's call. Once everyone gets out Andromeda whines to get back in the front. I want to tell her no, but I let her in the cab, she's a spoiled dog. We only get about a quarter mile down the road before Matt sees an old farm with a farmhouse and outbuildings.

"Hey, pull over here and let me out. I want to check that set of buildings out. The truck is too conspicuous so pull up about 200 feet out of sight and wait for me," he says as he opens the door.

"No, I am coming with you," I retort.

"Well Private, I outrank you and you will follow orders. We do things right, sister or not," he waits to see if I will listen, all he gets is another tongue and a raspberry. "Real mature. I'll be back in a minute," then turns and walks off.

I quickly open the door and let Andromeda out. "Go get him. Stay with Matt. You aren't in the military he can't get mad at you."

She looks at me for a second then turns and runs after Matt. As she runs off I pull the truck forward as he asks but I can hear the faint thank you in the air. Once I park I get out of the truck and get into the back. If anything pops off it is easier to get to each point or huddle down in the back. I'm not sure this is the right thing to do, but I have no training and it feels like something they would do in a movie.

It feels like forever before I see Andromeda running up to the truck. Her tongue is sticking out and she isn't barking so Matt must be ok, but I don't like that he isn't with her so I jump out of the back and start walking the way she came. I make it about five steps before I hear gravel crunching on the road. I step off the road into the bushes before I can see what is coming.

"I saw you move that bush, Ava. You're good, come on out it is just me," I hear Matt yell.

"Why weren't you with Andromeda?" I ask him as I get out of the bushes. Then I see why. He's pushing an older dirt bike down the road.

"Because I found this and she wouldn't wait for me," he says as he is huffing a bit.

I grab the other handlebar and help him push it to the truck. Matt tells me he will get it fixed later as it looks like it only needed some fuel.

"Once we load this up, we'll have to drive back there. I found some foodstuffs and some diesel. The transports can use that."

By the time we got all of that done the rest of the group was with us. Sgt. Hayes shakes her head. "Really Washington? Another bike? The last one didn't treat you all that nice," The other soldiers laugh. I laugh along but I'm not part of that inside joke.

"It was just fine when I wasn't around you guys. This will come in handy. I promise. I'll get it running later."

Sgt. Hayes just shakes her head and asks if anyone has anything to report. All of them shake their heads no, so we load back up and cruise down the road another mile and do it again. We do the same thing for the next couple of hours. The only thing that changes is the soldier in my passenger seat. Each time someone new would stay, but I was the driver all night. Hayes says it's for practice, but I think it has to do with the fact that she doesn't trust me out on my own yet. Which, to be honest, is completely fair.

Just after dark, Sgt. Hayes calls a stop to our movements for the night and has me find a place to stop for the evening. I pull off the road to an abandoned-looking house. I stop well short and the others jog off to check it out. I send Andromeda with them, although they probably don't need her. Once it's checked I pull the truck up closer and walk into the house. It used to be nice, but now it's just run down. The beds have sheets and the fireplace seems to work so we can cook some of the rations we found earlier. In the morning I'll drive the rations and gas back to the convoy then run back out here to follow their trail. That's a tomorrow concern, I only want to find a bed and lie down. As soon as I put my stuff down I hear Sgt. Hayes calling for me.

Damn.

You guessed it, first watch. She has me on the second floor of the house watching down the driveway. Every so often I have to walk downstairs and check around the house. In two hours I can wake up Oakley to take over. Ugg. I just want to sleep, but I guess I did drive all day while they walked. The draft should never include women. Well, not all women, just this woman. Some women, like Sgt. Hayes and Cpl Oakley, seem to be made for this stuff.

I am not a fan, I give it one star.

Days

In the morning I get up and take care of the usual morning stuff, then go looking for Andromeda. It's an odd feeling to have to look for her, but at least she enjoys being around the others. I take a guess and go to the kitchen table. I find her sitting and watching Oakley and Smith eat their breakfast bars. I look at them and Oakley nods towards a bag on the counter. I look at Andromeda and Smith shakes his head, meaning she has already eaten.

Weirdly, we all have gotten so close already that this is all it takes. I also find it odd that I don't know any of their first names. Matt has never told me and each of them only refers to each other by the last names. Luckily, they don't use odd nicknames like the military movies. As I sit down I hear a roar and someone yelling. I jump up quickly looking around for a weapon but the others just start laughing.

"It's just Washington getting that damn bike started," Smith tells me through a smile.

"What is it with the bike and all of you?" I ask as I sit back down.

"Did he come home with that bike as society fell?"

"Yes, he used it for supply runs when he got home," I say still confused.

"Did he tell you his story about how he came over from Washington and the Bay Bridge?"

"A little, but I always felt that he was holding things back," I say honestly.

"Well ask him about those couple of days. It'll explain it all."

"You mean you guys knew him even back then?" That's crazy news if it's true.

"Yeah, we met briefly before he made it home," Oakley starts then stares off a bit before she finishes. "A couple of times. It's a crazy story."

"Ava! Outside! Now!" Sgt. Hayes yells through the open window. Crap, I guess I have to hit the road.

I get up and walk outside to find out what Sgt. Hayes wants me to do. Once she fills me in I get in the truck and call Andromeda to me. I don't mind her riding with the others when I'm near, but not when I am going to be half a day away. We get on the road and head back to where I should be meeting the caravan. I get there before noon and meet up with the advanced unit. I want to check on Mom, but she's with the rear truck and I need to get back. I just tell the driver to tell her that I asked about her and that we love her, and then I get back on the road.

On the way back to the squad I have to pay a bit more attention so I know where to go. I memorized the markers, for the most part, but they would be easy to miss if I wasn't paying attention. I'm getting better with driving and, although I hate to say that Susie was right, it is easy when you don't have to worry about other drivers and speed limits. Just as I think this the truck starts to sputter and jerk. I look at the gas gauge and it says that the tank is half full. It can't be out of gas, right? I ride it until the truck comes to a stop then rest my head on the steering wheel, Andromeda whimpers beside me. I would like to think that it is because I am stressed but I have to check my surroundings. I can't get this far and let a dead truck get me killed.

I lift my head and slowly look around. I don't see anything but I still need to be cautious. I slowly open the driver's door and motion Andromeda out. She jumps down and disappears around the other side of the truck. I get down and work my way around just to see her peeing in the grass next to the road. Once she is done she trots back over and sits down next to me. Guess there isn't any danger.

I stand there and try to think about what my dad would do if he were here. The gas gauge says half, but I drove almost all day without putting in a full tank, maybe the gauge is stuck. I decide it can't hurt to put some more in. I jump in the back of the truck and grab the can. It's almost full so it is a bit heavy but I can drag it to the tailgate. I jump down and struggle with it to the ground. I don't spill any on the ground, my pants are a different story though.

I get the job done and get back in the cab. I place my head on the steering wheel again as I turn the key and push the gas pedal. The engine works sputters and dies, damn. I lift my head and try it one more time. This time it fires off and stays on. I have a small celebration and call Andromeda to me again. Another minute later we're back moving. It only takes a little while to catch up to the squad. Everyone is on the side of the road except Matt.

"Where is the dork?" I ask as I get out.

"Riding up and getting used to his bike. He should be back in a bit. Any problems?" Oakley asks.

I shake my head and look to see if we need to get supplies loaded up. Sgt Hayes tells me that we haven't found anything yet. She gets in the truck and tells me to drive on. As we leave the others behind, she tells me the plan for the next couple of days. Everything is going to be the same. If we find something we will load it up and once we have enough, I will make the trip back to the caravan. Otherwise, we stay ahead of them and make sure there aren't any problems coming up.

This is how it goes for the next five days or so. I hate to think that we've gotten lucky. I mean we lost 5 of our soldiers and two of the trucks in the first two days, but since then it's been very quiet. Andromeda has gotten used to riding in the truck with me. She may be getting a little lazy, but it's good for her. I have a distinct feeling that the trip isn't going to be this good the whole way. I keep waiting for the hammer to drop and everything to fall apart. Jordan would say I'm just being pessimistic, but she isn't here to say it.

Maybe I am, but maybe that's what'll save someone else's life.

Pittsburgh

The days pass slowly but the nights pass slower. We have to stop often to keep our pace just ahead of the caravan. We move left and right during the day but always camp within a few miles of where the caravan should be stopping. I've only been able to make one trip back since that second day. That one was good though because I was able to see Mom and make sure she's doing OK. The trip seems to be treating her all right, but she did look a little under the weather. I pass it off as not eating well, she's never liked to eat when she traveled.

As we settle in tonight Sgt. Hayes tells us that we should be hitting the outskirts of Pittsburgh the following day. With a city comes a high population, so there are bound to be people or Deaders in the area. We have to keep a little closer and stay together. I'm on first watch as usual, but it passes fast and I get in bed. I feel like I am already asleep as my head hits the pillow.

I am walking through the city. I have never been here so I am not sure what city I am in, yet I figure it must be Pittsburgh because we are so close. I look around for Andromeda or Matt but no one is around. The city is in bad shape, lots of fires have burned out the buildings. The city could be Gotham for all I know, it fits the bill. As I turn a corner I see the street lined with what appears to be electric vehicles. I know that people in the cities loved these things when they came out. Going green they used to call it. The electric cars are barely recognizable as melted metal husks. The batteries seem to have caught fire and then spread to the surrounding buildings. I knew those things were dangerous, but this many in one spot must have made the heat unbearable.

As I walk down the street I can see burnt husks that may have been people on the sidewalk, you would think an atomic bomb went off in the street. It was horrific. My fear peaks and I whistle for Andromeda. It takes a second but she peaks her head around one of the buildings up ahead. I smile at first but then something doesn't seem right. I take a second to look at her and notice that as she is moving towards me her gait is off. Is she hurt? It isn't until she is about 10 feet away that I can see that her eyes are glowing blue.

What!? How is she dead? How did she become a deader?

I am shaken awake by a hand on my shoulder. Bleary-eyed I see that Matt is kneeling beside me. I look and Andromeda is on the floor at my feet, her head up and cocked to the side as if asking if I was ok. That dream was crazy.

Since I'm up, Matt and I go down to grab something to eat. He'll be heading out before us to the city line. The rest of us will check the suburban areas around us before heading further west. If everything goes as planned we won't see Matt until this evening for dinner.

Here's to hoping.

As we finish our breakfast the rest of the squad is waking up. Matt gets last-minute orders from Hayes and he heads out. As the rest of them eat their breakfast I go relieve Smith from his watch so he can eat before we hit the road. The small house that we have stopped in used to be nice, but it was looted and broken in the riots that hit the cities before the fall. There isn't much left but a roof over our heads for the night. I take a walk around the perimeter to do one final check before we head out when Andromeda drops on her haunches and growls low in her throat.

I shout to the others and kneel next to her with my gun up and ready. I can hear Matt's motorcycle disappearing into the distance, so it can't be him. I lock in on where Andromeda is looking but I don't see anything. Reid and Oakley poke their head around a corner to see what was going on. I point to them and to where the disturbance may be, they nod and move out to flank the spot. As they hit the small tree line three Deaders run out towards Andromeda and me. We are the only two these things can see so we are the targets.

I pat Andromeda on the rump and call her to me as I turn and take off back to the house. The door is on the far side from where I am so it may be a close call. I call Sgt. Hayes to open the door and be ready for incoming. I can hear the other two chasing behind, but I am not sure if they can outrun the Deaders and get them before they are on me. I slip a little as I turn the corner to the front of the house and lose a little ground. I want to look back to see how much room I have, but I know that will only slow me down. Andromeda could outpace me at any second but she's staying between me and the threat.

I yell at her to get to the door so that I can close it as soon as I am through if I make it that far. The door is only feet away but I can almost hear the footsteps behind me. I hit the steps as Andromeda vaults through the door. I miss one in my hurry to get inside and it almost dooms me. The first deader grabs my shirt as a shotgun blast goes off, seemingly, in my ear. The hand lets go and I am through the door as Sgt. Hayes slams it shut.

"That was too close," Sgt. Hayes says. "The others will finish them off. Just give them a few minutes."

"Maybe I shouldn't be the one doing perimeter checks Sarge. I seem to be the bait," I say while bent over on my knees trying to catch my breath.

"That's why you are our driver. It keeps you the safest."

"I thought it was because I wasn't trained."

"That too," Hayes jokes.

Reid and Oakley come in the door and give us the all-clear. It seems so easy to them, while my heart is still racing from the fear. I guess that's one of the pros of becoming Unseen. I still haven't seen many cons. They tell me there are some though, so I believe them. You never can tell what is happening to people right under your nose.

Now that I have gotten my morning run in and my daily adrenalin boost I head to the truck and start loading the gear. We hit the road a few minutes later. A few hours more and we come to the suburbs of Pittsburgh. The city outline looks exactly like my dream last night, not good. We stop and check a few of the small communities in the 'burbs but find nothing of use. The cities rioted pretty heavily before the Fall because of the mask mandates and the curfews. Military law had to be enacted in larger cities like this one, so a lot of people moved out with friends and family in the suburbs. When they left they took everything, or everything was taken from them. Luckily, we hadn't found any pockets of humans trying to bother us.

It is kind of eery though, where did they all go?

We stop and check a couple of markings on the route to indicate which road Matt took to get into the city. Hayes thinks about checking another route just to be on the safe side but decides against it in the end. We only make sure the route that we take is safe, anything else is outside of our purview, she says. We follow Matt's marks until well past lunch. We're in the city proper when we find a city park on the side of the road, we stop and sit under the trees to have a bite to eat.

Like most city parks this one is pretty big, it has a soccer field, or what used to be one, buildings that probably used to be museums or something and even an ice rink. We don't walk it all but I find one of those kiosk maps still standing and it shows it all. Something else catches my eye though, the road leads to a bridge that goes to the heart of the city, but there is a small peninsula that seems to have been heavily populated. We have to cross through before we reach the bridge. It seems off to me and I get Minotaur vibes from it. I show it to the others and they all agree that that is a choke point that we shouldn't take. There are plenty of other bridges around to take and we can skirt the edge of the city instead.

Reid and Smith take the truck ahead to check for Matt's trail. When they return they say that he must have thought the same thing because his marks show him crossing the next bridge and skirting the city. He had also left a full fuel tank sitting next to his mark, he must have scavenged it along the way. We clean up, load up and get back on the trail.

"After we cross the bridge we will walk and start looking for anything that may be usable. There has to be a gas station that still has some fuel at least," Hayes tells us.

This is what we do for the next two hours. Hayes figures the transports won't get past Pittsburgh today so we'll stop just outside of the city limits for the night. In the morning I'll head back to about where we are now and bring whatever supplies we find. I have no expectations to find much other than fuel since the cities were the first ones to burn. Rioters took everything from televisions to toilet paper when they broke into stores. I didn't see that there would be much left.

A little while later my prediction seems to be coming true. We haven't found much of anything besides a few cars that still had gas in them. Suddenly, I look to our right and there is a huge island in the middle of the river with huge stacks. It looks to be some kind of factory area. I point it out to Hayes and she pulls out her paper map.

"It's a power station. Won't be any food there, but there may be some parts we could use and almost definitely some diesel. People stayed well away from the power plants after the NLBs fried themselves getting too close to the transformers. With that, there should be things we can find. Smith you three head over there and get what you can. Washington you and your dog will stay on this side of the bridge to keep an eye out and make sure we have a clear exit once they are done. Smith you take the truck, you'll probably need it." Sgt. Hayes orders.

Andromeda and I get out and stay at the edge of the bridge as the others head over to the power plant. The whole thing looks like it is one burned-out mess from here. I hope it's not a bust, I'm sure the transports are running low.

They always seem to be running low on fuel.

As I wait the morning clicks on towards noon. I haven't heard any gunfire, so I assume everything is going well. I keep a close eye on Andromeda to make sure that she isn't sensing something that I'm missing. She's good, just sunning on the bridge.

Man, dogs have the life sometimes, not a worry in the world. As I look at her I can see the truck coming up to the bridge. The bed seems loaded down, I guess they got a lot of supplies. As Smith pulls the truck to my end of the bridge, the lazy dog gets up and out of the way. He stops and gets out so I can get back in the driver's seat, I notice that he is covered in blood.

"Oh, crap! Are you ok?" I ask as I look him over for wounds.

"Oh, this. Yeah, not mine. The place was crawling with NLBs," he explains and he walks to the bed of the truck.

"Yeah, I thought as much that's why I left you on rear guard," Hayes explains. "Some of them probably never left after they came for the energy, nothing left anywhere else to draw them. No issue for us, but that's why no humans came near these types of places. Got us a good haul."

"You want me to take these back to the transports this afternoon?" I ask.

"Yes, but we'll wait for Washington to get back. With this much I want him to run security for you, I know we haven't seen anyone but that doesn't mean they weren't there. It just means we out-manned and out-gunned them. You running by yourself with a load like this could be a target," Hayes tells me.

I nod as I get back into the driver's seat. We move up the banks a little farther and wait for Matt to return, he wasn't supposed to be gone all day. I wonder if Hayes knew about this power plant and planned this run. Knowing her she did. About an hour later we hear Matt's bike droning in the distance. It takes about another thirty for him to reach our location.

"Man, that bike is loud corporal," Reid chides as Matt turns his bike off.

"Good thing the dead don't listen to it," Matt returns.

"But humans do. You being by yourself is a setup for something to happen," Hayes pipes in. "Anything you can do about the noise?"

"Not unless we find a motorcycle shop with new mufflers in it," Matt says as he puts the kickstand down and dismounts. "Plus, I can outrun and out-ride anyone out there. I'm good."

Matt has become cocky since he was gone. He was never the risk taker or the one with such confidence before. *I'm not sure if I like it.*

"Grab some lunch with Ava, then you two are heading back to the transports with our haul. You can out-ride anyone that tries to take our stuff hotshot," Hayes orders.

Matt just gives her a thumbs-up and grabs some food. He sits down in the truck with me as the others try and clean up from what I can only assume was a massacre of Deaders on the power plant island. I told him about my early morning run after he left this morning. He laughs and shakes his head like it was funny.

It was not funny.

I tell him as much and stick my tongue out at him. Andromeda agrees and chuffs at him too.

A little while later we are back on the road heading to the transport. Matt is riding a little ahead of me but keeps checking back on me to make sure I'm keeping up. You can tell he is used to being on his own. The day rolls on and we get back to the bridge we crossed. Matt is stopped on the other side as I approach. He's talking to a group of the military and waves me across. He seems agitated for some reason.

As I pull up and get out, Matt and another soldier are standing over one of the stick markings we use to tell the transports which way to go.

"No, we told them to cross here. The area ahead didn't feel safe and we didn't scout it out," Matt's telling the other soldier. He is waving his hands around like a madman. "Ava tell him that the way we just came was the way we went and what we cleared," I nod along in agreement, not much for me to add.

"Well Corporal Washington, the transport is ahead of us. We had a good day and people were moving well so they were trying to make up some time. They are about half an hour ahead of us and the walking people are about two hours or so behind," the soldier tells us.

"Shit," is all Matt says as he fixes the markers to the correct order and then walks back to his bike. "I'll scout ahead, you all come up behind, we need to find them and make sure they are ok."

Lost

It doesn't take us long to find the transports. We come up on Matt as he's crouched along the side of a building. The large transports are here but I can't see much else, the suburban is probably in between them

. "The area ahead of them seems to be blocked for some reason. I'm going to go up and check on them and see what's happening and see if we can get them turned around," Matt says as he heads off. The other soldiers and I set up a perimeter along the roadway. I look at Andromeda and see that she's very agitated, almost scared. I've never seen her this way.

I keep thinking back on the markers, were they moved by people or Deaders? I mean they set a trap for us at the Home of the Brave that took months to spring. Moving a few sticks around wouldn't be that hard, but how would they know the correct order to send the transports straight? Did people send them this way? I was thinking about this when Matt ran back to our position.

"Good news and bad news," he states. "The good news is that all of the people are ok, some small boy heard the trucks coming and stopped them before they got too far. The bad news is that this whole area is crawling with NLBs. It seems to be the largest den we have ever seen. The boy told us that at least 6 different clans are living in the local two-block radius."

"Can we just drive through and outrun them?" one of the soldiers asks.

"No, the bridge ahead is out. It was a way to keep the NLBs contained," Matt replies.

"Well, why don't they turn around and come back this way?" I ask as I pet Andromeda to keep her calm. The amount of Deaders in the area must be setting her off.

"The transports are too big to turn around on the local streets. We need to try and back them up, but to do that they need spotters. There aren't any Unseen with them, only regular soldiers. One of them already backed into a couple of parked cars and messed up the transport a bit. Nothing to make it undriveable, but they just can't see and there are too many turns and debris," Matt tells me. "I am going to head back and get my squad. Do you guys know why there are no Unseen with the forward transport?" Matt is now looking at the other soldiers.

"They all stayed back with the walkers because being around the scientists seemed to be making them sick. A couple of them even passed out while the research crews were making that awful-smelling chemical they brew. I know the smell is bad, but not enough to make you pass out," one of the soldiers, Pasqual by his name patch, fills in.

"Well, that's inconvenient," I reply.

Matt gets up and heads back to his bike. He pushes it back a ways and then starts it up to head back to the squad. It'll take him a while to get back there and then they have to walk back. Shit! They will never make it if he doesn't take the truck. I yell for him but his bike is too loud and he doesn't hear me before he takes off. I turn to the other soldiers and ask them to help me unload the gear and gas in the back of the truck. I have to head back after them if we are going to get them here fast enough. We unload it quickly. I call Andromeda to me then think better of it.

"Hey, you keep my dog with you. She can sense the Deaders, or NLBs. If she gets agitated you need to get somewhere safe. OK?" I tell them. The guy looks skeptical but nods. "Keep her safe. She is my best friend. I can't lose another." He looks into my eyes and nods again. I can see he feels the same.

I get the truck running and head after Matt. I know he took it easy on me getting here, partly because the truck was loaded down. I had to fly now. One to catch up to him, another to get the others back in time to help. The transports were keeping a low profile for now, but how long would that last? The truck was in good shape for running during an apocalypse, but it was not in peak condition. If I traveled over 65 mph the truck shook and it felt like it was going to fall apart. I kept it just under that as long as I could and hoped it would be enough.

I reached the spot where the squad was when I left, probably about an hour later. It was faster than the trip out, but not by much. I slow down so I don't miss any of the markers and hope they haven't gotten too far. My hopes are answered five minutes later when I come across them and Matt on the side of the road.

"Need a lift?" I ask as I pull up.

"I was hoping you would be smart enough to know we needed the truck to get back. This Washington didn't seem to be," Sgt Hayes says as she shoos me out of the driver's seat. "I'll drive this time. Washington get back there and do what you can. We will be right behind you,"

Matt nods and gets back on the bike. He takes a bottle out of his backpack and pours some gas into the tank. This back and forth is killing our fuel reserve. We're going to need to find more soon. Sgt. Hayes takes off like a bat out of Hell and keeps the truck at almost 80. I'm not sure how the damn thing is staying on the road or even staying together, but we make it back in about 45 minutes.

New track record.

Once we get close to the bridge she slows and comes to a stop, "We go the rest of the way on foot. If we park over there we will be in the way."

"Hey Sarge, can we go back a bit I think I lost a few teeth?" Smith yells out as he gets shakily out of the back of the truck.

"Yeah, and my liver. Holy crap, Sarge did you have to push this rust bucket that hard?" Oakley adds.

"Yeah, yeah. But did you die?" Hayes shoots back.

"Well, there was this one time," Oakley responds.

"I meant right now! Now clam it," Hayes orders.

"We have to get the supplies that we dropped off to come back and get you guys," I say as I get out of the truck. However, I looked at the others and silently agreed with their assessment.

"We'll load them on the first transport through. It'll be fine," Hayes answers.

As Hayes gets the information directly from the other soldiers and then gets the team ready to go I'm told to stay put. I start to protest but Hayes shuts me down. The team will be moving fast and there are a lot of Deaders around. I'd be a liability. She's even making Andromeda stay with me too.

"If the Scientists and others are smart, they are hunkering inside of the transports and keeping a low profile. We won't be seen, hence the name, remember. That's why these guys didn't go in. We will go in, and get them out. Be ready to roll out fast when we do. Got it?" Hayes tells me as she orders the team out towards the others.

Andromeda sits at my hip as we watch our team walk into a Deader nest. From what the boy told Matt there are a lot of Deaders around. As we set up to receive the transports I hear noise coming from behind us. The others do too and turn to face the new threat. It takes a little bit before we can see anything. As we do we all relax, it's the rear column of walkers finally catching up. I quickly tell the soldiers to stay put and wait for the rest of the team. I whistle for Andromeda and run back to catch the front of the column. The soldiers in the front are part of the Unseen. I recognize Sgt. Ragsdill.

As I approach he takes a second to recognize me, then he lets down their guard. I let him know the issue that we've run into and look at him for a plan. I'm not used to making decisions for others, so I'll let them do it. Ragsdill gets moving and swaps his team out with the other soldiers.

"Take the walkers over the bridge and about thirty minutes up the road. We'll wait for the others to get the transports back and catch up afterward. No reason for all of us to be in danger here. I'll send one guy back to inform the rear guard so they don't make the same mistake as the transports," he tells us as he passes off some of his gear to the others.

Andromeda and I stay on the north side of the bridge while everyone walks past us. I see Susie and ask her if my mother is walking, and she shakes her head. That means Mom is with the transports, surrounded by Deaders, great. Susie stops after we talk and waits with me for all of the others to pass. We don't talk but it's comforting to know that she's here. I know what she's capable of and how she reacts when things pop off, it's reassuring.

A while later the whole column is past us and we cross the bridge to stay with them. As we pass the truck I think about taking it with us, but I decide to leave it for Hayes and the team when they get back. I do grab a bottle of water out of the cab before I move on though. We walk for the prescribed thirty minutes and find a place to make camp. We start setting up what we can for the night. It's not late, but we don't know when the transports will catch up.

Might as well do something while we wait.

Everyone's on pins and needles as the whole situation is passed on from one person to another. I'm sure it gets worse with each telling. Two hours later, I hear the transports rumbling our way. I jump up and stand by the side of the road as they pull in. Matt's bike and the truck are right behind them. I look over the team and they seem a little worse for wear, I'll have to get that story later. First things first, I have to find Mom. I look in the back of the first transport, nothing but equipment and scientists. I jump down and head to the back of the second transport, before I get there the front door opens and Mom jumps out.

She grabs me in a hug and cries on my shoulder. "That didn't go well. I was so scared. I was scared for us and then for Matt when they came to save us. Something happened and everything went crazy, there were Deaders everywhere," she cries. She then tries to continue but it's nothing but gibberish.

I try to calm her down, but it's Andromeda that does the trick. She always knows how to calm us down. Matt comes by to join us, I can see that his shirt is ripped and he has blood on his hands. Thankfully, it doesn't seem to be his.

"Everyone ok?" I ask him, concerned.

He looks at me and nods. That probably means our team was good but not everyone was. Since Mom seemed to be calming down I decided to go and find Hayes to find out what she wanted me to do. On my way, I see a strange-looking boy sitting on the side of the road. The boy is about 12 or 13 and very dirty. It doesn't look like his hair has been washed or combed in months. Was he living there by himself? As I approach him he's eating something.

Suddenly, he breaks the silence, "Pickle!"

"Excuse me?" I ask, completely confused. Does he understand us and can he communicate with us? He had to have been able to say something because he told Matt about the Deaders.

"Do. You. Want. A. Pickle?" He draws out enunciating each word, while holding a jar of dill pickles. I guess he can talk just fine.

"Was that necessary?" I ask as I reach down and take a pickle. I'm not turning that down even if he was a bit of a jerk.

"You were thinking that I was dumb and couldn't talk. I could see it on your face. I'm young, not dumb." He stands up and hands me the rest of the jar. I notice that he is a bit small for his age. He's thin, of course, all of us are anymore, and a bit short. He is wearing clothes that have seen better days, along with a belt holding two wicked-looking hatchets.

"What's up with the hatchets?"

"My favorite weapon. They are very versatile. I can cut things, I can throw them, I can cut things."

"You said that." I laugh. I think I'm gonna like this kid.

For his part, he just laughs like he meant to say the same thing twice. "Hey, you want to meet my dog? She's with my brother and my mother. You can come hang with us tonight." I leave the invitation hanging as I turn and walk back to my family.

A few steps later he's running up beside me. "My name is Josh by the way. Thanks for inviting me. I haven't been around people much lately." He hangs his head a bit. He reminds me of

Jordan with his short stature and the sadness in his eyes. He does laugh a bit more though. A couple of minutes later I introduce Josh to Andromeda and my family. He sits down and we talk until dinner.

Josh

Josh told us his story, it took most of the night. He's lived a hard life but has learned more about the Deaders than most scientists know. He has seen them in the wild, not just in a lab setting. By the time he was about ten minutes into his story, I stopped him and ran off to get Testerman and Hayes. If this kid has this much information, these would be the people to hear it. Hayes listened to what I told her then went and got SGM Silver so he could hear it too.

Twenty minutes later, we are joined by the three leaders of the group. Josh seems a little less willing to talk until I tell him that everyone here just wants to learn from his struggles. He smiles and then tells us his story.

Josh speaks for the next couple of hours. He tells us all about his life in this apocalyptic world. He does have to stop several times to answer questions from a couple of us, but all in all, he's allowed to just talk his way through his story at his own pace.

I'll paraphrase a little.

Before the world fell apart Josh was living between Ellendale, DE, not too far from my hometown, with his Dad and Pittsburgh, PA with his mom. His parents had gone through a bitter divorce the year prior. He was in Pittsburgh with his mom when they heard all of the horror stories about the Walking Dead in the cities in Europe. His mother decided that it would be better for them to head to Delaware. She was from there too and thought that it would be safer than Pittsburgh. She never found out how right she was.

The night that they decided to leave was the same night that the power went out in the city. His mom packed him and his younger brother up in the car and tried to drive out of the city. With the loss of power came a loss of traffic lights. It also brought a mass exodus of people. Within five minutes of being on the road, the cars were at a dead stop on the highway. Two hours later people were leaving their cars abandoned on the road and heading out on foot. Josh's mom hadn't wanted to walk back to their apartment, but there didn't seem to be any other option.

Josh was a little short on the details of the walk back to their apartment. I think a few things happened that he tries not to think about. In the end, they all got back safe and sound. It wasn't until about a month later that disaster struck. Josh was told to keep an eye on his brother because his mother had to go and try to find some food. She had been checking the empty apartments in their building, but that was getting harder to do. She was going to try and walk down to the local store to see if anyone was still there.

Two days later, they still hadn't heard from their mother. Both Josh and his brother were starving and they were out of clean water. Josh got his brother dressed and they went out to see if they could find anyone to help them. They went through their building asking for help but received nothing but doors closed in their faces. His brother started to cry, but Josh just kept on pushing. They left the building. The streets were empty. Josh lead his brother down to the local corner store. The store's doors were ripped off and everything in the store was trashed. Josh was able to find a small bag of chips for his brother to eat, it was open and stale but it was still food.

The two of them wandered around the city for two days finding nothing but a few scraps here and there. They never came across their mother or any sign of her. Each night Josh would find them a semi-safe place to sleep, either in an abandoned building or in an abandoned car. After the second day, Josh's brother got sick. He couldn't hold down any of the food that they found. He became very dehydrated and died from a fever two days later. Josh was lost and depressed. He had tried his best to keep his brother alive but failed in the end. So far in just a week, he had lost his mother and his brother. His father was so far away that it might as well have been on the other side of the world.

At this point, Josh lost track of time. He wandered around and tried to eat enough to stay alive. He had found a small area that seemed safe. That was until a group of people moved in and acted like everything in the area belonged to them. Josh had stayed hidden for a day or two but was eventually found. He was taken to the leader of the group and asked to join them. Josh didn't like the look of them so he refused. At first, it seemed like they understood and would let him leave. Just as he reached the door a couple of them jumped him and beat him almost to death.

They thought that he was dead and tossed his body in the street a couple of blocks away. A nice man found him and took him in and nursed him back to health. Josh slept for days before he woke up in the man's house. The man told Josh that he had lost his heartbeat a time or two before he got him steady and stable. The man had been a pediatrician before The Fall and knew how to help him.

The next couple of months the boy and the doctor fell into an easy routine and kept each other company. The doctor had found a good stash of supplies that kept them both fed, not a lot for a growing boy, but enough. It was around March when the food started to run out. The doctor decided that they should go on a supply run. It had been a decently cold winter and they hadn't seen many people, dead or alive, moving around their part of the city.

They left early in the morning heading to a few smaller areas that may still have had food left. The amount of people that had been packed into this area led the doctor to believe that the food would be scarce. If so they would return by tonight and create a plan on getting out of the city. They never got that far. Around noon, they were attacked by a bunch of the walking dead, Deaders the doctor called them. The two of them were entering an old abandoned building that used to be used for storage until the smaller trucks could ship to the stores. Everything seemed fine until they got to the back offices. This is where the Deaders had made their den. As soon as the doctor opened the door, three of them attacked. Josh fell back in fear and waited for his end to come. It never did.

As they finished killing the doctor one of them looked up at Josh and cocked his head to the side, as if he was confused but then just shook it off and headed back into the office with the others. Josh ran to the doctor's side to see if he was somehow still alive. Even though he was young, Josh knew how to check for a pulse. The doctor didn't have one. Josh opened up his eyes and could see that life had left him. Josh was a little short on the details of what happened next, but I assume he sat there and cried for a bit before trying to figure out his next steps.

That's what I would've done.

As confused and lost as he was by the doctor's death, Josh was just as confused about why he was still alive. After he wept, he got up and walked around the Deaders to see if they noticed him. He had heard about them before but had never seen one. He knew that they were the same as zombies and should react to him in the same way a hungry zombie horde would. At this point, Testerman tried to correct the boy but the rest of us just shushed him and told Josh to continue.

All of the dead people completely ignored Josh. He took his time and walked around the warehouse to see if he could find anything to eat. He found a good little bit in the breakroom. Josh figured that he was safe there and found a small corner room to stay in until this food ran out. It worked out well because the Deaders kept the other people away and didn't eat any of the food that Josh had found.

A week or so into this new arrangement Josh made a critical mistake. He had gotten used to being around the Deaders to the point that the smell and the odd tics didn't bother him anymore. He had begun to look at each of them as friends of sorts. In his imagination, he had named them all and created little backstories for them. For instance, Georgia was from California. She had come here to be a Pittsburgh Steelers cheerleader. When she fell on hard times she married Kent in the corner who was the football team's waterboy. They were happy and liked their new living arrangement. This familiarity was his downfall. One day he let Jose get too close and his hand rubbed against Jose's bare arm. As soon as they touched Josh knew that something was wrong. He had felt a small spark, like being shocked after running your feet on the carpet and touching metal.

Jose knew something was different too. As soon as they touched and the spark was felt, Jose turned on Josh and tried to grab him. The others around started to gather and chase Josh too. Josh was a small boy, still was, so he was able to dodge under their grasp and run away from the building. He found another close by, locked himself in a room and hid. Jose and his crew didn't come after him, so after an hour or so Josh came out of hiding. He didn't feel safe going back to the old warehouse. He wasn't sure if they would know he was still alive permanently or just temporarily after the touch, but there was no reason to change it. Josh moved on deeper into the city.

Josh hadn't been in Pittsburgh long before the Fall so he quickly got lost. He had a vague idea where the warehouses were but geography wasn't his strong suit. Well, neither was math or science. Josh was more of an art and music kid. And video games. He loved to play video games. He had walked around for a few days hiding when he had to and struggling to find food and a safe place to sleep each night. That was how he ended up at the intersection of the rivers. The bridge had already been taken down by the time he had gotten there. He found that out the hard way. As he started to backtrack he looked into a couple of the buildings and found food stores. Not just a little bit of food either. It seemed like a lot of people had put the supplies together and stored them for a long-term survival plan. It was probably a gang of some sort.

This freaked Josh out and everything in him told him to run away quickly. He still remembers the beating he had gotten the last time he ran upon the living. He wasn't too keen on doing that again, plus the doctor was dead so there wasn't anyone to save him this time. His hunger won out though and he started to stuff a few packages in his pockets before he ran away. After he stuffed his pockets, he turned to leave and a Deader stood in front of him. The guy was huge but had been so quiet that Josh had never heard him approach.

As Josh stood frozen the Deader looked him up and down with his head cocked to the side like a dog. Josh was so scared he could barely breathe, let alone move. For a full five minutes, Josh stood there under the scrutiny of Jack, the name he had given the man. He reminded Josh of Jack Reacher from the television show. Just as quickly as he had come, Jack turned and left. Josh had passed the inspection. Knowing that Deaders lived in this area made Josh feel safer. If Jack and his group slept near here the food was probably safe. The living was probably run off by the dead and the food just sat there. Josh decided quickly to make this his new temporary home. One caveat was that he would keep his distance from his protectors so they couldn't touch him.

That was where Josh had lived since. He had found his hatchets in one of the buildings. It took him a few weeks but he practiced throwing them at a wall for hours a day until he got proficient with them. His dad had taught him how to sharpen a knife when he was younger, he taught himself how to sharpen the hatchets to keep the edges.

Over the months and years that he lived there, Josh had seen a lot of Deader groups come and go. He watched them all and learned their behaviors and habits. Each group acted differently than others, it seemed to depend on their leader. If their leader was smart the group did well, if they weren't the group didn't seem to last long.

Josh had gotten so used to the area that he knew something was wrong when he heard the trucks coming up the road. Josh knew that only the living drove trucks, so he left his area and hid along the route to see what was happening. No one had come up this road since Josh had been staying there. It was odd to hear anything from living people. He had almost forgotten what a living human being looked like. It had gotten so bad that his walk almost imitated the Deaders at times.

As the transports came up the street Josh could tell that they were military vehicles. His heart started beating a mile a minute. If the military was there they could save him and take him back to Delaware so he could be with his dad. That was why he ran into the street to stop the transport from going any further. Josh knew that if they went any further in, the Deaders would sense them and attack. With that many staying in one area, the living wouldn't have a chance, military or not.

That in a nutshell was Josh's life since the Fall.

An odd story for an odd little boy.

Habits

As soon as Josh finished, Testerman jumped in with a load of questions. The boy looked tired so SGM Silver cut the conversation so he could get some sleep. Josh's telling of his story had taken a few hours, it seemed like he could talk forever and not run out of words.

Sound familiar?

Everything broke up and Andromeda and I rolled up in our blankets to sleep. Since I was part of the forward watch, but not in the field, we would get to sleep the whole night without standing watch. Of course, I still woke up three times because I was used to getting up.

Stupid brain.

Over breakfast the next morning, Testerman started asking Josh questions about the behavior of the NLBs. Josh was confused by the acronym at first until I explained what it meant. Josh took the questions in stride and answered them the best that he could. The information that he had gathered would be invaluable to our journey. He didn't think that he was a smart kid, but he knew people and had watched the Deaders a lot. He knew just about everything about them.

For the sake of time and my hand I am just going to summarize the things that Josh found out about them.

1. All Deaders belong to a group of some sort. Almost like a gang. They report to one leader, an Alpha Testerman called it. The leader would run the group as they saw fit.

2. It seemed that some of the intelligence of the living person was retained in the Deader. If the person was a doctor or engineer, the Deader version would be smarter and have better reasoning capabilities.

3. Not all of the leaders were the smartest in the group. Some of them were all brawn, like Jack, while others had no distinguishing feature to make them the leader. Josh wasn't sure

why one led and the others followed, there wasn't any rhyme or reason he could determine.

Testerman surmised that it had something to do with charisma. Natural leaders tended to draw people to them. Even in death apparently.

4. Even if one of the group was smarter or stronger than the leader, they never fought for dominance. The leader also never seemed to defer to the others. So if a leader was dumb, but one of their people was smarter, the smarter one still deferred. A lot of times to the detriment of the group.

This may be a plus. If not they may have outsmarted all living humans by now.

5. A group typically consisted of 5-10 Deaders. Sometimes more or less, but typically in that range.

6. Even if two groups lived in the same area, they didn't interact with each other. Josh had never seen them hunt so he couldn't determine if they would hunt together or not. I had asked because it was more than ten Deaders that attacked the Home of the Brave.

Maybe they hunted together if there was enough prey. Or did they break into bands each under the leadership of one, like a squad?

7. In the winter the Deaders slowed down. It almost seemed like they were cold-blooded, like reptiles. Their systems slowed and they didn't need to feed as often. Josh had seen one group stand in the corner of a building for two weeks straight in the dead of winter. They never moved, it was like they were in suspended animation. "You know like in the space movies?" Josh added.

8. Deaders that fed often were more agile and looked more human. They were also smarter, or at least retained their intelligence better.

9. Deaders that were led by dumber Deaders usually rotted away faster because they didn't feed as much. If they didn't feed they rotted away like the movie zombies. As their bodies deteriorated so did their minds. Josh had seen a lot of groups come

and go because of this. He told us that even though jack was the biggest and strongest Deader he had seen, it had only been months before his whole group had started to rot away. They were finally run off by stronger and fresher, his word not mine, groups. He still wondered about that big guy.

10. As they deteriorated they became less active. This seemed obvious since they wouldn't have the energy to move.

11. One odd fact was that you could see their eyes glow, even when they were sleeping. The glow would emanate through their eyelids.

That seemed creepy.

12. They all slept in a pile touching each other. That way if one moved they would all know. The leader slept at the center to be protected.

13. They also slept a lot, kinda like dogs. If they weren't out hunting, they would sleep.

14. As the main part of the group slept, the leader would send one or two out to scout the surrounding area. There would also usually be one standing watch over the group. If either the scouts or the guard saw something, they would screech. It was a very high-pitched yell that humans shouldn't be able to make. This would alert the leader and he would decide on what to do.

15. Josh wasn't sure how they communicated besides the screeching. But it seemed like body language was part of it. He couldn't tell, but there seemed to be more to it.

Matt filled in that the Unseen had an innate ability to sense each other's motives. This had to be similar to what the NLBs did. Something through the spores.

16. Another fact that Josh told us what that at times one would "overeat". When it came back it would be twitchy and spastic. Like a kid when they had too much sugar. It would also cause the back of their neck to glow like their eyes. It wouldn't last long and didn't happen often.

It seemed super weird though.

The conversation with Josh and Testerman took most of the morning. Testerman couldn't seem to get enough. So much so that he asked Josh to ride in the first transport with him for the day so they could continue the conversation. Josh wasn't sure what else he could tell Testerman, but I knew that Josh would run out of words before Testerman ran out of questions.

As the two of them ran off, I went and got my stuff ready to leave. The team and I would be heading back out to the front of the column again to make a path for the rest. I did take some time to talk with Mom before I headed out. She didn't look well. Traveling had never been her strong suit, but she looked sicker than usual. I asked her how she was and she just waved me off and blamed it on motion sickness from riding all day. Leave it to Mom to worry about everything else and not her health.

Andromeda and I loaded up about thirty minutes later. Sgt. Hayes had me drive again, something about a vote among the others. I wasn't sure what I missed but I was comfortable driving now so I didn't mind. Matt was back on his bike and headed out as soon as Hayes gave him the OK. I put the truck in gear and started to pull off when Josh jumped in front of me and slapped the hood. I hit the brakes hard out of surprise.

"Maybe someone else should drive. I think Hayes wore off on Washington," Reid teased.

I just turned around and stuck my tongue out at him. I rolled the window down as Josh came up to the door.

"Can I ride with you?" he asked, "I felt sick in the other truck. It smelled weird."

I looked at Sgt. Hayes and she just nodded. I told him to jump in the back with the others but to not hurt anyone with his hatchets. I guess we had a mascot now.

Well, a mascot with a couple of deadly hatchets.

As he got settled I eased forward and then slammed the throttle down to toss the guys in the back around a little. Hayes laughed but the others decided to learn some quick sign language and told me their thoughts quickly. Pretty typical really.

Canton

A couple of days later we were in Cambridge, Ohio. I see signs for Canton being about 60 miles north. For those that don't know, Canton is home to the Pro Football Hall of Fame. This is a place that I have always wanted to visit. My dad was always talking about visiting here some day. As we reach the town limits of Cambridge I ask Hayes if Matt and I could head up to Canton to check for supplies and stop by to see if the museum was still standing. She wasn't keen on the idea but caved by telling me to ride the bike with Matt. This would allow the rest to stay on task.

I think Hayes is getting a little softer the more she's around me. But please don't tell her I said that.

The ride to the Hall of Fame only takes about 55 minutes. If we take an hour to look around, we could catch back up easily. As we ride up the drive, both Matthew and I are disappointed. I'm not sure what we were expecting, but the huge glass panels are completely shattered. Still, we stay undeterred and park the bike just inside the hall. No point in leaving it in the open.

A lot of the main lobby is covered in dirt and debris. As we walk the hallways into the history of the greatest sport in America, we see that some of the pieces have been defaced, but most are left undisturbed. It would've been amazing to see all of this before the Fall. Before this history meant nothing in the new world.

My father was a huge Bears fan. He never made it to the hall on George Halas Dr. The George Halas that created the NFL, the same man who was a player, coach and owner of the Chicago Staleys, which became the Chicago Bears. Walking through the hall that gave his history led me back to the days of football with my dad.

It was Sunday and the Bears played at 1:00. My dad was trying to get the streaming service to work so he could watch the Bears play their rival, the Green Bay Packers. This game was always important to any Bears fan as it was the oldest rivalry in the league. Unfortunately, since the time of Aaron Rodgers, the rivalry was less so. The Bears hadn't beaten the Pack in more than 5 years at Lambeau field, yet you could still hear the cheers of "Packers Suck" shouted through Chicago. My dad had never gotten to visit Lambeau, but we had gone out to Soldier Field last year to watch Philly beat up the Bears. That was a good time for me, and even through the loss, my dad was happy to have been part of it all. He had never been to a game where his team had home-field advantage. He was all decked out in his gear, Bears stuff from head to toe. I enjoyed seeing him take it all in, the win was just the cherry on top for me.

This Sunday though we were warm and snug in our house waiting for the game to start. Matthew was off in his room, no doubt playing D&D online with his friends. He was never much of a football fan. Which begs the question of why he came down to the Hall of Fame with me.

"Matt, why did you agree to come here with me?" I ask him suddenly. Almost like he could hear my thoughts.

"What? Oh, just because I didn't watch football with you and Dad all the time doesn't mean I don't like the history. I mean the man talked about football all of the time. I thought that we should at least see it before things like this are wiped from existence," he informs me. "Plus, Hayes would've never let you go on your own."

While he wasn't wrong about the second part, the first part surprised me. Matt hadn't seemed to feel the loss of anyone lately. I know he wasn't close to Jordan and Dad was lost so long ago now, yet he still seemed more distant than he had before. It was almost like he carried his emotions inside more, or felt them less. I wasn't sure. But at least he cared enough to help me do this.

We walked deeper into the hall and found the hall for the Super Bowls. This was where my dad would've shined. He loved the '85 Bears, Superbowl shuffle and all. I hung back and took all of the information in, well all that I could read through the graffiti, while Matt walked up and looked for the 2000 Ravens. It was kinda sad to see this place destroyed this way. Why take out your aggression on a place that was just here to maintain the memory of a time that was good for us? Yet as I've said before, people are dumb. They don't make sense most of the time. Like shooting at people who have helped you in a cafeteria. No! Nope, not thinking about that day right now.

We move on and find the doors to the outside. I know they have a full-size football field on the grounds somewhere. I want to see if any of it is still intact. It'll be nice if we can find a football and throw the pigskin around for a few minutes, like old times. It would be really good to honor my dad.

As we are walking down the hallway I remember back to the Bears vs Eagles game again.

We are leaving the game and walking back to our hotel. Soldier Field is odd to me because it doesn't have any parking lots connected to it. It is part of the city. Eagles fans are having fun, but being pretty decent even with the win. Just as I think this one young guy decides to be a jerk.

"Walter Payton ain't shit!" he yells near us.

"Excuse me, boy?" my dad says to him as he angles towards him.

"You heard me! E-A-G-L-E-S Eagles! PAYTON AIN'T SHIT!!" he yells again.

"OK, boy. Enough of that shit. Yeah, you won. Great for you. But respect the men that came before." my dad replies.

"Whatever that's why you ain't got a Superbowl."

"Oh, you're one of those dumb-asses huh? Don't remember anything before your dumbass was born. How about you shut the hell up before I shut you up and send your dumbass back to Philly eating through a straw?" My dad's mad now. He can't stand Philly fans typically anyway, let alone when they're dumb as hell.

Luckily, at this point, a few other Eagles fans break in and move the guy along. "I hope I'm not sharing a plane with this guy," another fan says as he separates the two.

My dad calms down and we finish the walk in peace.

"Hey Matt, did you see Walter Payton's bust in there? I'm not sure I saw it," I ask suddenly.

"I did. Why?" he asks as he looks back at me.

"No reason. I was just remembering the game I went to with Dad. He loved that man and what he did for the franchise. I just wanted to see it. I'm going to run back in. Go find the field and a football would ya?" I turn and run back in. I know Matt saw it but I want to remember it for Dad.

I run back in and hit a decent stride as I go back to the Hall of Fame gallery. I remember seeing the busts but it was thinking about other things at the time. I skid to a stop as I hit the hall. I catch my breath a bit, I am getting out of shape. I look through, it takes me a bit to find him. As I do I remember back to that same trip.

My dad and I are standing outside in 15-degree weather looking at a statue of "Sweetness". The statue is big and it looks to me like he is high-stepping into the endzone. My dad isn't sure that's what he's doing but agrees that would be a great image to see. He laughs at it again and just looks at it, maybe remembering a game he watched with him. He would've been young when Payton played, but maybe he saw a game or two.

As we walk back to the hotel he talks my ear off about the greatest players in Bears history. He brings up a lot of different players but always comes back to Walter. I guess there is a good reason that there is a Walter Payton Man of the Year award, I thought. He was a good man on and off the field.

I stop my thoughts from meandering and walk back to the fields to find Matthew. We don't have a lot of time left before we need to get back on the road. As I leave the building and walk out towards the field, the sight surprises me. I am expecting the field to be an utter overgrown mess, but it looks like it was mowed a month or so ago. That's odd. Matt is already on the field, punting the ball in my direction. It doesn't go far, and it's way to my left. I run to get it and feel the reason for my confusion as I hit the field. The field is turf. No real grass to grow and cover the field.

I lean over to pick the ball up and hear Matt running at me. I grab and duck at the same time. Matt rushes past where I just was. Since he misses I tuck the ball and start to run to the other endzone. I know Matt will catch me before I get there but I try it anyway. I get to the 50-yard line, at least where I think it should be, there's no paint left, before Matt catches me. I hear his heavy footsteps before he gets to me so I turn to my right quickly. Matt saw this move and launches himself to intercept. My foot slips and we go down in a heap.

I'm lying under Matt as we land but still start laughing hysterically. I have not released this much tension in a long time. Andromeda would love to run around with us like this. Matt laughs a bit and gets up then offers his hand to help me up. I go to take it but pull him back to the ground instead. He fakes a punch as he lands on the turf next to me. We both roll to our backs and lay there catching our breath. After a few seconds, we both just lay there occupied with our thoughts. Before I fall into a funk I get up and offer my hand to my brother.

He takes the offered hand and gets up. I walk over, pick the ball up and throw it to him. We lose a few minutes tossing the ragged, busted pigskin back and forth. We don't talk but I don't think either of us is doing much thinking either. Just enjoying the time. Matt runs a short route and I throw the ball deep to him. The ball doesn't go very far, partly because of the ball. He comes back and makes the catch, but something catches his eye.

"Hey, come check this out," he yells to me as he tucks the ball and walks off the field.

I guess the catch is over. I run to catch up to him as he enters a building attached to the field. When we walk into the building I gasp because of the staleness of the air. I cough to try and get my lungs working again, while also letting my eyes adjust to the darkness. It takes a bit for both, but eventually, I can see Matt across the way looking at something. I slowly make my way to him to see what caught his eye. As I get close I can see that he is messing with some type of cart.

What good is an electric golf cart going to do?

When I get close though I see it isn't a golf cart it is a four-wheel-drive side-by-side UTV. That might be useful if it works. As I think that Matt hits the starter and the engine almost fires up before it cuts out and the battery clicks. Dang, almost had it too. Matt looks at me then walks over and opens the garage door.

"If we push this onto the field we may be able to push start it. If we can the battery will charge," he tells me.

I'm not sure it'll work and we only have a little bit of gas with us for the bike. I swear Matt knows what I'm thinking because just as I think this he lifts a gas can and shakes it. It's full. He smells it, it seems ok so he fills the tank with it. After he fills the tank he throws the tank and two others in the back of the UTV. He grabs one side, I grab the other and we push it onto the field. As we get onto the field he tells me to get by the driver's door and put the key into the on position. Once we get it moving I am to jump in and kick it into gear as he continues to push. I'm still skeptical but I follow his lead. He has found two bikes in this broken world and gotten them to work.

We push the UTV until I'm at a good jog. Matt tells me to jump in, I do and throw it in gear. The engine coughs then catches. I punch the gas and take off quickly across the field. I turn and slow down, making sure to keep a little bit of gas down to keep it at a higher idle.

Yes, Dad taught me how to work on engines too.

I drive back to Matt and he's smiling. Well, we took this trip for a break and found something useful. Not bad all in all. Matt gets in and we drive around until we find a gate to let us out of the field area. Once there I drive back around to the front and get Matt back to his bike.

"I'm not sure how fast this thing will go, but get it as fast as you can and I'll match your speed. No point in getting separated now," he tells me.

I just nod over the engine noise and wait for him to get his bike started and back on the road. Once he does we head back down George Halas Drive and back to the team. Matt takes off and I get the UTV up to speed. It's moving over 40 mph so it'll keep up on the roads. We settle in and Matt leads us back to the unit. Time to get back to work. I did see though that Matt kept the football with him. Maybe we can use that again soon.

Spill

Matt and I hit Cambridge, Ohio a little over an hour after we left the HOF. Matt takes a second to look for the signs. We have started leaving two sets in different places to make sure the signs aren't being changed, we can't go through that again. It looks like they continued on I-70, as expected. Matt gets back on and leads the way. An hour later we come up on new signs telling us to turn south. Matt is confused and looks for the second sign, it confirms the route change. If we're heading to South Dakota, then south isn't the way we need to go, but something must have changed that we aren't aware of.

"Maybe they are avoiding the city of Columbus. If we keep pace we should catch up to them soon. They can tell us then," Matt must have known what I was thinking.

We continue and make our way southwest for a while. We finally come up on the rear guard. They take the time to talk to us for a bit, then we offer them a ride. If we are the last of our group there isn't any reason these guys walk the rest of the way. They hadn't seen anything following the group since we left Pittsburgh. The guys are tired so we give them a break.

We catch up to the group as they are setting up camp inside a metro park just west of Columbus. The trees are huge and everything is covered in pollen. I'd seen "green weeks" in Delaware where the pines pollinate all over everything, but this place is ridiculous. You couldn't step without seeing pollen puff up. I look at Matt and wonder if this is a good place for us to stay or not. As I look at him it looks like he has a headache. He's squinting and tries to clear his head.

"What's up?" I ask him.

"Nothing, the spores are everywhere here with the pollen. It's making it hard for me to see through the blue haze. I'm going to go out past this and catch up to everyone else. I'll send Josh or someone back with Andromeda if you like. Go find Mom and tell her about our day. I just can't stay here," he tells me as he gets back on the bike and slowly drives it out of the park.

I shake my head and wonder how the pollen is going to affect my allergies. Nothing to worry about for now, I look around and find Susie among a group of people. I walk over and ask her if she has seen my mom. She hadn't but pointed me towards the transports. Mom hadn't been walking well the last few days so she has been riding even more. I knew this trip wasn't going to be good for her. I guess it was starting to show. If she wanted to stop, would I want to now? That's all I wanted before... well you know.

Not going into that again here either.

I walk up at the same time that Mom is working her way out of the back of the transport. Dr. Testerman jumps down in front of her and helps her down. Not digging that.

"Hey, Mom," I call out. Testerman jumps a bit and turns around like a guilty man. I don't care if she dates, but not this weirdo.

"Hey honey, what are you doing here?" She asks with no guilt on her side.

I help her the rest of the way down and we walk away a bit as I tell her about our trip to Canton. She smiles a lot and cries a bit too. She knows how much Dad would've loved that trip even with the broken glass and graffiti. We sit down and talk for a bit, I can tell Mom is tired so I excuse myself and try to find Susie again.

Finding her isn't hard, she's near the food. As we both sit down and eat I ask her about everything that's been going on around camp. She tells me that everything has been pretty normal and smooth. Just as she says this we hear a loud bang and a huge commotion near the transports. We look at each other for a second, then grab our guns and head to the noise. When we get to the scene we find that it isn't anything dire. It was just a canister being knocked over as it was unloaded.

"Not just a canister," Susie tells me. "That's one of the canisters for the chemical we are making on the trip. That was probably all we have made this whole time. What the hell happened?"

One of the scientists came over and told us that someone sneezed from all of the pollen as they were unloading and it slipped. Not all of it spilled out, but it would take a while to replace. The chemical soaked into the ground quickly, so at least it wasn't going to be muddy. Well, the scientists screwed it up, they'll have to fix it. Afterward, the night wound down and we settled in by the fire. Since I'm forward watch I got to spend another night without a watch, which will be good. About the time I decide to get ready to go to sleep, Josh and Andromeda come running up.

"Pickle!" I yell to him and he laughs at my joke.

He smiles and walks up to hug me. Andromeda waits patiently for her love, which I give her quickly. Josh sits down next to me and tells me how things are going with the squad. Luckily, everything went smoothly while Matt and I were gone. I tell him about the new UTV.

"Can I ride with you? I like those things," he tells me. I nod and tell him that Hayes would have to approve it.

"I'll ask though," I tell him.

We talk about nonsense for a bit. He seems to be good at that. I guess when you spend that much time with only the undead to keep you company, you have to find ways to entertain yourself. He keeps droning on as Andromeda sidles up to my side and starts to snore gently. I guess she doesn't care what he has to say. Josh and I talk for a bit longer before he and I both start to yawn. We both roll over and sleep the night away like the young people we are.

When I wake up in the morning the camp is in turmoil. There seems to be a lot of confusion. I wake Josh up but he seems sluggish. I check his forehead and find that he has a slight fever. Before the Fall that wouldn't be too much trouble, but now it could be bad. I tell him to drink some water while I find the medic. It doesn't take me long to find a medic and send him Josh's way. Then I go to check on Mom.

Mom is awake and seems to be ok. She tells me that she has been feeling a little weak lately but nothing that a lot of traveling hadn't done to her before. I smile and nod but I'm still a little concerned. No one knows how these spores affect the body. It's been a little over two years now, how is this all affecting us? Mom and I talk for a little bit and I get us some food. After we both eat I head back to check on Josh with another plate for him. Before I get there I walk to the transport. It seems like this is where everyone had congregated.

I walk up and ask a young scientist what the concern was. He tells me that the ground around the transport, where the chemical spilled last night, was completely dead this morning. I work my way closer and see that he isn't exaggerating. Not only is it all dead, but the ground is just dirt. There isn't any grass or weeds left. The trees on the edges of the small clearing were starting to die too. The needles along the inner side of the pines are already brown and falling out of the tree. If this chemical killed the plants like this in the liquid form, what would it do once it's in the air?

"Hey, is this supposed to happen?" I ask as Testerman passes me.

He just shrugs me off and pulls a few scientists aside to talk about everything. After their little huddle, they start taking soil and bark samples from the area. Guess it isn't supposed to happen. I shake my head and make my way over to Josh. He's looking a little better but wants to get on the road away from the camp.

"I started feeling bad as soon as I got to camp last night. I think something here is making me sick," he explains. "I haven't been sick at all since the doctor found me. Hayes and Smith say it has something to do with the spores and being Unseen. They say it helps."

"If that's the case it probably is environmental. Let's get you back to the squad."

I whistle for Andromeda and we load into the UTV. Andromeda isn't too sure at first but gets comfy in the passenger seat. She makes Josh sit in the back. Typical. As we meet back up with the squad, Josh tells me he's starting to feel a bit better. We pull up and everyone gawks at my new ride.

"Daaang, Washington said you got a new ride, but that thing is pretty sweet," Oakley says.

"How was it driving out here? Will it handle ok?" Smith asks as he looks it over. He is always looking at the practical side of things.

"Yeah, it's been great so far. Even seems to be doing good on fuel. It'll be a good addition I think," I tell everyone.

I look around for Matt but don't see him. Hayes sees me looking and points to the cab of the truck. I tilt my head to the side with a quizzical look as she just shrugs. I walk over to the truck and peek in the window. Matt looks like he's either sick or hungover.

"Have some drink in you last night?" I ask him as I open the door.

"NNNNNNNN, No. I have felt like crap since I came back from camp. Tried to sleep it off but I'm still off," he tells me through half-closed eyes.

I close the door a bit and go talk to Hayes. I told her about Matt last night and how Josh felt this morning. She nods and thinks about it.

"Do you think it was that chemical?" she asks finally.

"It was a major spill. It killed all of the plant life in a huge area. Even started to kill a few trees. That stuff is potent," I tell her. I fill her in a bit more on how everything looked when I left.

"Haven't others told us that the Unseen can't be around that chemical at all? That's why Ragdsill's people are doing rear guard now and the normals are riding with the transports?"

"Yeah, we heard something about that in Pittsburgh. If that's the case Sarge, what's it going to do to all of you when they release that chemical into the air?" The question hangs in the air. Smith, Reid, Oakley and Hayes all looked at each other. No one knew what would happen to people who were half-Deaders when we released a toxin to kill the enemy. That was a bridge that would have to be crossed if we ever got there.

Sickness

A couple of days later, Matt's back on his feet. Whatever he was dealing with has passed. He has been arguing with Oakley all morning to get his bike back. She has been riding it since he went down and she doesn't want to go back to the old way. Eventually, they agree to take shifts with the bike. I laugh because I know Matt's compromises never work once he gets what he wants. If she gives him the bike he won't put himself in a position to give it back up. I keep my mouth shut though, she can learn the hard way.

As everyone else is getting ready to head out today, I am packing up to head back to the transports. We found a farm that had its own gas tanks yesterday and I need to get some fuel back to the transports. The others hate going back to the camp now, so it typically falls on me to go. It's fine because I can check on Mom too. Josh is riding back with me today. He doesn't like to go, but he will when I need him to.

Today's trip will be easy. It took us so long to clear the farm and get the gas out of the tank, the transports aren't far behind. In reality, I could probably just sit here and fill out my journal for a few hours and they'll catch up to me. But Hayes frowns upon that. *Party Pooper.* So I load up and hit the road. I think I'll run back to the rear guard today and check on them too. I like to keep us informed on what they're seeing too. Mainly to see if there is something we're missing that could cause them problems. So far it's all been good. How long will that last?

As I reach the transports I see that they haven't even broken camp today. I stop by and look for Testerman, but he isn't with the scientists. I find Mom, but she doesn't know why they stayed put today. She figured it had something to do with making the chemical. With all that they lost, they had been starting later and stopping sooner each day to try and make up for the spill.

With no further information, I look around for Susie. She always has her nose in everyone's business. She'll know the hold-up. I guess Hayes was right though, if I had stayed put I would've never seen the transports today. I send Andromeda off to find Susie as I get a small bite to eat from the food tent. A few minutes later, Andromeda and Susie join me. It's nice having a messenger dog. Susie and I forgo the pleasantries and get down to business.

"Why aren't you all moving?" I ask with a full mouth. Mom would be so proud.

"Testerman and a few other scientists are too sick to move. The medics are checking them but they don't know what's wrong with them. They have fevers and they seem out of it. I even heard that one of them growled at a medic to get him to go away," She tells me while stuffing her face too.

"Wow, sounds real mature. Did they get bit by a rabid squirrel or something?"

"No, but it may have something to do with the chemical spill. Since then a bunch of people have been complaining about feeling sick."

"Yeah, Matt was down for a few days with something after that. But he's Unseen. The spores run his mind and body more than anyone else," I explain as I finish my plate.

"Yeah, but as Doc told us before. We all have them running in our bloodstreams. If something is affecting the spores it can affect our immune systems and bodies too. Especially the older people, or the ones that were in clean rooms for the past two years, like the scientists," Susie weirdly raises her eyebrows. I'm not sure why. Maybe she thinks that is the reason why only the scientists are feeling it. Hard to say. Susie and I have been kinder to each other since the attack, but we still aren't what I would call friends so I'm not sure about her weird quirks.

I leave Susie and head back to the UTV. Josh is sitting in the passenger seat flicking the blade of a hatchet. It's an odd habit I've seen him do a couple of times. I have him unload the gas and I take it to the transports. No sense in sending him towards the chemical spill at all. After that's done, we load up and I head back to check on the rear guard again. They don't have much interaction with the main part of the caravan, and we have no communication devices that work any longer. That means someone needs to check on them regularly. I stop an hour later and wait to see if they have gotten this far. They shouldn't be far today since the transports haven't moved. I need to let them know that they may not move for a couple of days, or at least until Testerman is feeling better.

A little while later Sgt. Ragsdill walks out of the shadows. The man is creepy and silent when he wants to be. Since he left our squad to take over the new one he is definitely a different person. It feels to me that he likes being in charge, so it's probably a good move. I tell him about the caravan and everything going on. He nods and tells me that they will stay close, but won't enter the camp.

"My guys won't go near that chemical. I'm almost glad we're making it on the road so I don't have to be near it. It would be insufferable if we were in the basement with them making it," he tells me.

"Anything happening behind us?" I ask.

"Maybe. We aren't completely sure yet, but it seems like someone has been following us for a little while. They don't get close, but when we leave a trailer they usually report seeing something at night. I have two guys back right now, about a day behind us. They were instructed to hide for a full day, then trail us to see if they could come up behind them. I haven't heard anything back yet. The transports not moving will mess that up a bit too. I'll send word if we need help," he tells me.

I nod and say my goodbyes and get back on the road. I go around the camp to make better time back to the squad. No reason to stop back there today. I need to catch up and tell Hayes that the transports are stopping so we don't get too far ahead. It takes an hour or so before I catch up to the rest of the squad. It makes it a little easier that the world is so quiet. Weirdly, you can hear things for miles, especially Matt's bike. Once I get close I just listen for that and I can usually find them pretty quickly afterwards.

I tell Hayes and the rest of the squad about my day and the information that I found. Hayes isn't happy about staying put. She borrows my UTV and heads off, back to the transports. While she's gone the rest of us kick up our feet and start to build a fire for the night. We keep our guard up but relax for a bit. We haven't seen anything in a while. It's been pretty quiet all around. I would've loved to see this area before the Fall. But in reality back then I would've been bored or completely lost in my phone and wouldn't have seen any of it.

Luckily, we hear the UTV heading back before Hayes can see us slacking off. We all jump up and act busy as she comes around the last bend in the road. When she comes to a stop she looks at us like a mom. She knows we've been slacking it seems.

How do moms always know?

"The transports are hitting the road tomorrow morning. I don't care if Testerman's sick, and neither does Silver once he heard we may have people following us. We can't stay set for an ambush," She explains. "So get back to slacking off for tonight, but we will be setting a double guard tonight. No drinking."

"Yeah, like we have anything like that Sarge," Reid says.

"You saying that makes me believe you do, but I'm not going to ask. Just don't bring it out tonight," Hayes orders.

Knowing this team they probably do have something. Most likely found on one of our expeditions. I'm thinking about this when Josh walks off into the woods. Andromeda whines like she wants to follow him so I get up and do the same. A little way into the woods I watch Josh sit down on a fallen log and practice throwing his hatchets into a nearby tree. He throws both, hits his target then gets up and gets them. He then sits and repeats the act. He's pretty good.

I don't want to scare him so I wait for him to get up to get his hatchets before I call out. "Hey Josh, whatcha doing?"

I see him jump a little but he tries not to show it. "Just practicing."

"You know we could do that all together. Probably get a game going with it," I suggest as I approach him. I sit down on the log with Andromeda next to my feet.

"I just need a break from everyone I think. I'm not used to people anymore and I don't know how to act. That's why I talk so much. I'm trying to fit in."

"Ha! None of us fit in, bud. That's why we're out here and not back at camp. We all like being on our own. Did you know Andromeda and I spent a little over a year by ourselves?" he shakes his head and sits back down next to me. "Well, let me tell you my story."

I tell him everything. It takes a while, but in the end, he seems to feel a bit more comfortable. Maybe he felt odd living with the Deaders for so long. I think it was better than living in fear of them for just as long. We then get up and rejoin everyone for dinner. No one asks any questions as we return. They just nod and offer us our portion of the food they made. That's why we are all good. We have all been through it over the last couple of years. We know people need time alone.

The next morning we get ready to go. Hayes sends me back again, this time without Josh or Andromeda to make sure the transports are getting moving as they said they would. Sometimes I hate being the only non-Unseen. I think they use it to send me the crap details. Or is it because I'm the newest? I suck it up though and head back to camp. As I get there I can tell that something is wrong. The camp is breaking down to get moving, but there is something in the air.

As I pull up my mom walks out to meet me. I see that she has tears in her eyes. I wait for her to get her voice, in complete suspense.

"We had two people die in camp last night," she tells me.

"Was there an attack?" As I say it I know I'm wrong because the air would feel different than this. It is more mourning, less anger.

"No, They died from the sickness. Now everyone is worried that it's some kind of flu or something."

"Was it Testerman?" I had to ask.

"No, he's ok for now. He's still sick. It was Steven Nilroy, a scientist from the hospital, and George White, a mechanic from there too," she tells me.

"So both from the hospital, but I didn't hear about a mechanic being sick yesterday."

"No one knew that he was. They went to check on him this morning and he was dead, luckily he hadn't turned yet. No one is sure what caused his death. The lab guys are running a few tests to see what they can find out."

I nod and look around. "If he hadn't been found when he was, we could have lost a lot of good people. Have you thought about making sure that there is some kind of buddy system?" I ask.

"Until we figure out what is causing these deaths we're being extra careful. We're burning the bodies today. Once that is done we are going to get on the road. We're sending the walkers forward as soon as the pyre starts, then the transports will follow," Silver scares me as he suddenly appears out of nowhere.

"Won't that alert the people following us, if there are people following us?" I try to recover quickly so he doesn't notice.

"It's a risk we need to take. If there is a disease that these bodies are carrying, we need to get rid of it. Plus we can't just leave the bodies, it's not right. We don't have time to dig proper graves." Silver explains. He's right, but I don't like it. I know he has been out in the field working with the squads, but I've lived out here. I had to make sure no one followed me home where I was vulnerable. Silver never had to worry about that, I am worried that's affecting his decisions.

On the other hand, if they can't figure out what is causing the illnesses, we could have a mass panic on our hands. I already see a couple of people wearing masks around their faces. This could get bad. Silver is just as concerned as I am with it all. He wants me to stress to Hayes that this is a volatile situation and we need to keep close. It may be a good idea to find somewhere to hole up for a while out of the wilderness. The timetable is tight, but we've made decent time so far, we could set aside a day or two to get this under control. I tell him I'll pass the information along as I leave and head back to the squad.

Air Base

I reach the squad later in the day. I tell everyone about the happenings in camp and what Silver asks of us. Reid takes out a paper map, I wasn't sure we still had those, to look at the route. I figured we weren't just guessing our way across the country, but I hadn't seen anyone use a map. I guess I'm not too smart to not figure that out quicker. As we all read the map and figure out the best way, Smith points to Ft. Wayne, IN.

In a day we should be coming up to Fort Wayne, IN, home of Baer Field. This is a military base that housed fighter jets of some sort, according to Reid. The place was pretty secure, due to the nature of the airplanes there. I'm skeptical because Dover Air Force base was pretty secure too, look what happened to us there. Sgt. Hayes thinks it'll be a good place to check for supplies and maybe get a few new weapons. She wants Matt and I to run ahead to check it out before the rest get there. If it isn't any good we have to bypass it and head in a different direction.

Andromeda, Matt and I get loaded up with water and a few fuel tanks. The UTV gets pretty decent gas mileage,he trips back to camp over the last few days have shown me how good it is, but we need to make sure we have enough. We may not find any between here and there. I'm not sure how long we can keep the bike, UTV, truck, suburban and transports running. It would've only been worse if the Humvee was still with us too. Gas is getting scarce. The farther west we go the more spread out the towns get. It's getting harder to find what we need.

Once we are good to go Hayes tells us the general area to meet back with them in tomorrow afternoon. It'll take us all day just to get to the base so we will be on our own tonight. Andromeda climbs up in her seat as Josh saunters over carrying his ever-present hatchets. He has a backpack over his shoulder too.

"What's up Pickle boy?" I ask him as he walks over to my UTV.

"Going with," he says. Short, sweet and to the point.

I look over at Hayes and she just shrugs. "He's not old enough to be in the military. He listens to us well enough, but he told us he's going with you so I guess that's that. I'm not a mom, definitely not his mom, so there you go. As long as he doesn't do anything to get us hurt I don't care where he goes." She turns around and tells Oakley and Reid to get the stuff ready to go.

Well, I guess Josh is joining us on our adventure. He loads up and we hit the road. Matt has gotten used to the speed that the UTV can handle so he keeps pace pretty well. The trip is pretty mellow. Josh and I talk about a few things, practically yelling over the wind, while Andromeda sleeps in the back. I swear that dog can sleep anywhere at any time. As the day drags on, Josh and I run out of interesting topics to talk about so we just sit quietly as the miles pass us by. It takes us about five hours in all to get just south of Fort Wayne, IN.

As we approach the base it looks like it is in worse condition than Dover. The fences are torn down or missing, the buildings are mostly burnt husks. There appears to be one building that is still pretty much in good condition though. It's a large building, maybe a hangar of some sort? I look at Matt as we pull up to the building. He shuts the bike off and tells me to do the same.

"This place has had it rough," He observes as he gets off the bike and readies his rifle.

"Do we want to waste our time here, or do we want to go back and tell the others that this is a bust?" I ask as I follow Matt's example. Josh gets out and lets Andromeda out too. He doesn't have a rifle so he pulls out his hatchets and rubs his thumb over the edge again. A dangerous habit he has. I'll have to ask him about it sometime.

"Let's check this out. If this is clear we can get the transports and everyone inside, then secure the perimeter. It may work out perfectly, in all honesty. With the other buildings being burnt down it'll give the people following us nowhere to hide," Matt explains.

I guess he's right, I just don't have a good feeling about all of this. Why has just the air base been burnt down? Seems odd to me. I look at Andromeda to see if she has any of the same concerns as me. I know she doesn't care about the other buildings, but she may sense something that we aren't. She is sitting next to Josh as he pets her head. She seems calm enough, I guess that's enough for me.

We split up and walked around each side of the building. I send Josh with Matt since I have Andromeda. Matt rolls his eyes but allows Josh to follow him. As I watch Matt and Josh disappear around the far corner, I motion to Andromeda and we work our way along our side. There isn't much to see. The building is just metal, with no windows or doors. I look for any holes in the metal that could allow anyone inside, but I don't find any. I relax a bit as I turn the last corner. As I do Andromeda growls and something jumps out and grabs ahold of me around the shoulders. Whatever has me is taller and stronger than me. I freak out and struggle to get away.

In the second it takes for all of this to happen, I look at Andromeda and wonder why she isn't attacking the Deader. Suddenly, it dawns on me when I hear Matt laughing in my ear. It's Matt who's grabbed me as a joke I guess.

Not very funny.

As he lets me go I kick him in the shin. Hard. Josh's laughing too. I look his way and shoot him daggers with my eyes. He decides to hide his laugh and turns around. Now that my heart rate slows down, I assume that they didn't find anything either.

"So do we just open the big door and head in?" I ask the jerk and his little buddy.

"We saw a man door on our side. It's locked but I think I can kick it in," Matt says as he turns around, still laughing, to go back to the door. I'm happy to see that he is limping just a bit.

Good.

We line up at the door. Matt is in front of it, ready to kick it in, while Josh and I are on the catch side ready to go in hard. Hayes has had the team work with me on entries in this type of situation. Typically, we would have the whole squad, but we have to work with what we have. Matt nods, I look at Andromeda to see if she's calm. She seems intent, but not agitated. We should be good so I nod back to Matt. He steps back and puts his whole weight into his kick. As his foot connects with the door, it buckles a bit but holds. Matt falls over holding his knee. I can't help but let a small laugh slip out. Josh snickers behind me too.

"Ouch! How did that door not give?" Matt yells as he gets back to his feet and limps around a little.

The door must be braced on the inside. That's not a good sign. If someone is in there they know we're here now. I look at Matt and ask what the next plan is.

"Well if the doors are that strong, it'll be a good way to protect the transports. We need to get inside somehow," he says as he looks around for another way in.

"The only other way in I see is through the large hangar bay door. Did we check and see if it's unlocked? If people left they had to leave someway," I suggest.

Matt nods and we work our way back to the big door. I take the time to look at it more this time and see that the door is latched from the outside and locked with a padlock. The padlock looks like a heavy-duty one. I'm not sure how we're going to get it off. Just as I have this thought, Matt tells us all to move around the side and he raises his rifle to shoot the padlock. I'm not sure that'll work, but we move and let him try. Three shots later all I hear is Matt cussing. Josh and I walk around the side and see that the lock is still holding tight.

"I thought that would work," he says.

"Yeah. But...It didn't. A good thing is that I haven't heard any noise inside, No one has come out of the braced door and Andromeda is still calm. So we should be good, even with you trying to bring the whole town down on us. How about we try something the smart way? You wanna try that?" I ask.

Ok, yeah I was kind of a jerk, but he deserved it for scaring the hell out of me.

Matt concedes and I pull the UTV over to the door, hook the winch to the door lock and put it in reverse. I let the tension pull tight then goose the gas a bit. The lock comes flying off, along with the clasp and part of the door. Well, we aren't locking that closed again. I have to duck quickly as the lock whizzes by my head and into the frame of the UTV. Matt walks over shaking his head.

"The smart way huh?"

"Well at least I got it open," I retort as I stick out my tongue and get out of the UTV.

Josh doesn't seem sure how to act. I'm sure he was the same way with his brother, but that was a while ago and they were both younger. He also may be wondering why two adults are acting like children. I guess siblings just bring that out in each other. With that out of the way, Matt walks over to the door and sets us behind him. He counts down in a whisper then throws the door wide. He goes to the right, I go left and Josh hangs at the door with Andromeda. The doors are huge, so they let in a lot of light, but the building is big and there are still a lot of dark areas.

As our eyes adjust and the dust settles, Andromeda walks in the door and starts to lose her mind. She is barking and looking in every direction. I flip on the light on the barrel of my rifle. As I sweep across the open space I see bodies everywhere. All of the bodies seem to be dead, not undead but I can't be sure from this far away. If they've been locked up in here for a long time, they will be very weak.

"Well, now we know why the other door was braced. Someone wanted this building to stay closed. There isn't even a cool plane in here," Josh says. "If these bodies have been here long enough for the smell to disappear, they will barely be able to move. I've seen it before."

Matt walks in, and waves for Josh to join him and for me to stay put at the door. I start to say something but quickly remember that these things won't see him or Josh, they should be safe. Josh pulls out both hatchets again and rubs his thumbs across the blades.

What is with that?

The two work their way through the bodies in the open area. None of them seem to move at all. As they reach an office at the far end of the building I hear Matt cuss. The door seems to have been left open. As they walk out three other people follow after him. Matt's hands aren't up so it probably isn't living people. Andromeda growls low in her throat, yup, Deaders. Matt grabs Josh as they slowly back away from the others. Then another four walked out of another room, I thought that was just a closet.

The two groups mesh together and start walking towards the light. They are slow, they haven't fed in a while. But if these are here and the other bodies are dead, were all of these people left in here while they were still alive? Did some die and turn, then kill the others? What happened here? The answers will probably never come, but I like to ask them anyway. As I think about the scenarios, Andromeda's growl becomes a lot louder. Crap, the Deaders aren't walking towards the light, they are walking towards me. I realize this too late. I start to back up and bang into the door behind me. I try to get my bearings when two of the bodies fall, one quickly after the other.

Josh comes up and pulls the two hatchets from the necks of the two Deaders on the ground. He quickly pulls back and takes out two more with two swift swings. He's a short kid, but he can still reach the back of these things' necks. With every swing of his hatchets, another Deader falls. Long before any of them could reach me, Josh takes them all down. As he drops the last one he reaches down, grabs the Deaders shirt and wipes his blades clean on it. The Deader,(*is it dead Deader? Or just dead?)* rolls to the side and I see its white eyes as the glow slowly dies behind them.

Josh looks at me, I nod and start to ask him if he is ok. He looks different for a second, then the look fades and he smiles at me again. "I don't think this is a good place to bring the transports," is all he says.

"I agree Josh, I agree. Matt are you ready to get back on the road and break the news to Hayes?"

Matt doesn't answer. He just nods as he watches Josh walk out of the door and get into the UTV. As Josh gets in the back and starts petting Andromeda in the front seat, Matt looks at me with a quizzical look. He doesn't know what to think about what just happened either. I just shrug my shoulders and walk over to join Josh. This kid's full of surprises.

Separate

We load up quickly to get back to the squad. We haven't been here long, if we ride through the night we can make it to them before they get too far. We need a new plan because this one was just chopped all to hell. Matt has his, I'm thinking, look on his face possibly trying to figure out where to go to help the transports. About twenty minutes later Matt slows and pulls off the road. He reaches into his backpack and pulls out a paper map.

Am I the only one without one of these?

He tells me to hold the flashlight and traces out a route on the map. I may be wrong but it looks like he is tracing it away from our meeting with Hayes. He must find what he's looking for because he taps his finger near the top of Indiana.

"Westville. There is a large prison there. We could hole up there. It's only a couple hour ride from here," he finally says.

"It's in the wrong direction though. We need to tell Hayes about Ft. Wayne," I remind him. Josh has gotten out of the UTV and joined us. Andromeda doesn't let the bickering of humans bother her nap.

"You need to tell her. We can go our separate ways now that we each have transportation. Besides I can travel faster without slowing down for you to keep up. I'll go check it out then head back to meet you..."

"No way. You're not going alone," I tell him. I am dumbfounded by him even thinking about this.

"Well, Private. I can and I will. I've done several missions on my own and I traveled the whole eastern seaboard by myself before the Fall. I can handle it. *Little Sister.*" The last bit seemed like a bad slur to me.

I look to Josh for some help but he is keeping out of it. Of course, he is. I know I've lost the argument and he's going to do what he wants. He has always been stubborn. But he's also right that he can travel faster without me and maybe get back faster too.

"Well, ok. Leave your marks every mile or so. Don't go in. Just check it out and report back," I tell him.

"Yes ma'am," He starts to say jokingly.

"Or I'll tell Mom," I finish. He just shakes his head and gets back on the bike. He has memorized the first part of the route I assume so he is ready to go.

"Tell Hayes everything," He says as he starts the bike.

"Oh, I will. Including the part about this being all your plan and all your fault if it goes wrong."

I know he didn't hear all of what I said because he revved the engine louder as I talk. I just end by sticking my tongue out at him as he drives off.

After Matt pulls off, Josh looks at me for a second then gets back in the UTV. I guess it's time to go. I get in and head the rest of the way back to our rendezvous. Josh is quiet the entire ride back. He spends most of the time leaning back and petting Andromeda. I think he's capable of killing, but he's still young and it bothers him. He might need to talk to someone at some point.

I wonder if there are any psychologists among the doctors we have?

We reach the place where the squad was supposed to meet us, but we're early. I can wait here for them or try to find them along the road. It's probably safer to wait and I can talk to Josh, but I decide to continue and try to find the truck. Even if they are walking the perimeter the truck shouldn't be too far off the road. If I get too far I'll just head back. Hayes needs to know what we found, the sooner the better.

Thirty minutes later I came across the truck. It's pulled off the side of the road. I park the UTV next to it and keep the lights on. I want them to know it's me if they come back. I don't have to wait long, the noise of the UTV probably drew them back.

"Where's the other Washington?" Hayes yells from behind me. I didn't hear her coming and it scared the crap out of me.

Yes, I did jump a bit.

"He went off on his way Sarge," I try to simply explain. She doesn't like the simple explanation so I go deeper. I told her about the entire trip and where Matt was heading.

Hayes doesn't say anything at first. She assaults Reid as he shows up and takes the map out of his pocket. She doesn't seem happy with Matt's brilliant idea. I knew she wouldn't be. Reid holds the flashlight for her as she maps out Matt's supposed path. I see her nod her head a few times, obviously talking to herself. After a few minutes, she folds the map up and hands it to Reid. She doesn't say anything as she walks over to the UTV. She shoos Josh and Andromeda out and takes off towards the transports with it. Smith is the first to speak.

"I just got back, but what just happened?" he asks.

"Matt," is all I say. He laughs but nods.

"Well, I guess we need to finish up our checks here and head to the next rendezvous point. Hayes will meet us there and tell the transports the plan. Where's Oakley?"

"Here," she yells from the woodline. "I found a house with a ton of supplies. We need the truck. Oh hey, Washington's back. Where's the other one? Also, where did Hayes go?"

"Long story," Reid says. Oakley nods and gets in the truck.

"Load up everyone. We found the mother-load," she yells into the night.

She's always been a strange one. But I like her energy. Five minutes later we are pulling up a long decrepit driveway. It's dark and it feels like we're driving straight into a horror movie scene. Oakley never hesitates and drives straight to the house to park the truck. She quickly gets out and walks to the garage door. The rest of us get out a little slower and follow behind. Andromeda doesn't care what we're doing, she walks off to find a place to pee. Afterward, she wanders around the yard. I watch her for a second to make sure everything's ok, then follow the others. As I enter the garage I can see what Oakley was talking about. The garage is full of cereal, soap, disinfectants, toilet paper, and many, many more things.

"What is all this? Was this a prepper's place?" I ask as I try to take it all in.

"I don't think so. I think I saw a show on these types of people, back when we had shows. They were extreme couponers. They would get all the stuff they didn't need just because buying it in bulk like this made it free." Oakley explains as she starts grabbing things off the shelves.

"I think I remember hearing about that. I never understood how using coupons for things could get you them for free. It was just too much. But didn't they then try to sell the items on Facebook and things like that?" Smith added.

"I don't care," Reid says. "This is triple-ply toilet paper. Have you ever used triple-ply? I haven't, but now that's all I'm using."

Everyone laughs at that. We cut the conversation and got to work loading the stuff into the truck. Luckily one of the items that they stored in the garage was a tarp with tie-downs. That would help us cover the stuff so it didn't blow out of the back of the truck as we drove back. I wish Hayes hadn't gone back to the transports yet, we could use the extra storage space of the UTV to help. All of this stuff is super useful in today's world.

After we loaded up everything we could fit Oakley drove the truck back to the main road. She told us the shortcut that she had used when she found the place. We would all have to walk since the truck was so full. We did manage to get almost everything in it though. We would be set for a lot of things for the rest of the trip. As we hit the main road, Oakley was just pulling up. She told us that she would drive up about another mile and stop for the night. It was getting late and with all of us walking we wouldn't get a whole lot further tonight. There was no way Hayes had been by yet, so she would see us on her way through.

As Oakley started to pull off Reid yelled, "Stop. Stop for a second."

He then ran up to the truck, reached under the tarp, and rifled around for a second. Then he pulled out his hand and held a roll of toilet paper in the air, "Got it, you can go now. Also, you guys go ahead, I have some business to take care of. I'll catch up."

I shake my head and so does Oakley as she drives off. Andromeda wanders over to Reid and sniffs the TP. She doesn't seem to care as she ignores him and walks back to me. Not a big deal to her. She craps wherever and whenever she wants. A couple of minutes later Reid comes running to catch up to us. Since phones aren't a thing anymore it doesn't take men as long to use the bathroom as it used to I guess.

It doesn't take us long to walk the mile and meet up with Oakley, it is a nice pull-off area to park the truck. There is a nice fire going to keep us warm through the night. It's still early September but nights are getting chilly. After a while we all settle down and Reid takes the first watch. He will wait for Hayes to pass through if she even does tonight. The rest of us try to get some rest.

I look over at Josh as he settles in. He takes off his hatchets and sets them under his jacket which he uses as a pillow. He sighs heavily and lays his head down. He seems heavy tonight. I hope he's better tomorrow. I'm sure he knows this already, but he saved my life today. It was gruesome and grisly but it had to be done. The knowing of this doesn't make it any easier but hopefully he can find some solace in it.

I lay down to get some z's, I don't like the fact that Matt is out on his own and Hayes took off without anyone accompanying her. We are all broken up. I was that way for too long. I like being part of something now. I thought it would make me weaker, like it did to people at the Home of the Brave. But this group seems to make each other stronger. To pick up your weaknesses instead of emphasizing them. It's a feeling I don't want to lose.

Death

Hayes finds us later that same night. She doesn't say much, just tells Oakley to take the next watch and then found her bedroll. The next morning we all get up and go about the usual chores. Hayes is ecstatic about Oakley's find. She knew how much it means to our trip to South Dakota. After breakfast's made Hayes sits us all down and tells us the next steps.

"So, Testerman is still very sick. He may not live too much longer. Luckily, most of the scientists know how to make the chemical and how to make it into an aerosol that we'll need for the launch. The bad news is that the rear guard is completely sure that we are being followed. Sgt. Ragsdill's team made contact with them, thinking it was a small group. It wasn't. The team barely got away with their lives. They did lose one soldier. They then recruited another from the group with the transports. Ava, I think you know Susie. She was the one they picked. What do you think?"

"She's good. She knows what she needs to do and she has a mean streak a mile long. She might put Ragsdill in his place a bit," I said. Everyone laughed at the last part.

"He needs it," was parroted around the group.

"We are going to keep the original course to Fort Wayne and past. Hopefully, Washington can find something at that prison. And hopefully, the group isn't riled up enough to come after us sooner. We do have a new plan though. We are splitting up and covering a few new details. Reid, Smith, and I are going back to reinforce the rear guard. They are going to stay closer to the transport, basically right on their tails. Ava, Josh, and Oakley are going to stay out front with the UTV. You will not venture off on your own. You will stay close to the road. We have these supplies. So the only thing you need to look for is gas. We should be able to resupply that ok in Fort Wayne so don't venture too far for it. Everyone stays mobile in the vehicle. Got it?" Hayes ordered.

There were a lot of nods and yeses around the group. We were separating more it seemed.

"When your knuckle-headed brother gets back, Ava, you will let us know back at the transports and we will decide further from there. Right now it's speed to get away from this group. We can't run fast, but the rear guard will be setting some things up to slow them down and maybe get them off our trail. Hopefully, we find somewhere to fortify. An open war out here won't be good. Any questions?"

Hayes asked knowing there wouldn't be any. We all follow her orders quickly and easily. We break down the camp and load up in our prospective vehicles. With quick goodbyes, we head our separate ways. Hopefully, not for the last time. Things are starting to get a bit real. The first part of this trip seemed hard but went pretty easy in all actuality. Now it may not be so easy. I sigh and look at Oakley, Josh, and Andromeda. Now there were four. The others pack their gear and squeeze into the cab of the truck. As they hit the road, Andromeda lets out a small whine. She knows it wasn't good for us to separate like this, but it's what needs to happen. Our job is to protect the transports.

The three of us finish cleaning up the campsite and then load up into the UTV. I know that people used to name their cars with female names, before the Fall. I had been thinking about what to name my new UTV. I know it isn't a car, but I spend a lot of time driving it so it should have a name. I ask Josh and Oakley about it as we drive slowly down the road. Oakley asks serious questions, like where I found it, and if I had any names that were special to me. Josh on the other hand had stupid suggestions. He names a few fruits and vegetables, then names a few Pokemon that he likes. As stupid as his suggestions were though it did help me decide on a name. Evee was one of my favorite Pokemon. It was doglike and the name rhymed with UTV. So Evee the UTV was born.

Well, the name was born anyway.

The rest of the day is a slow slog to Fort Wayne. I had traveled this way before and knew that there wasn't much for us to investigate. We did find a few small areas that we stopped to check, but we found nothing worth talking about. As we got to the outskirts of Fort Wayne we stopped and waited for the transports to catch up. Since the fiasco in Pittsburgh, we didn't want to move on and have a similar incident happen, so Oakley figured we would wait for them and escort them through the area. As we wait Oakley and I talk while Josh vegges out in the back of Evee. As we're talking a thought suddenly comes to me.

"Oakley, what is your first name? I don't think I've ever heard it." I blurted out.

"HA. No, we don't use our first names too often. It's Lyla by the way," she giggled as she told me.

"Yeah, why is the military like that? With my brother and I, it would be easier to use first names, yet you all still call us both Washington. It's kind of annoying really. You know what though. I just had another thought. Josh. What's your last name? I don't think you ever told us." Oakley, Lyla, and I both turn to look at him.

Josh looks at us sheepishly. He looks like he is going to ignore us before he speaks, almost in a whisper, "Would you laugh if I told you that I don't remember?"

Lyla and I look at each other for a second. Lyla speaks first, "How don't you remember? I know you were young when you got separated from your mom, but not that young."

"Well, to tell you the truth I'm not sure that Josh is my real name. It's what the doctor called me and what was on my jacket, but it could've been found and I just wore it. When I died and the doctor found me, I had some lapses in my memory. I remember my mom, dad, and brother, but I couldn't tell you their names. It's been that way for a while now. I remember that I went to school and where I used to live. I'm not sure if it was dying or just the time I spent with the Deaders that caused my memory to lapse so bad. "

"Wow, that's tragic," I say although it's obvious. "The memory can be an odd thing. I find it hard to remember things sometimes too. I found my family which helps. So maybe now you have found your new family, would you like to be a Washington?"

"How about an Oakley, that names better and there aren't already two of them," Lyla inserts.

"I like Cpl. Reid's last name. It sounds right. Maybe that was my name before or close to it. Do you think he would be ok with that?" he whispers.

"Of course he will. He'll love it," I answer.

"And if he doesn't I'll make sure he's ok with it anyway," Lyla says as she punches one hand with the other.

We all laugh and Josh tries out his new last name over and over. Reid will love it, he is a softy when it comes to the kids. After that, the conversation dies off. Nothing seems important enough to talk about anymore. I'm worried about Matt. I know he can handle things and he is Unseen, but that doesn't mean that the living can't be an issue for him. A prison is an odd place to go alone. I laugh to myself, almost everyone in history who has gone to prison has gone alone. Though true, it's not a comforting thought.

The hours pass and finally the transports could be heard trudging along the roads. I wake Josh and Andromeda from their naps and call to Lyla. She's walking a perimeter to make sure no one is stalking the transports as they travel along the roads. She hollers back but says that she's going to walk one side and catch up with the rear of the transports. She just wants to be sure, she'll catch up in a bit.

The idea has been for us to wait until we can see the transports then keep pace about a 1/4 mile ahead until we're clear of Fort Wayne. I'm hoping we would've heard back from Matt by now so we would have a better plan. Of course, we haven't. As the first truck comes into view I start Evee and pull away. I have Josh standing on the back seat to keep a higher lookout around the transports. I figure I'd stay with the plan and Lyla would catch up. Now that we are back on the road I guess I should think of her as

Oakley again. I need more military bearing, or at least that's what Hayes always says. I wonder if she'd be mad if I started using first names.

Probably.

The stop for tonight was only about another hour out. There we'd set up camp and wait for the stragglers and rear guard. We're all camping together at night until we can get these stalkers off our tails. Smart, I guess, more guards to keep watch at night. After a bit, I start to show Josh how to operate Evee so he can drive and I can take the top watch. He's hesitant, but like I was told, there aren't any cops or other people around to make driving dangerous. He would have to learn sometime, might as well be now. *That's something my dad always said.* After a few hesitant starts and stops he has the idea and we swap. He gets better, but he still needs practice. There's no way he's watching for the road signs along with driving he's too focused on staying on the road.

When we hit the area that was designated for our stop I have Josh pull over and I take the wheel back. We need to find a place suitable for everyone to camp. Another thirty minutes down the road we stop at an open field that's backed by a woodline. It seems ok, so we wait for the others. As the first transport pulls up so does our truck. Reid's driving and Oakley's sitting shotgun. I guess she made it to the back of the line.

As they get out Reid picks Josh up and gives him a big hug. Oakley smiles at me and I know that she told him about our conversation. Reid's so happy that he gives Josh a patch that has his name on it. I guess that makes it official. We now have two Washingtons and two Reids. Less than two minutes later Reid's waving goodbye and heading back to the rest of the squad. Oakley joins Josh and me waiting for the transports to get settled. As soon as they do we would set up a patrolling watch with the other soldiers that traveled with the transports.

Everything gets settled and Mom comes up to find us. She doesn't look happy, but at least she doesn't look sick either. When she reaches us she has all three of us sit down. With Mom that was never good.

"I have to tell you that Neal passed away earlier today," she says somberly.

"I'm sorry. But who is that?" I ask.

"The doctor."

"Yeah, still not helping." Mom looks frustrated with me.

"Testerman," she sneers.

"Oh, why didn't you say so? That sucks. I know you liked him. Are you ok?" I ask her as I put my hand on her shoulder. She looks at me oddly but nods her head. "What was it caused by?"

"Also, I hate to ask, but was he taken care of afterward?" Oakley asks. Fair question in these times.

"Yes, we aren't sure of the cause of death yet, just like the others. They plan on burying the body as soon as we are set up. It's just awful that all these people are dying," She barely finishes the sentence before she starts coughing.

"Are you ok?" I ask her as I have her sit down in Evee.

"Yeah, allergies I think. I've felt bad since the pine tree area. It'll pass."

I look at Oakley as she and Josh back away. I knew this would happen. When people get sick for an unknown reason people get scared. It gets worse when the same people start to die. We need to find the cause. Soon.

I walk Mom back to camp after she catches her breath. She needs to rest but I know she'll just start helping everyone around her with the preparations instead. I kiss her cheek and wish her a good night. I'll see her in the morning after I finish my rotation on the watch. Hopefully, Matt will be back by then. We'll reach Westville by tomorrow afternoon either way. We need Matt's intel.

Westville

As Hayes and the others catch up, she tells Oakley and me that we will be taking the last watch tonight and reporting to Sgt. Ragsdill. Last watch isn't bad, it means you had to get up a few hours earlier, but you don't have to break up your sleep. Because of this, we need to get to sleep as quickly as we can, before tomorrow comes too early. It would be dinner then bed for the three of us.

Unfortunately, we have to deal with Dr. Tersterman's funeral pyre first. They sent all of the soldiers out to get wood to build the pyre. It was being built closer to the road so it didn't catch the trees on fire, but this would also act as a beacon to those following us. If we light it quickly it may fade with the setting sun and not betray us completely.

That's the hope anyway.

I bring back my armful of wood while dragging a long stick about as thick as my leg. I think I'm doing well until I see Josh and Oakley dragging a whole tree out of the woods. Always someone showing me up. A little while later we are all gather around so that we can say our goodbyes. One person, whom I still don't know, reads a bible verse. I'm not sure if that thing still pertains. If God was going to save those who were his sheep, wouldn't they have been called up by now?

Maybe they were and we were too busy to notice.

After the fire was lit and burned down to a respectable level, people leave to get dinner started or to take their watch. I hang around for a bit, I didn't know the man well, but I stay for my mother. She stays until she can't see the body any longer. She touches my arm and walks back to the transports. I think those two got close over the last couple of weeks. I guess he was a nice man. He always seemed too nerdy to me though. As I walk back through camp I can see people breaking off into pairs and small groups. No one seems to want to be part of a large group any longer. I figure it's time to check with the scientists to see what they think.

SGM Silver must've the same idea because I run into him as I approach the transport. I'm still not sure if I should salute him, like in the movies, or not. I usually just side with not. He looks at me fidgeting around him and just tells me to relax.

"Unfortunately, there isn't a real military any longer. What we have is a good representation, but it will never be what it was. In some ways that's a good thing," he explains as he walks up the stairs to the truck.

"Does that mean I can use everyone's first names then?" I ask quickly. I know the answer before he says it.

"No," is all he says as he disappears inside. "Also you never salute an enlisted member of the military, only officers. We don't have any of those, so relax," he calls back.

"Well, if he's checking on that I can go and check on Josh and Andromeda then hit the sack for a few hours," I say to no one in particular.

All's good with everyone so we quickly eat, then try to get some sleep. Of course, Josh and Andromeda are asleep within seconds. I swear kids and dogs have it easy. Lyla, yes I started thinking of her by her first name when we weren't on patrol, and I talk about Testerman for a bit before she starts to drift off. After that, I don't remember anything until I'm shaken awake by the previous watch.

"Up and at 'em," he says as he shakes me.

"It's Atom Ant," I reply. He looks at me weirdly and just walks off. I guess he wasn't a '60s cartoon fan.

I get dressed and feed Andromeda before we meet Ragsdill for our assignments. As we all gather around I can see the previous shift drifting in to get a few more hours of sleep before we hit the road. I can see that Hayes used the transport guards for the mid-shift. Which works because they can ride for a bit of the day if they are too tired. Ragsdill assigns Josh with me and Andromeda, I'm guessing Hayes had something to do with that. We are to keep a roaming perimeter just outside of camp. It's easy and with

Andromeda keeping her ears and nose out it would be an easy shift.

We all break up the meeting and head to our assignments. About thirty minutes later I hear a loud obnoxious buzzing droning toward camp. My heart jumps into my throat. If that's what I think it is then we should have a plan soon. It takes Matt another thirty minutes to make it into camp proper. He's stopped by a few of the patrols but they all know him on site, once he takes his mask off.

Why was he wearing a mask? I'll have to ask.

I can't leave my post to see what the news is, I don't think Hayes would forgive that, but at least I know Matt's safe and that we would know about Westville before we get there. Knowing he was back though made the night drag on. By the time the sun started to rise and camp started waking up I was on pins and needles.

Have I ever mentioned that patience wasn't a strong suit of mine? I'm sure I have.

After we are told to return to our regular assignments I send Josh to get Evee warmed up while I find my brother. As usual, I find him around the food. He's stuffing his face while trying to tell everyone around him what he has already told Hayes, Ragsdill, and Silver. I guess that order was probably wrong, oh well. That's the order that I like them in. Anyway, I walk up as Matt is saying something...

"So the towns of Plymouth and Bremen are both completely clogging up the roadways around them. You can't get in or around them. I had to find new ways and some small backroads to get from here to Westville and then back. Even though they're blocking the roads they aren't messing with anyone. They kind of remind me of the town in *The Walking Dead*. They hide behind the fence and hope things go away," he explains.

"Yeah, that doesn't work for very long," I refute. "Or at least it didn't for us."

"Well, not our call. We just have to avoid them. Which ain't easy since they are both on the only main roads heading west from here. I found a route but the transports aren't going to like it. It's tough sledding the whole way, even on my bike. Those things are going to get beat to death by the time we get there.

"It'll slow us down, but will it damage them?" Smith asks him. Also while he had food in his mouth.

I guess it's a man thing.

"Shouldn't. I heard about hte one's following us. maybe it'll also slow them down. By the way any news on that front?" he looks around as he asks.

No one has any new information so we just shake our heads. He nods and tells us the plan that the three heads came up with. Matt, Josh, Lyla, and I would stay in the front and map the area, keeping the transports in our sight the entire time. The rear guard would do their thing and try to keep the stalkers off our backs for a while. We need to get moving and get somewhere that we can defend, these jokers could attack us at any time.

In all reality, I'm not sure why they haven't.

With that done we all help break down camp and load up. The four of us hit the road with Matt in the lead. Oakley decides to ride with Matt so she could mark the roads and Josh can have a seat in the front with me. Andromeda seems a little mad about this, but she deals with it fine. It was nice before, riding without having to listen to Matt's loud bike droning on all day. Yet, it's nicer to know where he is and that he's ok. The ride goes well for a while. It isn't until we start seeing signs for Plymouth, IN that we have to detour to smaller roads.

Matt wasn't kidding that these roads are junk. They never had any real shoulders to them before the Fall, and now that the vegetation had grown up in the last two years, they were even worse. The tree roots pushed up the asphalt in more places than I could count. The fields had overgrown to the point that we almost need a machete to cut our path. I could send a kid out with a couple of hatchets if need be. The transports would have an easy time with that, but then they wouldn't see the tree roots in time and could break a wheel or axle. They had to take it slow. An hour's drive will take all day at this pace.

It takes all day. We had to stop a few times to find another route because the roads got too bad. The transports could've handled it but it would have risked spilling the chemical or losing supplies. Matt and Oakley would take off while I waited at the intersection to tell the transports where to turn. With all of the overgrowth we couldn't leave signs, they would never see them. While I wait, Andromeda gets down and runs through the fields for a bit. If it were any other dog I might worry about them getting lost, but she won't go far and she needs to burn some energy. Riding all day is making her lazy. She comes back several times and brings us a total of three dead rabbits and a pheasant or bird of some kind. I guess she's having fun.

As the transports catch up to me I hear Matt and Oakley yell that they found a route. I get the driver's attention and follow the path that they set for me. It goes on like this all day. It's grueling and the fact that I have been up since four hours before dawn doesn't help. About halfway through the day, I let Josh take the controls and drive for a bit. Just resting is nice.

Since we discovered this tail, they have had all the doctors, medics, and civilians riding in one transport, while the scientists are all in the other now. A few people are riding in the suburban, which is somehow still running. Good thing we brought a few good mechanics. The lack of supplies, and the loss of a few people, has allowed more people to ride and we don't have to wait for the walkers. The only ones walking throughout the day now are the soldiers keeping the perimeter.

If that's the case though, our supplies must be lower than I thought, or we lost more than I have counted.

About the time that the sun starts to set, we come back to a main road and head to the town of Westville. A half an hour after dark we pull up just outside of the prison's gates. There's no way we were going into a prison that hasn't been cleared, at night. We will have to wait until morning to get that done. We do notice that a couple of the buildings, have lights burning. That means that someone is there and that they have kept a generator running for over two years. Had Matt seen this before, he couldn't have. This is a dead giveaway that there are people here. They will most likely fight to protect it too. I don't have time to think on this too much, let the big brains do that. We need to get camp set up and I need some rest. I think tomorrow is going to be a very long day.

As we all get done and I settle down, I look at Matt and Oakley. Matt just sighs and hangs his head. He missed it. He thought it was clear. Oakley just shrugs her shoulders, like whatcha gonna do? The three Sergeants will have tonight to figure it out. Hopefully, we all survive tonight and will hear the plan in the morning.

With that thought I curl up next to Andromeda, who's still crunching on some rabbit bones, and try to rest my eyes before my watch. It doesn't take long for everything but her warmth to fade away. I guess I am getting better at that too.

Plans

The sun comes up while I stand my watch. It's a pretty sunrise, but the sky is red. That means a storm is coming. My dad always quoted some adage *Red sky at night, Sailor's delight. Red sky in the morning, sailors take warning.* If we don't find a way into the prison early, we will most likely have to do so as it rains on us.

Speaking of which, the Sergeants just came out of the transport, so they may tell us what the plan is. I tap Josh and point back towards the camp. He and I have already talked about it. When they came out he would take my watch and I would go see if we have a plan to get into the prison and find out what's going on in there. Josh takes most of my watches with me anyway. Since he's so young SGM Silver doesn't see him as mature enough to stand watch himself. All he has to do is spend a few minutes with this kid and Silver would know how wrong he is.

Josh nods to me and I tell Andromeda to stay with him as I walk back to camp. I run into Hayes and Matt on the way to the meeting. Hayes looks at me like she's going to yell at me for not being on watch, but I just mouth Josh and she nods. I still don't think she's happy, but I get away with a lot. I know the real military wouldn't run like this.

I'll take advantage if I can.

As we all get settled Silver stands and tries to get everyone to stop talking. All of the remaining soldiers are here, with the few exceptions of those on watch. I see Susie and nod in her direction. Since she joined the rear guard I haven't seen her much, but I don't miss her either. As everyone settles down I realize that there are only about 20 of us. That's not a huge force to try and storm a castle. I'm hoping that's not the plan.

"OK, settle down. You know some days I miss the bearing of real military soldiers," he starts. It's not a good start as a few of the soldiers around shout that they were in before the Fall too. Silver laughs a bit, just trying to break the tension I guess.

"Yeah, Yeah. Ok. Settle. I know everyone is ready to do something about this group tailing us. They have been there for about a week and from what Sgt. Ragsdill and Hayes tell me it is becoming a force to reckon with. We need to get in here and put our backs to a wall to fight this group head-on. Do we agree on this?" Silver waits and looks at each of us and watches all of us nod in agreement. Running like we have can't continue. They will attack us soon and most likely when they have the advantage.

Silver continues to tell us the plan. He'll have a small group go into the prison by finding a hole or cutting one in the fence on the back side away from the buildings that were lit up last night. Once in ,this group will clear the buildings quickly but efficiently. While they do that, the transports will move to the main gate and try to draw the attention of anyone there, plus being able to put their backs towards the fence and leaving only one direction for the other group, stalkers, to attack from. Prisons have always had good sight lines from the towers and had land cleared far from the fences. The area wasn't as clear as it was before the Fall, but there weren't any trees or wood lines for the others to hide in. They would have to show themselves and confront the caravan head-on. By the time that happens, hopefully, we have figured out if the people in the prison are going to help, hinder, or hide.

Of course, the insertion team was Hayes's original Unseen team. They have been together the longest, they have the Unseen advantage and they were mostly military trained. Others who have joined later, like me, don't have the training for this type of situation. I'm not   happy that my squad is going into a dangerous situation without me, but they had done this for years before they rescued me, Jordan, and Andromeda in Dover. It's hard to believe that wasn't years ago. It felt like it had been so long, but it was just months.

Time moves differently after an apocalypse.

I walk over to relieve Josh as the meeting breaks up. He asks me what the plan is, so I tell him the basics. He isn't happy that he isn't going with the squad either but understands. He's still sitting with me when my relief is sent over. I almost tell the watch that we hadn't seen anything all night and to get ready for a boring shift but thought better of it. You never curse someone like that. If you tell them the shift will be boring, or that it's been quiet it is destined to be the exact opposite. We don't need that today.

Josh and I tap Andromeda to pull her away from the new watch and the breakfast that's in his hands, and head to get our breakfast. Andromeda follows us, reluctantly, as we walk off without her. The area around the makeshift kitchen looks like the meeting that we just had. It's almost all soldiers sitting around talking about what Silver has just told us. I find Matt and Lyla sitting with Reid and Smith. Josh's eyes light up as he sees Reid and hurries over to him, almost forgetting to get his food. I hope all of these guys make it out of the prison ok. I'll have enough of a problem, but Josh will be lost without a few of these people. He's just starting to come around and becoming a normal kid again.

After I get my food I sit down and hear the end of a conversation.

"Hayes just doesn't want them there," Matt's saying.

"Who doesn't she want there?" I ask as I sit down.

"You and Josh," he tells me bluntly.

"Why is that? We have proven ourselves multiple times."

"She knows that. She also knows that Andromeda would be a huge advantage. She's just worried about how you'll work with the others that are coming along. It's not just us this time," Matt shrugs and looks to the others for help.

"I know Ragsdill is going, he was part of your original team. Who else is going?" I ask. I wasn't mad before, but I was starting to get there now.

"A few of Ragsdill's team members that Hayes has seen work too. They're good, but they don't know you guys and what you can do. I think it was Silver's call," Matt explains.

I let the subject drop for now and eat my breakfast. It would be good to spend the day with Mom and not have to worry about moving too much today. We're going to be running double watches since we're putting ourselves in between two groups we don't know much about. It's still better than being on the move all day long. Mom could use the rest too. She hasn't been looking good lately. I hope it's allergies like she keeps telling me it is.

The squad finishes up their meal and heads off to gear up. There isn't a lot of reason to wait any longer in the day. With a plan in place, we might as well get it done. The people in the prison probably already know that we're here. That's why they're sneaking in the back door. The storm clouds are moving in too. It could get wet quick.

Matt can't take his bike, since it's so loud. The truck will take some of the group and will be left near the hole in the fence for a fast getaway. I volunteer to take others on Evee so they don't have to trek through the grass. It'll make it a little easier.

After everyone gears up, Matt hands me a bag and a rifle. I stuff them away on Evee and watch as everyone else loads up. My job is to take them and wait until they make it into the first building. I'll then return here and wait with everyone else. As we start to leave, Josh runs up with his hatchets and jumps in the back of the truck with Reid. Reid just smiles and points to him as he looks at me. I guess he's making sure I saw him so I can bring him back with me. I give Reid a thumbs up as we pull off.

We get to the back of the prison, but we can't see any opening in the fence. Whoever's living here has kept the fence repairs up. You can even see where a few holes have been fixed or filled. Are they trying to keep people out, or in?

A couple of guys jump out of the truck with cutters and start to cut an entry hole. As they do, the others get out of the truck and get set to enter the fence line. In no time, the hole is big enough for the team to walk through. They all nod to me as they pass and then they get their game faces on. It's been a while since they all walked into a situation like this.

It's like riding a bike though. Right?

Josh comes over and sits with me absently stroking Andromeda's neck. We watch the team enter the first building and close the door behind them. There isn't any yelling or commotion so they should be good. Since that's my cue to head back, I sit up and start Evee. I put it in gear as Andromeda jumps off and runs to the fence. She stops at the entrance that the team just cut and growls. Her body is stiff and her hackles are up. If something is around the door the team may not see it until it's too late. Josh looks at me and I nod. We aren't leaving if Andromeda senses something wrong.

We get up and set up behind Andromeda. I tell her to find and she looks back at me before walking through the fence. We come up to the building that the team had entered without finding anything out of place. I tell Josh to stay at the door as Andromeda and I check the far side. I follow her as we round the corner and find myself face to face with a Deader. I stumble back before I figure out that it isn't a Deader, just a dead body tied to a pole. I check the back of its head and don't find a hole. This person was tied to this pole and then killed by a Deader. Was he bait, or was this punishment?

Andromeda has completely bypassed the body and kept moving. I shiver as I pass the body but keep up with her. She starts to sniff the ground and weave back and forth. It's odd behavior for her, but I wait her out. She then lifts her head and takes off back around the corner towards Josh. As we turn the corner again she stops quickly. I see why. Josh is leaning on the door so it can't be opened while a Deader stands directly behind him looking confused. As soon as it senses me and Andromeda its eyes come alive, per se, and it tries to leap at me but Josh is quicker. As it passes him Josh cuts the Deader achilles tendons, dropping it to the ground. It hesitates then digs its hands into the ground and pulls itself towards us. Andromeda is barking now and jumping at the Deaders face, trying to intimidate it. Josh slowly walks up next to it and puts a hatchet into the back of its neck, stopping all of its movement.

Just as he does, the door pops open. Matt and Hayes push their way out with their guns up. They relax for a second when they see us. Well, Matt does, Hayes seems to get angrier. I start to tell her what happened, but she just holds up her hand.

"Don't. Just don't. You're here now. Since you are, follow us and join the squad. We could probably use your help anyway. But this is not over. We'll talk about all of this later," Hayes simmers as she looks at the dead Deader at Josh's feet.

I look at Josh and shrug as we fall into line behind Hayes and my brother. I guess we get to come along anyway. I hold the door for Andromeda and look around as the rest of the squad looks at us. Some are smiling, some are laughing while others just shake their heads. I guess there could be worse reactions.

After I look at the squad members I look around the building. The sights make me want to turn around quickly and take Evee back to camp. I can't do that though, so I just swallow hard and try not to shiver visibly.

Prisoners

The scene isn't one that I would have expected. The hallway is lined on both sides with cells. The cells are the types that you see in the movies. The fronts and door were nothing but bars that held the person inside. Each cell had a metal bunk, a toilet, and a sink combination. There's a metal desk with a small stool attached to it. This isn't the unexpected part. In each cell, there is a Deader. Each one has their grotesque differences but they are all in a deep level of decay. They made the *Walking Dead* zombies look alive. The few that I look at before I stop are pretty disturbing. Some of the Deaders ware stumbling around the cells, while others had apparently hung themselves at some point and are still swinging from the bars.

That wasn't a memory that I needed to relive.

One other has three different pieces of metal sticking out of his chest as he walks around. You can tell that a few of the Deaders had died from starvation. Their faces are gaunt, while their stomachs are bloated. We slowly walk through the rest of the cells. As Andromeda and I pass they all reach out towards us, trying to feed if they can. I make sure that we stay in the dead center of the hallway. No point getting any closer to these things than necessary.

Matt slows and walks next to me.

"It looks like this was a maximum security building. These people were left here during the Fall to starve. No one came by to let them out. I mean maybe there wasn't anyone to do that, but it still seems cruel," Matt's talking to me, but I feel like he's talking himself through it all.

The hallway stretches on until we get to an office at the end. I jump as a Deader slams itself into the window. The window looks down the hallway, most likely used to keep an eye on the prisoners. It's smeared with blood, mucus, and other fluids. *Ewww.* The Deader walks towards the door but it seems locked. At first, I think it's one of the prisoners, but it's wearing a uniform. I wondered if the officers were left too, until it turns and I see a piece of metal sticking out of its neck with blood caked around it.

I slowly approach the window and look in. Two other Deaders are lying on the floor, barely moving. These two are in prisoners' uniforms. There must've been a fight and they all lost in the end. I look at the team and Hayes tells us to turn around.

"We go out the way we came in and try the next building. Hopefully, the transports are keeping the guards busy," she explains.

As we exit the building the team all turns the corner to head to the next building. Hayes stops me, Matt, and Josh. I figure this is where she is going to tell us to go back through the fence and leave like we should've before. I'm wrong.

"You three and the dog are going to go with me," she explains then turns to Ragsdill. "With the extras, we can split up and cover these buildings quicker. Give me Reid too. I might need his strength." Just as she turns it starts to drizzle just a bit.

Ragsdill seems like he is going to say something, but just points to Reid and flicks his hand towards us. He then points to two different buildings. We go to one, his team goes to the other. The building they go to is another long and skinny building, but it seems to have three wings in total. It'll take them a bit to clear all of that.

Our building on the other hand is a set of two buildings that look more like barracks than a prison. Matt approaches the door and checks it, locked. He stands on his tiptoes and looks through the dirty window. He says it looks clear, so he looks to Reid, who lifts a lock pick out of his pocket and gets to work.

Since when can he pick locks?

In a few seconds, he has the door unlocked. We set up with me and Josh in the back of each line. They count down and throw the door open. The line with Matt leading heads in first and he sweeps the entry. It's odd seeing Matt like this, even after all of this time. He's more focused than I have ever seen him. The cells here are actual doors with small windows in them. As we pass I stand on my tip toes to look in. A few have dead bodies, and a few have Deaders in them. All of the doors are locked, so we should be safe.

As we approach the center of the building it opens up to what looks like a lobby with a large front door and a big desk. This must've been where the officers sat. Everything looks clear, but Matt rifles through the drawers anyway. He finds a spray can that says OC Spray. It's a form of mace the officers must use. He pockets it being careful to stow it where the trigger won't go off. It probably won't do much good against a Deader, but a human will hate that stuff.

Reid finds a baton that slides out with a flick of the wrist. That's convenient. He pockets that too. Joshua and I don't find anything, but Andromeda is chewing on something she found on the floor. How gross is that, I don't even want to know what it was. We clear the building to the other side and Reid has to pick the lock at the far end for us to get out. Too bad we didn't find a Deader officer here with some keys.

As we exit the building the rain has picked up dramatically. Hopefully this doesn't stay too long. We make our way to the next building. It's much of the same, without the cool, or gross finds. As we exit that building I see lightning streak across the sky. We need to meet Ragsdill's team at the largest building.   When we catch up to them, everyone is soaked. We have a quick conversation as we wait for Reid to pick the lock. They tell us that they hadn't found much other than Deaders and junk, like us. The building we're entering is huge. It has one main building and four offshoots connected through breezeways. Once we enter we are going to break into four teams and take each wing at the same time. Once this is done we are on our way to where the lights were on last night. That's where it's all going to get interesting.

Reid gets the door open and the troops storm in. As we get inside everyone stops and checks the surroundings. All I can hear is wet boots squeaking on the tile floor. The lobby looks clear. There are stairs that lead to doors, probably to prisoners' cells. There are four stairwells so we break off to check these before we go to the other buildings. We all wait and enter the hallways at the same time. It takes a bit of time. We haven't found any keys so Reid has to go around and unlock each hallway door.

As we enter our door, Matt leads while Josh is behind me with Andromeda following. As soon as the door opens, she growls low in her throat. It takes a second for my eyes to adjust, but as they do I hear Josh whisper, "They're hibernating."

The 'they' he's talking about is around 40 Deaders all looking the other way. They are huddled tightly together. Unbeknownst to us the door we opened has a spring on it. Josh lets go of it to grab his hatchet and it slams shut with a loud bang. All of us cringe, forgetting that Deaders don't react to sound. I slide behind Matt to mask any electrical signal I might put out as we get turned around to slide back out of the door. Josh slides around me and walks towards the Deaders. I try to grab him, but he's small and quick.

Matt backs me to the door and waits to see what Josh is going to do. Josh slides around the bodies, being careful not to touch any of them. He tells us that he is trying to figure out why they are all huddled at the end of the hallway like this. It's odd behavior for them. He gets almost to the front of the bodies when he yells.

"It's a vending machine. I bet it comes on at night without the guards realizing it. It does have some food in it. I can break the glass and get them."

"Not our mission right now," Matt calls back.

"There are M&Ms and Skittles though. Just a handful?" Josh pleads.

"Just hurry up," Matt says.

As quickly as Matt has that out of his mouth I hear glass break. Josh was going to do it anyway. The little bugger. I can see Matt's face and he knows it too. Josh gets what he wants and works his way back to us. All is good until he trips on his shoelace, slips in his wet boots and stumbles into one of the Deaders.

As soon as Josh falls into that one Deader it wakes up. It taps the one beside it and the rest follow suit. In a second all of them are awake and turning towards Josh, who's picking himself up off his knee and trying to get his hatchets out. Matt doesn't waste any time as he runs down the hall and jumps in front of Josh before they can attack him. With the speed of it though, he ran directly into another Deader that was lunging at Josh. Now both of them were exposed.

All 40 of the Deaders turn and scramble after the two who are running back down the hall. I don't think, I just react and pull my rifle. I aim clear of my two brothers and start taking potshots at the encroaching Deaders. I know that I won't kill them, I'm just trying to slow them down. I also know that any chance of stealth is now gone from our excursion.

I drop a few Deaders causing others to trip and slow down the whole group. Josh and Matt make it back to the door with plenty of time and by looking at Josh's pockets, with some candy too. I send a few more rounds down to try and slow them further, before we shut the door. As we put our backs to the door to keep the Deaders in I call out for Reid. He's heading our way quickly. He must have head the shots.

What am I saying? Everyone heard the shots.

Reid scrambles out of his hallway and down the steps. He runs up our steps two at a time as we strain to keep the door shut. Forty Deaders pushing from the other side is a lot of weight to stop. Reid throws his shoulder into the door and sets a charge on it. Matt and Reid push harder and tell me and Josh to get to cover. As soon as we're clear, they hit a button and jump clear themselves. Quicker than I would've thought, the explosive goes off with a thump. A bright light flashes and I feel a little wonky.

No, I don't have a better word for it.

I remember this feeling though. I felt like this when Matt rescued me from the Dover Air Force base. This was an EMP explosive. I look around and everyone is dazed but seems fine. Hayes calls out and tells us to get out of the building. We wobble to the door and exit the building. As everyone is gathering their heads together, we look up and see the business end of fourteen gun barrels, well it may have been less but I was seeing double a bit.

My brain had just been razzled, OK? Is that a better word?

Either way, the officers or people running this place had just found us and they didn't look happy.

Guards

We had to be a strange sight. Not only had we just caused an explosion and a gunfight in one of their buildings, we were also dizzy, disoriented, dripping and drained. We didn't look like a group of people here to take everything over. That may be what saves us.

"What is going on here?" the man in the front asks. He's a large man, but you can see signs of starvation in his eyes and around his face. He used to be fat, but now his skin hangs on him a bit. He isn't going to die soon, but he isn't healthy either.

I look around at all of the others, twelve in all, and see similar signs in them too. A couple used to be muscular, but now their clothes hang on them loosely. The skinny ones have bones showing through their clothing, especially around their collarbones. This is a group that is getting to the point of desperation.

"We were just coming to see you," Ragsdill chimes in. "We wanted to see if we could use your nice facility for a few days to help scrape a bug off of our back. And possibly dry off a bit?"

"If that was the case, why did you sneak around in the back and start blowing stuff up?" The guy asks. Rightfully so.

"Well, you see we wanted to take a tour first to check out all of your lovely amenities. Like the nice NLB shop you have here," Ragsdill's pointing to the building we just came from. "You have what 200 or so in there?"

The guy in charge doesn't seem to be humored by the responses given. "Are you with the group that just backed three trucks up to our main gate, blocking us in?"

"Yes, but they aren't blocking you in. They are protecting your front gate. As I said, we have a very large bug on our backs that we need scraped off. To do that we need somewhere that our back isn't exposed. This place fits the bill pretty well. On the other hand, we have plenty of food and supplies that we could share with those who help us. Soap maybe?"

The guy in charge doesn't flinch, but I can see several of his men do, at the thought of food. Josh pushes his way forward and handed a guy in the front a bag of Skittles.

"Here, you can have this too," he says in a sweet little innocent voice. The kid pours on the charm.

The man takes the Skittles and several of his buddies drop their barrels down and put them on their backs as they reached out their hands for a taste of the rainbow. I also notice that Josh doesn't give up any of his M&Ms. Good kid.

With the rest of the team worried about the candy in their hand, the main guy gives up and joins them. No use in trying to act tough when you don't have any backup. Afterward, the man just waves his hand to the sergeant and walks back to the main building.

"Might as well get out of the rain. Obviously you know we need food. It's not hard to see," he looks down at his body as he says this.

Along the way, he points at a few things and says something about them. I'm not really paying attention. We won't be here long enough for me to care about this place. It's a pit stop at best. What we need is access to the towers outside and more ammunition if they have it. The quicker we can get these stalkers off of us the quicker we can get back on the road to South Dakota.

Once we get the main gates open, we get the transports, Matt's bike, and the suburban in and parked towards the center of the compound. Matt and I go back around to get the truck and Evee. A couple of Ragdsill's team go out back with two of the officers to fix the hole we cut in their fence. All in all the guards are taking everything pretty well, especially after we offload some of the food supplies that we had found in that hoarder's home.

As we walk around to the vehicles the rain slows then stops. I watch Matt, he seems off, distracted. I decide to ask him about it.

"So, what's bothering you?"

"What? Nothing," he replies.

"Well, tell that to your face. It disagrees," I tease. All that earns me is a shove sideways. I counter with a shoulder to his side, which doesn't move him an inch.

"I'm just thinking about things. Are we moving fast enough to get to South Dakota in time to beat winter? Will all of this work, be worth it?"

"So, now you're questioning the trip. Not before when I had the same question? I see." Matt smiles but it doesn't reach his eyes. He's worried and about more than he's letting on.

We reach the truck so I let it drop. We race a bit around the prison to the front gate. I win, but only because Evee is smaller and can take tighter turns. Matt's laughing with me when we get out. A real laugh too. Maybe he just needed to brood for a minute. I can relate to that. As we get to the main building Josh and Andromeda meet us. The Sergeants have met with the officers in charge.

The guys that we met were all officers assigned to this prison when the world fell apart. They had no families to get back to or had already lost them, so they just stayed on post. At first, they tried to run the place, but a few officers died, and a few were killed by what they called life-suckers. A couple of prisoners got out of their cells for one reason or another and decided to try to get out, through the officers. They were sad to say that a few made it too. By the time they got down to about twenty people, they had given up. They locked all of the outer doors to the buildings and cut the power to them. They tried to conserve food and energy as much as they could. There wasn't anything close, and a few officers that they sent on forays never came back. Since then a few others had left which took them down to the twelve they had now.

I figure that it would be similar in other places around the world. People living at what used to be their jobs because they got stuck when the world fell. Not glorious, but maybe safer than being at home. The officers agreed to help us against our stalkers if and when they showed themselves. But we had to leave them some of our supplies, mostly food and gas. It seemed like a fair trade, so we took the deal.

The next couple of hours were taken up by the Unseen clearing a building to house all of our people. They lure them out of the building and slowly and efficiently killed them one by one. The officers watched in horror as they let the Deaders out, but that turned to amazement when our people walked among them without attracting their attention.

"Can they clear all of the buildings like that?" One of them asks.

"Yes, but it would take a long time. You have a lot of undead prisoners here. We don't have the time. Sorry."

"Can I become like them? Is there something I can do?" He asked with fervor.

"You can die, then be brought back to life. Then you can lose all of your emotion and drive to live," Josh says blankly. He looks up after he says it, apparently saying the quiet part out loud. He looks sheepish for a second, then adds, "Or something of the sort anyway."

"It would be nice to be able to stay in a larger building though," the officer doesn't look as enthused to become Unseen anymore. I don't blame him.

I look at Josh to see if he's ok. That was a dark statement from such a young child. But I guess he has endured a lot. Add to that the fact that he can only remember loss from his life before. I can see why he has some darkness to him.

As the deadly game of cat and mouse winds down and the rest of us get started on moving the necessary items into place. The civilians and scientists work on putting things in or around buildings so they don't get damaged if there's a shootout. The soldiers add guns and ammo to key places while setting up watches in the towers. We all take some time getting used to the conditions of the whole area. As darkness sets in a strange calm falls upon the institution. Everything seems quiet, we are done with the preparations and we are now waiting on the storm to come. Everyone keeps moving and doing what they should, but it seems like all conversations are held in whispers.

Radgsdill's squad is sent out to work their way along our trail. They are looking for the stalkers. We need to see them before they get to us so we can be ready. I almost wish that we were sent on that patrol. Yes, this squad has worked around these guys for a while now and had even lost one of their team members to them, but I hate the waiting. The only plus is that since we aren't moving we can spend some time as a family. Mom, Matt, Andromeda, Josh, and I all huddle together and try to play a game of cards to pass the time. The game goes fine, but I spend more time looking around at the people than I do at my cards.

My only true wish is for Jordan to be here with us. The next wish, since I can't have that one, is for all of us to get out of this fight alive and travel the rest of the way together. I have a sinking feeling that not all of us are going make it to the end of the line. The world just doesn't work that way anymore. I'm not sure if it ever did.

Stalkers

What we thought would take hours, or a day at most, takes more than two days. The days of waiting at high alert take their toll on the soldiers. Your body can't stay under stress like that with no relief for a long time without burning out. Unfortunately, it's almost at that burnout stage when the runner for the rear guard comes up to the gate. Maybe that's what the stalkers wanted? The rear guard had found the stalkers and hidden themselves so that they could get in behind them if anything broke off. It's a solid plan, not the original plan, since it did shorten the number of soldiers we have in the prison.

The news only gets worse from there. It seems that it took them as long as it did because they stopped in the towns around us and recruited new people to their cause. What that cause was? I'm sure we will find out soon. When the runner gives us his rundown, he has only limited information. As soon as the stalkers had been seen, he was sent off so that he was safe and had no way of getting captured before making it back to us. It was a good idea, but now we have to run on limited information. SGM Silver's not happy about this change in plans and the lack of information.

When he had left, the runner had counted more than 60 people in the group. That's almost a 3-1 odds for us. We have less than 60 people and more than half of them aren't soldiers or officers. The runner says that he was about a half a day out from the prison when he left.. If they're that large and not running, we have probably about another half a day before they make it to us. It's not much time, but it's enough. Silver tells Hayes to enact his plan and get everyone into position. We will be swapping our guards every two hours now, just to keep everyone safe. We are also paired up at all times so we can be sure that everyone is on alert and there aren't any blind spots because someone gets distracted.

It was almost 8 pm when the runner arrived. I hate the fact that I still don't know the guy's name. He's always with Ragsdill on the rear guard so we have never spoken before. Still, I should know their names. Hopefully, this group will take a break and sleep through the night. That would put them here in the morning sometime. That's better than in the middle of the night. I'm on a later watch, partnered with one of the prison officers. He seems nice and competent enough. We shall see what his training is like and how much these guys are willing to put on the line.

Josh is working with Reid on the first watch so I will see him later. I go to the safe building to catch some sleep and maybe talk to Mom for a bit. When I get into the building all of the civilians ask me questions about what's going on. They don't have any representation with the soldiers so they are in the dark on things. I tell them what I can to calm their fears. After I finish with them I pull Mom off to the side to make sure she's feeling ok. She lies to me and says that she's feeling better, but I can see that she's worse than before. I have taken some time over the last day to talk to the scientists, Matt had too. They confirmed that there was no illness going around affecting people. It's spore sickness. The people that have been in the clean air of the hospital for the last few years, had very minimal access to the outside, they weren't inundated with spores as those of us that had lived outside. When they were outside in the wilderness for the first time, the spores were stronger and affected their immune systems more. The younger and healthier people are able to fight it off with minimal effects. The older ones, like Testerman, had a tougher time and the spores eventually won out.

They also said that this is going to happen to all life on the planet at some point. The spores will overpower the immune system and kill the host, only to then reanimate it. It seems counterproductive for the spores to kill off their only means of food but if this was sent by an alien race bent on takeover it would be beneficial for the world to be Terra-formed and cleared of all sentient life at the same time.

Did I watch too many sci-fi movies?

So if the sickness isn't contagious, why is Mom's condition worsening? Are the spores taking over her immune system too quickly? She had spent the time after the Fall outside, she should have immunity. Or is there something else affecting her? I don't want to lose anyone else. But, there's no reason to dwell on it. There isn't much we can do. I just talk to her and spend as much time with her as I can between rotations and sleep. I have been leaving Andromeda with her a lot too. Just in case something happens, she won't be alone, and Andromeda can tell us that something happened.

I sleep and am woken up for watch after what felt like only five minutes. I can tell it's later when I walk outside and the moon has already set. The night is dark, there is a light cloud cover so there's no starlight shining down. With no light pollution from cities any longer, when it gets dark, it gets dark. If the stalkers decide to attack tonight we won't be able to see much at all. Unless they use torches or something to light their way and point themselves out to us.

Ok, not likely, but you can hope. Right?

My watch comes and goes with no issues. Matt and his partner come to relieve me as the sun starts to come up. I let the officer go but hang around with Matt for a bit before I leave.

"Have you seen Mom?" I ask him.

"Yeah we spoke a few times over the last couple of days," he replies, not too engagingly.

"How do you think she's doing?"

"She says she's fine. Other than that she's just like the rest of us, worn out."

"I think it's more than that. I think she's really sick," I plead with him. He seems distant.

"Well..." he starts before a call goes up. The stalkers have been seen. I look at Matt and take up the extra gun and he pulls out the binoculars. He slowly scans the area, then passes them to the officer with him, who then hands them to me. I see a massive group coming out of the woods on the edge of the prison's fields.

It'll take them an hour to cross the fields, so we have time to get ready.

I look around the prison behind and below me. Everyone is running around and getting into their positions. I knew we were going to be out-manned but watching the number of people pour out of the woods is a bit disturbing. I decide to wait with Matt and be his runner if he needs one. I'd rather face this with my brother than anyone else. If Mom is as sick as I think, it may just be us soon. I push the depressing thoughts aside and concentrate on the possible battle ahead. We've hyped it up as a battle, but we really aren't sure what this group of people want and why they're following us. When they get close enough we'll try to establish communication before the first shot is fired.

That chance comes faster than I thought it would. A large part of the group stops just past the woods line, almost like a show of force. Are there more in the woods? We really don't know. With the intel that we have, we can assume that this is all of them, but we haven't heard from Ragsdill's group since the runner came in last night. As the main group stops a few of them break off and head towards the prison at a run. It's an easy jog, more than a run. The kind of pace you would set for a 5k, not a sprint. They seem to want to get here faster, but not be too tired when they do. Matt and I watch them come towards us until they stop just outside of the main gate.

"We know you are prepared for us!" The first guy yells. "We are not here to start a war with you. This isn't television. We just want you to hand over your vehicles, weapons, and supplies. We'll then go away happily."

"You must be joking!" Silver yells back from behind the main gate. "You want to take everything from us and then expect us to be ok with that?"

"Well, you took everything from us and left us behind with nothing. It would just be returning the favor. We even waited for you to have a safe place to stay before we approached. We knew that eventually you would figure out we were behind you and take refuge somewhere. I really didn't think it would take this long though." the guy isn't really yelling but his voice carries well. He must know how to project. As he talks the others around him stand tall with their hands on their guns, but they keep the barrels down. It's a show of force without being hostile.

"I don't know how we took everything from you and left you behind. We haven't taken anything from anyone. We supplied our vehicles and resources to cross the country." Silver sounds as confused as me.

Just before the other guy starts to speak again Matt jumps up and yells, "Dante! Is that you?" I look at Matt confused. He just waves a hand at me, like he would explain later.

"Ahh, so at least one of you remembers me. Do you remember leaving me behind to fend for myself now SGM Silver?" Dante yells.

"I remember the name, you were the failed Unseen. That's why you were left behind. You weren't a soldier, you weren't Unseen, you didn't have anything to contribute. I'm sorry but people had to be left behind. You have to realize that." Silver tries to explain.

"We'll make you realize that you took the wrong soldiers. We're better than yours and since you obviously won't give up your stuff willingly, we'll just take it from you by force." As Dante says this the group from the woods starts moving forward and spreading out along the prison's perimeter. How did they know to move? I didn't see a signal and they are too far away to hear him speak.

"It's not worth this Dante," Matt yells. "It's over Anakin, I have the high ground!"

Really Matt, a Star Wars quote? Now?

"You're going to quote Star Wars? Right now?" Dante echoes. "But, you do underestimate me."

"Don't try it," Matt counters. "Seriously, it's not worth it. We have fences and fortified walls. You may have the numbers, but nothing else. Just give up and go away. We left you in a safe place. We left you with food and shelter."

"Food and shelter? Maybe, for a time. It was only two days before the generators cut out. With that, half the food supply spoiled a day later. Shelter? Once the lights went out what were we supposed to do? Sit in the dark like bats? Shit on the floor? We had to leave. We had to find a purpose. You left us without one, so you could go and find safer harbors and glory." Dante starts to seem delusional. Is it me or is he actually foaming at the mouth as he screams at Matt and Silver? He's screaming now, not just projecting his voice.

"Glory? No, we aren't looking for glory. Yes, we have a purpose. We are looking to save the population that is left from the NLBs. We are trying to take out all NLBs at the source; the spores. Even if we succeed, which we may not, our names won't be remembered. Who's left to remember us anyway? We are doing this so the world can survive." Matt's almost tearing up explaining this to Dante. Silver has just let Matt handle him. He's doing what he can.

"We could've helped you with that. But you left us behind. You left us to die a slow and miserable death. A death that in the end will mean nothing. You took any purpose from us. We are here to take that back from you! I'm done trying to explain this to you. I've been done listening to you try to explain your reasons for leaving us behind. Ten more mouths to feed wouldn't have hurt you. We could've helped. We tracked you. We stayed behind you for weeks before you even knew we were there." Dante lifted his rifle, one that had been hidden behind his back, and aims it directly at Matt. "It all ends now. Now we will prove that you are the weaker soldiers."

Dante pulls the trigger, but Matt doesn't even flinch. The shot goes way wide as Matt stands there watching Dante with sorrow in his eyes. The officer with us aims and shoots Dante. The shot is a little off, or Dante moves because it only catches him on the outside of his left arm. Dante spins and runs under the tower's line of sight. It'll be up to the ground forces to keep an eye on him now. Matt takes a second then shakes his head as he reaches down and grabs his rifle.

"Ava, go help the ground forces. They are too close now for the towers to do a whole lot. Mark and I here can do what we can."

I look at Matt for a second to see if he's ok. His eyes soften just a bit, but the blue glow has also intensified. Matt looks at me and mouths, Go! So I do. I run down the stairs with my rifle on my back. I did leave all of my extra magazines in the tower for them. They may not be able to do much straight out, but they can shoot to the sides. The way the stalkers spread out will let them shoot from multiple angles and give us separate targets, but it also spreads them out so the towers have more sight lines.

After the first shot rings out, many more follow it. Everyone's shooting at everyone else. As I come out of the door of the tower a shot ricochets off the concrete at my feet. I jump back quickly, but that still would've been too late. I look out and take a few potshots in the direction the round had come from. I'm not sure if I can shoot someone in a battle like this. Sure, I have shot Deaders and shot at people before, but that was to save my life. This felt wrong, it felt like murder.

Was it murder if you killed someone in the heat of battle?

I really hope not. They attacked us. They followed us. I should be justified in protecting my group, and my family. But I still don't feel right shooting at these people. As I run and contemplate this another shot whizzes by my head. This all might be mute. It's kill or be killed right now. I don't want to be killed. I run down to the main gate to see where Silver and Hayes want me.

"Where have you been Washington?" Hayes yells at me.

"I was with Matt in the tower when they showed up. I should've left earlier, but I thought that Matt might get through to Dante," I confess as I keep my head low.

"I was hoping. Dante seems gone. If they only left with ten people, where did the other fifty come from?" Silver asks as he tries to concentrate on what's going on around us.

"He recruited them from the towns and cities we passed I guess," Hayes adds.

"But we didn't see that many people as we came through," I state.

"We avoided them as much as we could. Then add to that the large group and military trucks they all probably hid from us as we came through. Better hide than fight against an unbeatable force. That's probably why Dante didn't attack until now. He didn't have the numbers. He thinks he does now." Silver analyses. Silver seems like he knows what he's talking about so I take it as truth.

"Where do you want me?" I ask finally.

" Find Susie. I need you two with the truck to head out of the gate if anything goes wrong. And get that dog of yours too. She'll keep you outta trouble." Hayes orders.

Great another battle that seems unwinnable. I am to be the runner if things go wrong, aaannndd I am working with Susie again. This is a bit too much Deja Vu for me.

Battle

The battle rages on as I get Andromeda and find Susie. Susie's already at the truck and has a few extra magazines for the rifles. She looks a bit nervous and mad at the same time. I look in the back of the truck and see it has barrels of chemicals in it. What?

"What is that? And what are we doing?" I ask Susie warily.

"You know what that is. If this goes sideways, we are to run the truck through the fences and out of here. We are to take the chemical as far from here as we can. If we can find the rear guard we are to pick them up and we are to finish the mission. If we can't find them, we should wait until the battle dies out, then sneak back and see if any survivors can go with us. That's our order," Susie tells me.

"No! No, No no no no. That's not what I'm doing," I start to get out of the truck, but Susie grabs my arm. "You agreed to become part of the military, just like me. This is part of it. You do what you're ordered to. Especially if you don't like it. This is important and I can't do it alone. I'll need a gunner. I requested you. If we have to finish all of this together I need someone that I can trust. That's just you," Susie says then turns her head away.

That has to have been hard for her. I relax and sit back in my seat. "Ok, but if we have to run I control the radio," is all I say.

"No way. Driver picks the music, shotgun shuts her cake hole."

We laugh a bit and it breaks the tension. The shooting around us hasn't slowed down a bit. I wonder what's happening. Andromeda doesn't like the shooting and is sitting in the middle anxiously. I can see people run by at different intervals. The medics are to take anyone hurt back to the building that Mom is in so the civilians can help take care of them as the medics return to the battle. I haven't seen anyone rushed to the building yet, but that could also mean that the wounded aren't able to be saved.

About that time I hear a thumpf of flame hit nearby. "Are they throwing Molotov cocktails? We don't have enough gas as it is and they're wasting it on Molotov cocktails?" I say to Susie. I jump out of the truck to look for the fire and possibly an extinguisher. About that time I see Matt running by holding his shoulder. His clothes look singed.

"Matt! Over here. Are you ok?" I yell.

Matt turns and runs over to me. "Yes, I'm fine and so is Mark. We both made it to the stairs before the cocktail hit. Can you believe they are throwing gasoline at us, and while it's on fire?"

"I said the same thing. Where are you headed?" I look him over and see that he is good.

"I think we need to resort to plan B. I'm going to head to Silver and let him know. These guys are good shots, we can't set up properly without risking a shot at our heads. I almost think Dante missed that first shot on purpose," Matt loses himself in thought for a moment. Then gives me a quick shot to the shoulder and runs off to find Silver.

"OK," I turn to Susie. "What's plan B?"

"You'll see. If they do that we need to wait and then get out front for clean up. We won't be driving this thing out of here. Hopefully, the rear guard is far enough away. It's not good. It was supposed to be the last resort," she half explains.

A few minutes later I hear a siren go off in the compound. It's loud and seems to come from everywhere at once. I look at Susie and she just nods. Whatever plan B is, it's happening now. She and I get out of the truck. I wait for Andromeda to stretch and jump down before I close the door. So we aren't driving out of here, now what? I wish I had been told these things. Already this is the second thing that I am to be part of that I have no idea about. I guess this is what it's like to be part of the military. Listen and do, don't ask.

Susie and I run over to what the officers called the auxiliary gate. It is fenced off and near the minimum security building housing the almost 200 Deader inmates we woke up earlier. As I see the makeshift fence that was constructed from the door of the building to the gate I instantly understand what the plan is. We are going to release the Deaders to do our work for us. Then what? We let them leave? But what is the cleanup that Susie talked about?

I stop thinking about the future as the door to the building opens. Two soldiers run out of the front and towards the gate. Behind them are four Unseen holding long sticks keeping the Deaders from catching the soldiers, without touching them directly. As the soldiers get to the gate they jump up and out of the way along the fence line. When they are safe, the Unseen let the Deaders go. The Deaders see their freedom and run outside of the gate as quickly as their decrepit, rotting bodies let them. Not long after they clear the gate, I hear their squeals of delight. They have found food and it's stretched all along the fence-line.

The stalkers have come right up to the fence and started to cut their way in as the Deaders clear the gate. It didn't take the stalkers or the Deaders long to figure out what was happening. The stalkers turn their fire upon the undead, but it was mostly inefficient. Their fear and adrenalin stop their shots from being true. Their number of sixty dwindle to 50,40 and 30 before much can be done. By this time several of the stalkers turn to run back to the woods. As they do, shots ring out from the woods taking them down just as quickly. The rear guard had set up in the woods to stop them from retreating.

This battle has turned bad. The soldiers had lost one of their own before to these people, they aren't going to let that happen again. One by one the runners are taken down by the rear guard, long before they can reach the possible safety of the woods. Along the fence line, a few have started to climb the fence, only to be cut up by the razor wire. They scream for help, only to receive a bullet from one of the soldiers inside to end their screaming. I don't know if we have lost anyone, but the stalkers are being decimated, quickly.

The thought of how this is going down makes me sick to my stomach. This is quickly becoming a massacre. I can see the reasons behind it, but it still doesn't feel right to me. Couldn't we take them prisoner? We are literally inside a prison right now. But we couldn't feed them, they would just die and turn into Deaders like all of the others in here. If we let them leave, would they go or come back with another army to fight us again? Larger and stronger this time.

It isn't long before the human screams die off, only to leave us with the screams of the Deaders. Matthew has come back in with Oakley and Smith. They have taken a few prisoners to question, Dante's one of them. The other two I recognize from around the hospital, but I don't know their names. After they drop them off with SGM Silver and Sgt. Hayes, they gather up some gear and head back out of the gate. All of the Unseen are gathered together, including Josh, to go back outside of the gate. I look at Susie.

"They are going out to take the Deaders down. No one wants that many swarming around the prison when they know there is food for them in there. Some may run off, but the Sergeants want most of them taken care of, hence clean up," she tells me.

She and I go to the front gate and watch the Unseen work. Some of them like Oakley are moving like dancers. She's making sure she is in position for the kill but doesn't accidentally touch any of them. That wouldn't be good for her. Josh and Matt are more like bulldozers than dancers. They run in, swing hard for the kill then spin to look for the next target. Reid and Smith are a different sort altogether. They stand back to back and wait for a Deader to get into range. When they do they swing long poles that have knives attached to them at the back of their heads. Sometimes they stab with these poles at a long distance, sometimes they swipe the knife along the back of their necks. Both ways are pretty efficient. All the while their staying pretty still and just racking up a body count. It's amazing to watch them work. Being able to be out around them Deaders like that and have little fear of being chased or drained would be amazing.

A few Deaders sense those of us watching the ordeal and smack themselves into the glass. Josh is usually close when this happens and he will swoop in with his hatchets connecting to the back of their necks. It's gruesome to watch, yet mesmerizing all the same. When the Deaders get too spread out, one of the regular soldiers runs out into the fields to attract their attention. The Deaders are so rotten from not feeding for two years that they are easily outrun back to the gate.

This game of cat and mouse goes on for two hours. In the meantime, the rear guard has come and joined the clean-up effort. The massive amount of people and Deaders killed this morning was astonishing. Later we may learn about our losses. That idea scares me as I think about it. If some of our people were killed during the battle, they would have risen again by now. The civilians and scientists are safe inside the building, but regular soldiers are exposed and focused on watching what was happening outside of the fence.

The likelihood of a Deader inside the gate two hours after the shooting has stopped is small, yet not zero. It's never zero. I call to Andromeda and tap Susie on her shoulder. I nod my head to the side asking her to follow me. She squints her eyes but gets up to follow. I tell her about my sudden fear and my idea to use Andromeda as an interior guard. If there is one lurking about, she will sense them. Susie nods. It may amount to nothing but walking the compound but I will feel safer after it was done.

Susie agrees and we take a walk, letting Andromeda lead us. A few minutes later we find a few charred remains of soldiers near the rear guard tower. The tower's burnt and blackened. The bodies are cold and too far gone to rise again. This still means that we lost at least two more soldiers today. We can't keep taking these losses. Thirty minutes later we complete our check of the entire compound. We only found one officer that had started to rise. Luckily, their leg had been shot, which is how they had bled out, but it was damaged so badly that they had to drag themselves along the ground. That's what stopped it from attacking anyone in the compound. If not for that, today may have been worse.

So two soldiers and one officer had been killed. When going up against a party of approximately 60, that was a small price to pay. I guess some people will find that acceptable anyway. As we walk back, I want to check on Mom and the rest of the civilians. Susie keeps going to see if she can be any help at the gatehouse. I tell her that I won't be long,and that I would bring Evee around for the clean up. The officers want us to clean up the Deader bodies around the fence line before we leave so that the stench of rotting flesh isn't as prevalent.

Solid ask I think.

As I walk into the building, Mom races towards me and grabs me into a bear hug. She asks about Matt and everyone else. I tell her and the others who have gathered around about the battle. Then I tell them that it seems that we had only lost three of our number. A few ask who they were, but I tell them that I wasn't sure. I don't want to tell them that I couldn't recognize them in their burnt condition. I tell everyone that Silver will probably be asking for volunteers to help with the cleanup, but those who don't will probably be asked to prepare a meal for the others. Many of them nod their willingness for one or the other.

I return to the rear of the compound to retrieve Evee from her hiding place. I don't like her being used to haul bodies, but it's better to do that than carry them one by one to the woods.

Afterward

The cleanup takes until after dark to complete. During this time we only take short breaks to get food and water that the civilians, like Mom, bring out to us. It's hard, disgusting work that has to be done. The most disturbing are the fresh bodies of the stalkers that had been fed upon by the Deaders. It's hard to keep my emotions in check. I've never wanted to see the loss of life on this scale. I hope I'll never have to witness it again. Andromeda even seems subdued with all of this death surrounding her. It's a hard day, but it's over quickly enough in the end.

After the work is done we report to the sergeants for watch assignments. The officers had stayed in to watch the prison while we worked outside the fence, so they volunteered to take the first four hours of watch. With the stalkers gone, we can go back to four-hour watches, but we still need to be on the lookout. We can't be completely sure that there weren't any left behind in reserve that are just biding their time.

Ragsdill's team says that they had never seen any more than what we had killed and they had stayed a half a day after everyone passed. Silver agrees that they are most likely gone, but most likely isn't good enough. As we continue to talk about what needs to happen. the prison officers tell us that all of the Deader screams got the inside prisoners riled up. We should stay out of any buildings that weren't cleared before as they are looking for food, I guess hibernation mode is over.

I look at Josh and ask him, "Have you seen these things come out of hibernation like this before?"

"Yeah, once. The whole group was hibernating when a small group of people had been run to the ground by another Deader group. When the other Deaders started screaming, they all woke up and ran to the apparent food source. It was scary. It was the only time that I would say they acted like zombies instead of the creatures that they are," he explains.

"Noted, don't wake a hibernating Deader," I joke.

Not really a joke though.

We break up the meeting and go our separate ways. I stop by the building with the civilians to check on Mom. When we get there I notice that the building is almost empty. Out of the almost thirty people that had been in here during the battle it seems like there are only 10 left. As I look around I can tell that all of the medics and scientists are gone.

"Where is everyone?" I shout as I walk through the echoing building.

"Working, or so I'm told," Mom says from her bed. "The scientists wanted to make as much chemical while we weren't moving as possible. They say that we almost have enough if we stop spilling it. The medics and doctors are either helping them or tending to the wounded. I don't know where the mechanics went. Doing whatever mechanics do I guess." Mom stops talking and breaks down into a racking cough.

"Why aren't they looking after you too?"

"They were. I told them that they had more important things to worry about than an old woman with a cough."

"That's not just a cough Mom. You're sick. You need something. I bet this prison has antibiotics or something." I get up to go look for one of the officers but Mom puts a hand on my arm and stops me.

"They do. The medics already talked to them. We are leaving here with a good supply of things like that, just less food I guess."

"Well, you need some. Or something. You need to get better," I say as my eyes start to well up with tears. Andromeda senses something is wrong and pushes her head under my arm so that she is touching me and Mom at the same time. I pet her for her effort and dry my eyes.

Mom doesn't say anything. She just lets the emotion work through me. I think she knows how sick she is but just doesn't want to admit it. I'll talk to the doctors myself and see what we can do, if she wants it or not.

Maybe I can wrap the pills in cheese like I used to do with Andromeda.

Since I was already here and no one seemed to need the beds I decided to bunk down here for the night. I have the morning watch, so I can actually get eight hours of sleep. If the memories of today will allow that. Hopefully, the fatigue will overpower the cringe and I'll sleep.

I wake up a little before my time for watch. I look around the building and see a few more people, but still not all of them. I rouse Andromeda from her slumber and sneak quietly out of the door. The only sounds were a few snores, my boots, and Mom's sporadic coughing. I stop by the cafeteria area to see if there's anything out for breakfast yet. It seems like there are just a few pieces of bread and peanut butter. Good enough. I grab enough for Andromeda and I then head to the main gate.

Silver and Matt are there talking about Dante, the leader of the stalkers. Apparently, he didn't just talk, he squealed about everything that we had done to him and the others. How we left them behind, blah, blah, blah. It sounds like this guy has some kind of complex. I barely listen while I wait for a break in the conversation to ask where I'm going to be posted. Before I can ask, Silver points to the front tower and waves. I wave back and head on. Since I'm in a tower I tell Andromeda to stay with Matt. I know he'll feed her a second breakfast, but she could use a few pounds. It won't hurt her.

I get to the post and relieve Oakley. She looks worn, but the middle shift is always rough. You only get to sleep a little before and after your shift. I hate it. She pats me on the shoulder as she passes, but doesn't say anything. I smile and tell her to get some rest. She just raises one hand with her thumb up as she exits the door. The other soldier here is from the rear guard so I don't know his name.

"Do you know where Susie is?" he asks

"No, I slept in the civilian building last night. Is that who I'm on with?" It would be her.

"Supposedly, I just want to get some sleep."

"She won't be late, I'm just early. I know her she'll be here soon." I barely got the words out before the door opens. I can hear her boots clanking on the metal stairs all the way up. I turn and smile at the guy as he grabs his stuff and runs out of the tower.

"Wow, does he have a hot date?" Susie asks looking at the door slamming shut at the bottom.

"With his rack apparently," I tell her.

The day goes on without much to talk about. I figure we would leave a day after the battle, but it seems like we are here for a bit. Hayes told me that it is partly because the scientists say that they can make up the chemical faster when there aren't any bumps spilling chemicals all the time. If we stay here for a bit we may be able to make up the time and travel faster because they aren't making the chemical every day. The sergeants have been discussing it but hadn't come to an actual plan yet.

Of course, the fact that the body count didn't come out correctly after the battle didn't help either. If you add up the Deaders we released and the number of stalkers and then subtract the number of bodies, we are missing about 15. That means that there are either 15 stalkers, 15 Deaders, or some combination of the above out in the surrounding woods. Silver assigned Ragsdill and Hayes to run patrols in the woods to see if they stuck around. Until we know it's safe we are going to stay put.

After my watch I go around looking for something to get in to. There really isn't much to do in a prison. I play a little basketball with a few guys, but other than that it was pretty boring for a couple of days. I spent a lot of time arguing with doctors and Mom about her condition. She isn't getting worse or running a fever so they just ignore it. All of them ignore it. It's getting very aggravating, to be honest. But I decide to let it go and let them make the decisions.

Even though they are the wrong decisions.

We end up staying at the prison for a whole week after the battle. I don't think that staying here is good, we have so far to travel and so many more things could go wrong. In the end though, it's not my decision and I have to abide by the one that was made. I just hope that it doesn't hurt us in the end. We are halfway through September now. It gets cold in the north a lot earlier than where we're from. You can already feel it at night. One good thing about the time we took here is that we were able to get cold weather gear from the prison. They had a uniform supply for the officers on site. It gives most of us a chance to get a good cold-weather jacket, boots, and gloves. That's a plus.

After the week's gone we load up to leave. As we start to head out a few of the people from our group are standing with the sergeants and seem to be saying goodbye. I see them all shake hands and part ways.

As Hayes catches up to me I ask her what happened. We keep moving to load up as she tells me. "We lost a few of our people. They want to stay here. Their scared and didn't know what they were signing on for. They feel safe here and the officers have agreed to let them stay. We lost 2 of our medics, which isn't good, a mechanic, and 3 of the family members that were along. Their brother, mother, or son died and they don't want to continue without them. They feel that this is far enough. With the loss of people though, we can now travel in the vehicles full time, which will make the trip faster." she explains.

"Well that's a plus I guess," I reply. I'm not sure what to think. I mean I get the family members but the medics and mechanics are needed. It's their decision though.

Here we are again with that.

We head out with our squad leading the way in the truck, Matt's bike, and Evee. The transport and suburban will follow behind us. The rear guard has a truck now too. It was given to us by the prison officers. They said that they couldn't use it so it might as well get some use. At least no one would be walking now. As soon as we are out of sight of the prison and we make sure we are on the correct road our squad takes off and speeds down the road. We send Matt ahead the furthest, then the truck with Oakley,

Hayes, Reid, and Smith. Josh, Andromeda, and I will stay back and try to keep the transports in sight.

We are back on the road and back to being the forward guard. I look at Josh and nod, he's happy to be back on the road too. So much so that he isn't even flicking the blades of his hatchets, yet. The next few days will just be getting back into the rhythm and making sure we keep the correct distance for the transports. With no one walking and no one stalking up behind us, we should be able to make better time.

Hopefully.

Peanut

A couple hours into our drive we come close to Lake Michigan. For those that don't know it's one of the Great Lakes. I had seen it before when we visited Chicago. It looked like the ocean to me instead of a lake. The thing is so massive that you can't see the other side. As we were looking at it I remember that it's fresh water. In essence, we could stop and gather some water if we needed it. I brought the idea up to Josh and he agrees that it would be good for cooking at least. There isn't anyone around to tell me no, so we divert and find a road to lead us to the lake.

Since Evee is a UTV we don't stay directly on the roads and take a few shortcuts through fields. When we get to the lake I assume it's going to be grown over and green with algae or something but the lake is clear. It's a bit murky like it was when I saw it from Chicago, but there isn't any extra plant growth. When I was at the state park I noticed that the bay and the ocean hadn't changed much, I just thought that was because of the salt water. Maybe it was just something with large bodies of water. On the trip so far we have seen swamps, ponds, and small lakes. They were all overcome with algae and lily pads. While we filled up a few containers, Josh pointed out that you could see fish and other sea life in the water. At least the spores didn't affect everything.

Could you imagine a Deader shark coming after you?

I know there aren't sharks in the Great Lakes, I was just wondering.

After we filled up and Andromeda plays in the water for a bit, we load up and head back. Since we aren't exactly sure where we are, and I don't have a fancy paper map, we head back the same way we came. As we pass through one field, Josh suddenly yells out. "Land Dolphin!"

"Excuse me," I look around and can't tell what he's talking about.

"It's a land dolphin. I can see a little gray something jump up out of the field and then fall back, then it jumps again. Like a dolphin," he tries to explain.

I almost blow it off when Andromeda jumps out of the back of Evee and runs into the field. Maybe it's a rabbit, but I veer in her direction to be certain. When we finally catch up to her she has cornered a small little dog. The coat is grey but molted. Maybe a little Australian Shepherd? I get out and go to the poor thing. It's scared and it hasn't been getting enough food. I bet it was a pet and lost its owner recently.

The little one lets me pick it up and carry her back to Evee. As I do, Andromeda gets jealous and jumps in the back to stick her nose into my business. The little girl is cute but shy. I hand her to Josh as I stand up on the back of the UTV to see if I can see a house nearby. There's nothing but woods and fields.

"Well, I guess you're coming with us now. We'll have to come up with a name for you since you don't have a tag. I'll show you to the squad and we can see what they think. How about you Josh?"

"I like Dolphin," he says excitedly as he pets the poor dog to death.

"I bet you do. I don't think that quite fits though. We shall see," I say as I blow the idea off. I'm not calling this dog Dolphin.

We head back to the road and pick up the trail easily enough. We shouldn't have lost too much time. With the addition of the water and the dog, it was a good side quest. *Really, side quest? I've been hanging around Josh and Matt too long.* I look over and the dog seems to be enjoying the ride, that's good. Andromeda is fine with her now that she is in Josh's lap instead of mine. She can be a bit protective. As the day disappears we catch up to the squad and show them what we found. I try to tell them about the lake and the water we have, but the little one gets away from Josh and runs over to the group. She quickly sniffs everyone but stops at Matt and jumps in his lap. Hmm. I'd never seen a dog like Matt that much. Most don't mind him, but they don't usually choose him.

Matt seems to be just as surprised as he smiles and pets the little girl. Everyone wants to get pets in and talks about how pretty she is. Hayes says that her coloring is called Blue Merle. I'm not sure where the blue is, but ok. As they all fawn over the new arrival, I explain how we found her and what we were doing. Hayes isn't happy that we deviated from the plan, but she does like the water and the dog. After we all get done with the little girl she hops down off Matt's lap and lays at his feet. *Well, I guess she picked her human.* Josh is a little sad until I remind him that she can't ride with Matt all day, she can ride with us though. He smiles and cheers up a bit.

We all agree to pick a name for her.Everyone has their own grand idea. A lot of stuff was thrown around, including Dolphin, but none seemed to fit. Matt's quiet while he's thinking but finally says, "Well we're near Chicago. My Dad's favorite football team. His favorite player was Sweetness, but that doesn't fit, nor does Payton. But another favorite of Dad's was Charles Tilghman. He went by Peanut."

As Matt says the name the little girl perks her ears up. "Well, I guess she approves. Peanut it is. The best cornerback in the league!" Matt yells. He seems happy. Happier than I have seen him since we got back together.

Maybe there is still a small bit of emotion in there.

The rest of the night calms down. Andromeda and Peanut even curl up and sleep together near the fire. I hope to myself that Peanut won't run off. I think Matt would be hurt if that happens. She seems comfortable and if she learns from Andromeda she'll be good to go. I look at them as I drift off to sleep. Hoping for more days like today ahead.

I wake up in my room thinking I'm late for school. It's almost 7 O'clock and I have to catch the bus at 7:10. No way I'm making it with a five-minute walk. I run out of my room and see Matt standing in the kitchen, still in his pajamas making waffles.

Mom is on the couch watching a show, playing on her phone, and drinking coffee.

"You forgot it was a holiday, didn't you," Matt teases as the toaster pops up.

"No!" I protest as I steal a waffle and shove it in my mouth.

"Hey! Just because you're dumb doesn't mean you can steal my waffle," Matt yells as I run away from him. My mouth was burning the waffle was way too hot. I'm not telling him that though.

I run to Mom and hide behind her. Mom looks at me, "Waffles are hot huh?"

"Yeah," I say with my mouth full of burning lava that was supposed to be a waffle.

"Forgot you were off school too," she says in her tone. I'm not sure how to describe it. It's not menacing or condescending, but you can't lie to her when she uses it. It's infuriating really.

"Yeah," I admit.

"HA! I knew it. Dad owes me five bucks. I knew you'd forget," Matt yells as he does his happy dance around the kitchen and makes a new waffle for himself.

"Dad's at work and Matt has some computer game thing he's doing today," she starts before I interrupt.

"Yeah, Dungeons and Dorks! Or is it Virgins we will always be?" I tease. Not my best.

Matt sticks his tongue out at me covered in syrupy waffle. "As, I was saying," Mom continues. "We could do a mani-pedi day. Just the two of us."

"That sounds great Mom. Can we do the afternoon though?"

"Sure honey. Why?" She asks with a concerned look on her face.

"I'm going back to bed. That's why." I throw up the peace symbol and saunter off back to my room to get a few more hours of sleep. No reason to be up this early on a holiday. Whatever holiday it is.

As I'm dragged out of sleep in the real world I know I don't have to get ready for school. School is a thing of the past. Now I have to get ready to set myself up to not die today. Hopefully, help others do the same. I roll over and see Andromeda and Peanut sitting by the fire next to Matt. They are both sitting nice and watching Matt's every move. I wonder why, then the wind shifts and I smell cooking meat. Fresh meat if I'm right.

"Whatcha cooking?" I ask as I try to get up.

"Rabbit and squirrel. Shot them both this morning. The rest of the squad is out on patrol they told me to let you sleep until you either woke up or the transports passed us. You woke up first," Matt tells me.

Suddenly I am embarrassed. How did everyone else get up, eat, and leave before I ever woke up? "Why did they let me sleep?"

"It looked like you needed it. You had some weird dream or something last night and you tossed and turned for a while. We have nothing pressing today so it didn't hurt anything. They all just left about thirty minutes ago. It's not really that late." He pulled the meat off the fire, set some aside for me, and gave bits to the two dogs.

It's still odd thinking that we now have two dogs.

Matt and I talk a bit as I get up and get ready to go. He's going to stay back with me today and meet the rest later, before sunset. He wants me to head back later today and check on Mom. He agrees that she wasn't looking good and that we need to stay closer to her. That's probably why he isn't running point. I tell him that it's a good plan for the day and it would be nice to introduce Mom to the new puppy. It would make her happy to see her.

"By the way, where's Josh?" I ask thinking about having to ride alone today.

"He went with Reid and Smith. He said he wanted to walk today and learn some things from them. I don't know," Matt scoffs.

We break down the rest of the camp and bank the fire. I load up the two dogs into Evee and we hit the road. We should end up near the outskirts of Chicago by sunset today. After this, we should be able to stay away from all the major cities from here on out. The day goes well with the exception of a cold drizzle all day long. The temperatures are starting to stay low even in the sun, so a cloudy day full of rain makes the cold unbearable. I stop a few times to let the dogs get down, pee and play for a bit. Andromeda's used to the long rides, but I'm not sure about Peanut, so I err on the side of caution.

As sunset approaches, not like we could see it, I slow and wave to Matt. I head back to the transports. I don't expect them to be too far behind so I take it slow. I start to get worried when half an hour goes by and I still haven't seen them. I stop and check the signs that I could see, nothing's amiss. I look at the dogs, like they can give me an answer, then pick up the pace. An hour later I finally came across them. They were slowed to a crawl. I pull up and don't see the suburban with the two transports. I stop the soldiers and ask them what the hold-up is.

"Suburban started acting up. We left the last of the mechanics with it and piled everyone else in to the transports. We are slow because *we* soldiers have to walk again, there isn't enough room. I hope they get that thing fixed," he says. He's soaked through and looks completely miserable. I get it, I mean I have a cab on Evee so I'm not wet, but I still get it.

I let the transports pass and turn around to follow them. As true dark sets in they stop for the night. I help them set up in the rain and then look for cover as soon as my help isn't needed. I find Mom helping with the food and introduce her to Peanut. I explain the name and she tears up and holds the dog tighter. I know the name brings up memories of Dad, but the dog never knew him, why hug the dog tighter?

Moms are weird.

Loss

In the morning I wake up and Peanut is nestled in tightly with Mom. Mom sounded a bit better last night and she seems happier this morning. Maybe she was right and whatever was ailing her has passed. We hit the road and I decide to stay back with the transports today. I don't know how far the squad got last night after I lost an hour and a half just looking for the transports. If they got an early start they could be hours ahead by now.

We pack everyone in where they can fit. I leave Peanut with Mom, both seem content with that. The suburban had shown up late last night with the mechanics. They said that they got it running, but they aren't sure for how long. As we go to leave I do report to Silver and let him know why I was here and why I was staying close.

"If they get worried they'll send Washington back on that loud bike of his to look for you," is all Silver says. He then gets back to whatever it is that he does all day.

The ride's slow but by midday, we hit the outskirts of Chicago. It was a big city so skirting around it would still take all day. I run Evee to the lead to make sure we stay on target with the road signs that the squad has left. Funny enough I find a handwritten note.

Stay with the transports today. I'd like extra security with them through the city. It's also nice to know that you can run your UTV to catch us if there is a problem. After tomorrow night catch back up with us.

Sgt. Hayes

Well, that's solved.

I make sure to keep everything on course. I look for both sets of signs before committing to a path. We don't need a reenactment of Pittsburgh, although we did find Josh. The day passes slowly. As we get near the outer edge of the city I hear a horn blare from behind me. I wheel Evee around and headed back to see what the problem is.

As I come around the first transport, the problem is obvious. The suburban is hissing steam out of the front grill and liquid is pouring onto the ground from beneath it. A mechanic opens the hood as I pull up and that's when I see smoke boil out too. The truck is fried. Unfortunately, it's between the two transports and this road, if you can call it that, is very narrow. We're going to have to push it off the roadway to get the transport by.

Silver comes by to see the problem for himself. "So, now what?" he asks simply.

"She's fried sir. This is what we were worried about. Our fix just made it worse. We just have to push it off the road and leave it here," one mechanic says.

"We can't have people walking. Take some unnecessary supplies out of the transport to make room for the eight people. Pack them in this thing and then get it off the road. We need to keep moving," he then spins on his heel and walks off.

It takes us two hours to get all of that done. People kept arguing about what was necessary and unnecessary. The medics wouldn't give up medical supplies, the cooks wouldn't give up food or water, and the scientists wouldn't give up any of their equipment. It finally took Silver getting in the transport and chucking things out of the back to get people moving. Sometimes that's the only way to compromise.

After the suburban's loaded we push it off the road and into the bushes. It's hidden from sight almost instantly. Even though I know that we most likely won't ever come this way again, even if we did this will most likely be ransacked. Still, I mark the area with our signs to tell us where it is with the supplies. Better to be safe than sorry.

The lost time cost us and we have to stop for the night just outside of the city. If it had been before the Fall, the city lights would have stopped any stars from appearing in the night sky. Now you can see every part of the Milky Way. It's beautiful, but I would still prefer my phone and some electric heat myself. We set up camp and set the watch. I get the mid-shift tonight since they knew

I had gotten out of a shift last night. It's fine, I'm feeling good and things are looking ok.

I lay down with Mom, Andromeda, and Peanut a bit early so I can relax. As Mom lays down she has a racking cough again, but she waves me off. "Lingering effects," she says. I let it go because, during the last two days, she has seemed good. After she calms down, both dogs curl around her and we're all asleep pretty quickly.

What seems like five minutes go by and I am woken up by Andromeda whining and Peanut barking her head off. I'm groggy and can't tell what time it is. There's no moon out, that I can see, and it's pretty dark. I tap Mom to wake her up, but she doesn't move. Andromeda's looking at me then at Mom and whining more. My heart rate kicks up to 1000 and I shake Mom to wake her up. No matter how hard I shake her she won't wake up. I started screaming at her to wake up.

People come running over and pull me away. The medics check her breathing and heart rate. From the looks on their faces, I know that she doesn't have either. At this point, I melt into a puddle of tears. I feel Andromeda lean into me and hear Peanut whining a sad little whine. People are all around me and talking to me, but I can't see or hear them. My world fades out to the two dogs and the body of my dead mother in front of me.

I watch one of the soldiers grab Mom by the shoulder and roll her over towards me. At first, I have no idea what he's doing. Why is he moving my mother? Then I see the knife in his hand. I know what has to be done but I can't let him do it. I jump up and attack him, pulling the knife from his hand and putting it against his throat. Andromeda and Peanut jump up with me and bare their teeth. They growl at anyone that comes near me or Mom's body.

"YOU STAY AWAY FROM MY MOTHER! YOU HEAR ME! YOU WON'T TOUCH HER!"

I feel a gentle hand on my shoulder. I spin with the knife out towards them. I have no idea what I'm doing, but I can't let them stab my mom. They can't kill her. I know that she's dead. I know they need to do this. My heart is broken into so many pieces that I can't make sense of anything. I focus and see SGM Silver in front of me.

"Call off the dogs and give me the knife Washington. You know this is necessary. We can take the body away if you'd like. So you don't have to see it," he speaks calmly and plainly. I know he's right.

"Andromeda, Peanut. Down. It's ok." I hand the knife to Silver. "Don't take her yet. I'll turn away as you do it. But I need to see her for a bit longer."

Silver nods as I sit back down and lose focus again. I think that I hear Evee start up and take off, but I'm not sure and I couldn't have cared less at that moment. I continue to be catatonic for a long time. I have no idea how long. It isn't until Matt bends down in front of me and holds my face in his hands that anything feels real. I focus on him and see that it's my brother. My only family left. I pull him into a hug and let new tears fall onto his shoulder. Matt doesn't say anything, he just holds me and pets the dogs as I cry and scream and yell at the world. I'm not sure if any of it is out loud or just in my head. It really doesn't matter. I just need the release.

A while later I finally pull back and let Matt get off of his knees. He pulls his legs out and sits down next to me, pulling me into a side hug. "You good?" is all he says. I nod, knowing I'm not. "We need to get on the road but we have to burn Mom's body first. We'll get it set up, then the two of us will stay behind to watch it burn. Afterward, we'll catch up with the group. OK?"

I nod again, not knowing what else to do.

Emotions

As the day progresses I'm lost in my memories and imagination. The emotional fog that I am in is hard to navigate. When Dad was killed and Matt was lost, I had to step up to keep Mom safe and moving. She was the one that wanted to shut down. I couldn't blame her, she lost her husband and son on the same day. Her world had shattered, just like mine just had. I know Matt's still here and I have Andromeda, but in the past month, there has been too much death. Jordan, Testerman, and all of the people at the battle of the prison. This trip wasn't supposed to be about death, it was supposed to be about saving lives. About getting rid of this disease of the spores.

In the moments that I'm lucid, I watch the squad. Matt, and other soldiers build a pyre to place Mom on. It isn't big, it didn't have to be. It just has to burn hot enough to cremate her body. Cremation was the only way nowadays. Even though this seems to take a long time to put together, it only takes an hour or so. Digging a true grave is not as easy as television made it look. To dig something like that it would take a whole day.

I keep wondering why I was so broken and Matt seems fine. He's walking around and joking with the others. He stops a lot to check on me and take the dogs for a walk with him. Peanut stays with him often but does stop to check on me too. I think about how much worse this morning could've gone without those two. They couldn't do anything for Mom, but they saved lives by warning us of her passing. We were able to react before she was reanimated and tried to steal someone's soul.

By the time the pyre was ready and Mom is wrapped in a blanket and placed on top of it, I have recovered enough to move on my own and function, almost like a human being. A couple of people say a few nice words, then walk off to get ready to leave. The words pass over and through me, without really meaning anything. It's not that I don't appreciate the gesture, I do. It's just that it can't do anything to dull the pain.

Everything comes to completion, the only thing left to do is light the fire. Matt lights a torch and holds the handle out to me. "Do you want to do the honors?" he asks.

Honors? Is it really an honor to set your loved one's body on fire? Is that what'll take the pain away?

"No," I say. I manage to keep my tone even but Matt seems to know what I mean.

He nods and turns the torch to the pyre. A loud thwump, and the fire is burning brightly. The flames get hot quickly and I have to step back because of the heat. I hear the transports and other vehicles start-up and head out. I feel a hand on my shoulder that brings me a bit of peace. I turn and see Sgt. Hayes standing behind me.

"The rear guard will be here soon. Stay as long as you need. They will give their respects and move on quietly I'm sure. Catch back up to the transports by tonight. There isn't any reason to be out on your own after dark. Ok?" Hayes says this calmly and evenly. It's the words that aren't spoken that I hear the loudest.

I nod and touch the hand on my shoulder. She lets it rest there for a minute then slowly pulls away and disappears into the distance. Matt steps up to me and stands to my right. Peanut and Andromeda are lying just outside of the range of the heat. I don't blame them it is kind of stifling. I stay there until I can't stand it anymore, then walk over to Evee and take a seat. Matt sits next to me and doesn't say anything at first.

Finally, he breaks the silence, "Josh wanted to stay with you too. Hayes said that we needed to do this. Just the two of us. He was really sad to see you hurting. He wanted to make sure I told you that."

"Thank you. I'll talk to him later and tell him you told me," I reply.

We sit in silence until the pyre is nothing but red, hot embers. "We need to get on the road," Matt says.

"Where's the rear guard? I thought that Hayes said they would be by soon," I ask confused. I started to get a little worried about them. It shouldn't take them this long to catch up.

"They were by over an hour ago. You were zoned out on the flames and they passed through silently. I saw them and Ragsdill stopped to make sure I knew they were there. There didn't seem to be a reason to break your revelry," Matt replies.

Wow, I must be out of it. I didn't realize any of that had happened. I turn to start Evee and call for the dogs at the same time. I don't realize they were both already in the back. Matt looks at me and tilts his head to the side. I just nod and get out so he can drive. I am in no condition at this point. When we get back on the road I wonder about Matt and how he is handling everything.

"Matt, how are you doing with all of this?" I ask without looking at him, hoping he'll open up.

"Unfortunately, it's part of life now. I mean it was always part of life to die and to lose others. Now it's more immediate, I guess. That's probably the wrong word," he rambles.

"This isn't just someone. We lost our mother today! We lost Dad two years ago. You weren't even there for that," I scream at him. I didn't know I had held that anger towards him for not being there. "I had to deal with Mom, alone, after she lost Dad. After WE lost Dad. You were out gallivanting and just left us to join the military. You didn't come back to check on us. Ever!"

Matt was seething with anger. "I didn't check on you. I found Dad in the driveway. I ran into the house to try and find both of you. You had gone. There was no one around and I had to leave on my own. I heard Dad's last words. Not you. I watched him die."

"You're lying! You never came back, we'd have heard you."

"No! Dad's last words to me were to 'Get the girls'. He was worried about you two. I failed in that. I failed miserably and took it to heart so badly that it's how I ended up almost dying. I was lost and rambling. I froze to death after being tortured by the assholes that caused the   problems the day that killed Dad. You want emotion. That's emotion. You think you're traumatized right now. You don't know anything. I let Dad down on the last thing he ever asked of me!" I was at a loss for words.

Weird, I know.

We ride in silence after that for a few hours. Matt's talking it slow to not jostle us around too badly, the roads are bad. From what I understand, they were bad around Chicago before the Fall, so it only figures they would be even worse now. I take the time to think about the good times with Mom. How I felt the day I found her at the Home of the Brave. I like to think about how Mom loved Jordan from the moment she met her, and Peanut too. A light went out in an already dark world today. I'm not sure I will ever get over it.

As the sun was going down, I figure enough time has passed to talk to Matt again.

"Look, I'm sorry alright. I had no idea about you finding Dad still alive. I shouldn't have called you a liar. I know you would've come back if you thought you could've found us."

"I tried to come back multiple times. Hayes and Silver wouldn't let me. Not until months later. I think you and Mom were separated by then. You were probably already at Cape."

"Wow," I say as I turn in the seat to see him better. "It was really that long."

"It was a far way to go and they were still trying to figure out how to harness my...you know. My ability. My difference. I guess."

"OK, but why have you seemed fine today? With everything, you just trudged through like it was a normal day."

"Because it was a normal day for me."

"What!" I start to scream at him again, but he shushes me.

"Let me explain. Please. It was a normal day. I have dealt with death for the last two years.."

I didn't let him finish. "But not the death of your mother!"

"Would you let me explain?" he looks over at me with anger in his eyes. I decide to stop and let him finish what he wants to say. Although I don't want to.

"The other part, I have kind of explained before. Being Unseen has its disadvantages. One of those being a loss of certain emotions and an amplification of others. Anger is amplified. Sadness, melancholy, and grief are all muted. I don't feel them. They are not an emotion that keeps you alive." He slows Evee to a stop so he can turn and look at me.

"So you don't feel anything? Nothing, even though you just lost your last parent? I call bullshit!"

"It's not my choice to be this way. It's not my choice to anger easily and not feel regret like I should. It's the spores. It gets worse all the time. Like the spores are taking over, more and more."

I jump up and look at him. "Like the spore sickness that Testerman died from? You're saying that every day the spores are taking over more and more of our bodies. Until someday we won't be able to stop them and they kill us, like the others?"

"That wasn't what I was saying," he says as he starts moving again. "But, that's true. The scientists saw it in people who spent a lot of time outside, like you and me, over the last two years. They knew this was happening."

"And they didn't tell us?"

"In a way they did. That's a lot of why we couldn't wait the winter out. The other reasons were true, but this was additional. And more important."

I sit back in silence until we pull up to camp. We are a little later than sunset, but I think the time was needed. I'm still not ok with Matt saying that he doesn't feel the loss of our mother. I am willing to give him time to grieve in his own way though. Not everyone grieves the same way. It may hit him later, we'll see. In the meantime, I have to find Josh and apologize to him for ignoring him this morning. The rest of the squad too. They came back from forward watch to help with everything with Mom. They didn't have to do that. I need to make sure they know it was appreciated.

Appreciation

I catch up with Josh and sit down with him, Andromeda sits by my side and Peanut next to Josh, to get all of her pets in. I sit with him for a bit, both of us just petting the dogs. I'm trying to figure out what to say. I don't know where to start.

"I lost my mother too," he says. "I never got to see her after she left. She may not even be dead. Kind of like your mom when you were at Cape Henlopen. It's different when you see them die I think. I hate it when I see people die. I couldn't break down when Mom left, I had my brother to help. But I cried at night after he went to sleep. I still miss her."

This kid has been through a lot, but he can put this into words when I can't even think.

"I know. It's hard not knowing. It should be easier knowing, but it's just too much. I had to hold it together when my dad died. I had to take care of Mom. I don't have anyone to take care of this time. I can let the emotions roll over me," I tell him. At this point Josh leans over and gives me a side hug.

"You have a lot of people to take care of. We all have to take care of each other. So come back to us soon. OK? We need you. The real you that is good at what we do. We are missing something when you lose yourself. Take your time, but come back to us," with that he pets Peanut one last time, gets up and walks away. Peanut looks after him but seems to know I need her more. She moves over and lays down with her head on my knee, looking up at me with her bright eyes.

As Josh walks away, I'm crying. Not an ugly cry like before, but a healing cry. That little boy is right. This team needs me to be at my best. Mom's gone, but she will always be with me. Just like Jordan. I need to carry them with me to make me stronger, not weaker. I need to put my head on straight and get on with it. It's easier to say for sure, but I know what I need to do now. After another minute I get up and join everyone else by the fire. I stand and look at each member of the squad. As they lock eyes with me I nod my head slightly and they nod back. I'll have to let them know more later, but right now this is all we need. They know what it means. They know I appreciate everything they did for me and Matt today. There isn't any use wasting words on it right now.

Hayes takes me off watch for the night. I eat then lay down with Andromeda and fall asleep within seconds.

"You're burning it!" Matt yells. "Why is there so much smoke!"

As he says this the smoke alarm starts going off next to my bedroom. I'm just trying to make pancakes and bacon. But the bacon got away from me and I forgot to flip the pancake. I turned to it just as Matt started yelling. My dad comes out of the bedroom and just looks at the two of us. I was just trying to make Mom breakfast in bed for her birthday. I wasn't trying to burn the house down.

Matt takes the pancake and throws it in the sink while I take the bacon off the burner. I start to cry a bit because I screwed everything up so badly. I'm only 8 years old, but I thought that I could do it. Mom comes out and tells me to get dressed.

"Daddy is going to take us to breakfast. How about IHOP?" she says sweetly. "Thanks for trying honey."

With that, I'm a bit happier.

I'm blinking because there is smoke in my eyes. I squint to get it out and my eyes water like crazy. As my vision starts to clear I can see Mom surrounded by flames. I blink again and see that she is just sitting across the campfire from me. I have a marshmallow stick in my hand, Matt is next to me holding the chocolate and crackers for when my mallow is done. I look at the end of the stick just in time to see the marshmallow melt, catch fire and fall off of the stick.

"Good job dummy," Matt says snidely. "That's the second one. Would you pay attention we don't have all night."

"Matthew, leave your sister alone. She is only 5 and hasn't done this as much as you," Mom tells him from across the fire.

I look up and see her sitting in her camp chair. A drink in one hand and a book in the other. This is when she is the happiest.

"Ava. Ava. Hey lazy butt, get up already," As I open my eyes I can hear Matt yelling at me. It takes my groggy brain a bit to register where we are. Are we camping? If so where's Mom? I don't see her chair.

It's only a second before I realize where and when we are. Mom's chair isn't here and neither is she. She won't be sitting across from me again. But I refuse to fall into that again. "Alright, alright. I'm up, I'm up," I tell Matt as I push his hand off of me.

"Well, you could've fooled me. We are moving in five minutes. Your plate is right here, getting cold. Put something warm on. It doesn't seem like it's going to warm up today," then he's gone. Andromeda comes over and licks my face.

"Ok, ok. Not you too," I say to her as I push her away.

I get up and get ready to go. It may not have been five minutes, but it was less than ten. I need to be better. Sgt. Hayes isn't going to let this go on much longer. As I walk over to Evee, she is there holding my key. She doesn't say anything, she just holds the key up and arches an eyebrow at me. Basically, she's asking if I'm good. I nod and take the keys. She smiles and turns around to get in the truck. As I get the door open to the driver's side, I look in to see if Josh is riding with me. I'm surprised to see the other Reid sitting there.

"It's my day to ride in the back of the squad with you. Hayes wants someone to keep an eye on you, without keeping an eye on you. She doesn't trust Josh for that. We do have Peanut and Andromeda though," he explains. That's when I notice that he is holding Peanut so close to him that I didn't even see her at first. He's a funny guy. You wouldn't think that a large guy who stands over six feet tall with tattoos over his arms and legs would be such a softy. I love it. But it's not what you would think just looking at him.

Guess that's why Mom always said to not judge a book by its cover.

We get on the road and I get back into the pattern of work. I never understood my Dad when he said that work would clear his mind. But I understand now. I have a lot to think about, so my personal stuff has to get pushed to the back. I still have to sort through a lot, but it can be done at the right time. Right now isn't it. The day goes by pretty normally. Weirdly, I find this normal now. It wasn't that long ago that normal was sitting in the bunker and playing with Andromeda all day. Then before that, it was sitting on my phone. Life changes fast.

Nothing much of note happens for a couple of days. Hayes has a different person ride with me each day for the next three days. It's nice because it gives me a chance to really tell each one how much I appreciate what they did. The guys just blow it off and change the subject. They don't seem comfortable talking about things like that. On the third day, Lyla is riding with me and she lets me really open up about it all. It's a good talk and it really helps me put it all into words. After we talk she asks me a question out of the blue.

"Have you talked to Matt about all of this?" she asks. "He isn't hiding his feelings as well as he thinks he is."

"He told me that you all don't really feel it the same as you used to. He says it's all ok," I explain to her.

"It's true. To a point. But something that deep is still going to be felt. He probably just doesn't want to talk about it," she looks at me for a second then lets it drop.

Maybe she's right.

Rockford

Four days out from Chicago we reach Rockford, IL. It was a medium-sized city, before the Fall. With the supplies we lost to make sure everyone was in a truck, we need to take the time to scavenge the area. The day before Hayes had taken Evee back to the rear guard and spoken to Sgt. Ragsdill about combining the two guards for the scavenging team. We could cover more ground quickly. Ragsdill's team hadn't seen anything behind us since the prison, so one day shouldn't hurt, he told her.

In the morning their team meets us in front of the transports with their new truck. I wave to Susie when she gets out of the truck. Andromeda lopes over to her and says hi herself. Matt is told to leave his bike with one of the regular soldiers with the transports. He's not happy but he understands that if something happens this guy can run into the city and find us. The transports aren't moving today since we aren't setting the trail. We have both trucks and Evee, they only have the two big transports now, not really the best to set the path.

The two sergeants talk about the day over a paper map. Once that's done we break up into three teams and head into the city. I'm driving Evee with Josh sitting shotgun. Reid and Matt are in the back with the two dogs in the bed. Andromeda isn't too happy with this scenario, but she deals with it better than her friend. Peanut whines the whole drive into the city. So much so that Matt reaches back and puts his hand on her to calm her down.

Our task is to hit the main downtown area and look for gas stations or vehicles in parking lots and get fuel. We pretty much know that there won't be anywhere with food supplies around, but from what I understand we are still pretty good there. A couple of soldiers have been hunting at night to bring in fresh meat now and then. Rations may get a bit thin, but they should last us to South Dakota. The main problem is getting there with all of our vehicles running. Hence, our trip today.

Rockford was built with Rock River running down the middle of it. It's pretty easy to find a path and follow it. As cities go this one doesn't look too destroyed. That bodes well for our mission today. Until we get to the river and try to find a bridge to cross. Each bridge we come to has been barricaded. Not just fences or wooden pallets. They have moved heavy operating equipment and large trucks to block the bridges completely from the east side. We stop and look at each other, wondering why someone would take the time and the equipment to block this many bridges with this much equipment. It was like they were building a new Berlin wall between east and west Rockford. In the end, we decided that it wasn't really an issue that we needed to pursue since we were just looking for fuel. We would have to get the transports to travel further south to cross the bridge, but it didn't hinder anything too much. We put it in the back of our minds and travel north along a main route looking for gas stations. We run upon a few larger trucks that ran on diesel, so we stop and siphon gas from them. Matt's trick of blowing into the tank with a second hose made it a lot better than what I used to see in movies and TV shows.

With some diesel in hand, we head north, keeping the river to our left. Matt figures that we should follow the river north then angle east and head back south that way. Reid has his paper map so we should be able to find our way back without any problems.

A little way up the river we come upon a city park. *We seem to come across these often.* As usual, the park is overgrown.

As we go to the roadway, Reid notices that part of the park used to be a golf course. "If the course used gas-powered golf carts, they may have a lot of fuel on hand. Who would think to look at a golf course for gas? Food maybe. But not gasoline. Let's go look there," he points out.

"They may even have some containers we can use too," Matt chimes in.

I agree but look at Josh to see what he has to say. It probably won't change the decision but it's nice to include everyone. Josh looks at everyone in turn and nods in agreement. While he smiles and agrees I also see his hands slide to his hatchets and he starts flicking the blades. That tells me that he's nervous about our decision. I keep that in mind as I look for a way to get to the course. It takes a minute to find an off-ramp. It's highly overgrown but seems safe enough. I take it and follow old beat-up signs to the course.

As we turn into what used to be the main road to the golf course, we hear gunshots in the distance. It sounds like it's coming from the west, I hope all of our teams are ok. I look at Matt but he just shakes his head, meaning we can't leave to help. We have a job to do, we have to rely on the other crews doing their job too. Before the Fall we would be able to communicate by radio to see what was happening. Nowadays, we don't have that.

I haven't been to too many golf courses in my life, neither has Matt. We rely on Reid to tell us how to get to the clubhouse and find the golf carts. It's not too hard and we pull up soon after entering the property. The clubhouse looks like it's in good shape. The building still has all its windows and doors. That's a good sign. When people come to look for things and don't find them, they usually take it out on the building itself. I'm not sure why, but we've talked about this before. Josh and I decide to go into the clubhouse itself to see if we can find some food or water while Matt and Reid go look for the golf carts.

As Josh and I approach the doors, I can tell that they are chained together on the inside. They are glass doors so Josh just walks up and hits the corner of the glass hard with the back of his hatchet. The glass shatters but stays in place, safety glass. Josh laughs then hits the center and clears the glass out of the jamb, just enough for us to walk through. Andromeda goes in first, while Peanut hangs back hiding behind Josh's legs. I haven't seen her in a situation like this before.

I hope she doesn't do anything to put anyone at risk.

As we enter, Andromeda leads us to the right and down a hallway. I'm hoping she is leading us to the kitchen, the locker rooms aren't going to help us much. A minute later I shake my head, I should've known that she would lead us directly to the kitchen area. Everything seems clear. Josh goes to the freezer and starts to pull the door open.

"Stop!" I yell.

Josh jumps back with his hatchets at the ready. "What?" he asks.

"You never open a freezer or fridge anymore. There is nothing good that is going to come of that," I say.

"Oh, makes sense. Sorry," he casts his eyes down and walks to another closed door.

I didn't mean to make him mad, but a freezer that's been off for two years can hold disgusting stuff that will stay in your nose for hours. I let him sulk for a bit as we look through the kitchen area. There isn't anything here worth taking but a few spices that were left behind. The cooks will love this stuff. I shove it in my backpack and decide that we should go check on the guys. I push open an emergency door and breathe in the fresh air. The air in the kitchen wasn't bad, but it was stale from years of disuse.

I send Andromeda off to find Matt. As she lopes off, Peanut cowers behind my legs and whimpers. She is looking towards where Andromeda just ran off to. I lean down to see what is bothering her when I hear Andromeda bark. It's a clipped bark, but it means that she has seen something that she doesn't like. I tell Josh to stay with Peanut and get back to Evee.

"When you get to her, get Peanut inside the cab and bring it back here. If something is here we may need to get out of here quickly," I tell him. After he nods, I take off at a run towards Andromeda and the others.

As I round the side of the building that holds the golf carts, Andromeda is just ahead of me baring her teeth and growling low. That means Deaders. I peek around the corner and see Matt shooing us away. I take a quick look around and see 4 Deaders wandering around. They must have stirred them up when they were checking things out.

Good thing they're Unseen.

Just as this thought goes through my mind I see one lurch forward and knock into Reid. Reid tries to react quickly enough, but the Deader's hand grazes Reid's bare hand. The Deader's eyes comes *alive* as he sees Reid for the first time. Before anyone can react the Deaders attack him all at once. Matt jumps into the fray and tries to kill one with a shot to the back of the skull. He misses slightly, the Deader keeps moving. Andromeda rushes in to help Reid too. Just as all of this is happening Josh pulls up in Evee with Peanut in the back.

The new electrical signals from the dogs distracts two of the Deaders long enough for Matt to get a good shot on each of them, killing them instantly. Reid has been under this pile too long to not have sustained any injuries from these things. Hopefully, he can keep them from contacting his skin. Andromeda whines as she is thrown off of one of the Deaders. Instead of going after her he drops down and tries to drain Reid again. Reid seems to be holding his own and is still moving around.

Good. That's good.

Josh makes it into the fight and swings at the topmost Deader. His swing isn't accurate, but I think it was more for effect than accuracy. Whatever it was supposed to be it worked by drawing the attention of the topmost Deader for just enough time for Matt to end it's afterlife. Only one left to go. Matt and Josh seem to have everything handled with that, so I check on Andromeda. She got up from where she was thrown, but she seems to be keeping her weight off of one rear leg. It probably got hurt when she landed awkwardly. I have her lie down and look back at the fight. What I see is something that I had never in my life expected to see. Matt and Josh had stopped fighting and were trying to make sense of the sight too.

Reid and the Deader are locked together in their own fight. This fight doesn't seem to be physical, but mental. The Deader has one hand on Reid's face. Reid has one of his hands covering that and the other on the Deader's face. The Deader's other hand is covering the hand on its face. I have seen people get drained, I have been personally affected by it before. It does not take a Deader long to drain the life out of you completely. A few seconds and you usually lose consciousness. We stand there and watch this battle for a good thirty seconds before anyone can think enough to react.

It seems like Reid is stopping the Deader from draining him, or he is draining the Deader at the same time he is being drained. Kind of like an energy transfusion? I have no idea. Luckily, Josh reacts enough to break our revelry.

"Matt! Kill it!" Josh screams.

This wakes Matt up and he stabs the Deader in the cerebellum. The Deader falls to the pavement a second later. We all rush over to Reid to make sure he's ok. Reid pushes the remnants of the Deader off of him and stands up. His reaction scares us. He jumps up, looks away from us and yells into the air, "Whooooo! What a rush!"

"Umm. Excuse me?" I ask quietly. "How are you not dead?"

"I saw you being drained," Matt chimes in.

"Yeah! Yeah! I was. But I was draining him right back. I think I won too because I have more energy than I think I ever have," he informs us. As he turns around to explain we see his eyes glowing brighter than I have ever seen a Deaders glow.

"Holy shit!" Matt exclaims as he jumps back and pulls his rifle.

"Whoa, what's up?" Reid asks as he puts his hands up.

"I've seen this in Deaders before," Josh interjects. He puts his hands up in front of Matt to stop him from shooting Reid. "When the Deaders overfeed their eyes glow brighter. So much so you could see the spores in their neck."

"If Reid is dead and a Deader, how is he talking and how did he turn after being drained?" I ask as I slowly work my way out of the way and closer to Evee.

"I'm not dead, or an NLB. I swear. That Deader tried to drain me, but something inside of me kicked when it did. I knew that if I grabbed it, I could stop him from draining me. I was stronger than him. I guess I also stole some of his energy too. I don't know. Does anyone have a mirror?" Reid looks scared now.

"Reid, I have never seen anything like this. Nor have I heard of anyone being able to drain an NLB. I don't know what to think," Matt says as he's thinking as fast as he can.

"Kinda like seeing a kid come in and his eyes glow? Or like being able to see spores, being able to see animal outlines or tell if something has an electrical charge? All of this is new man. It's me. I just beat the Deader at his own game," Reid pleas with Matt.

As Matt thinks about it, Josh walks over and pushes his gun barrel to point at the ground. "He's right Matt. It's just new." Then he walks over and hugs the big man.

Josh is a force of nature. One second he's a small kid then other times he does things like this. He's a hard one to figure out. But Reid loves it and drops to his knees to hug Josh back. When Reid looks back up his eyes have less of a glow to them. As he looks at me I can almost watch the energy fade from them, until they only have a dim blue glow.

"Well, Testerman would have loved this tidbit, wouldn't he?" Matt pipes in as he helps Reid to his feet.

"Yeah, but we have to tell the others and let them know. It may be something that more of us can do."

"I don't think any of us are volunteering to try it out anytime soon. If we don't have that ability it may go bad," Matt responds.

I shake my head and help Andromeda into Evee's bed. She seems to be getting better, it was probably just a reaction to hitting the ground. No real damage done, hopefully. As everyone else loads back up we head out of the golf course and back onto the road. All of this happened and all of the golf carts were electrical, so there was no gas to be had. Jeez, this world made the small things difficult sometimes.

Ready

The rest of the day passes without incident. We were able to get a few more vehicles to give up their small remaining amounts of fuel for our reserves, but the gas stations are a bust. Two hours after the incident with Reid and the Deader, Reid gets really tired and falls asleep in his seat. I have never seen that man sleep while on duty. Taking the extra energy was good for a boost, but it was apparently like a sugar high. Once you were done, you crashed hard. We let him sleep for a while but wake him up as we approach the rendezvous spot. The sun is setting as we pull up. It looks like we're the first ones here. As we settle in to wait, we hear the truck pull up. Smith, Hayes and Oakley get out. Matt starts to tell Hayes about Reid's new ability, but Reid puts his hand on Matt's shoulder to stop him.

"Let's wait until everyone gets here so I only have to tell it once," Reid says.

The others have odd looks of concern and confusion on their faces but roll with it . We unload all of our supplies into the truck for easier transport as Hayes asks Matt if the mission was good. He nods and says that we ended up finding diesel and regular gasoline. Enough for a few days anyway. Hayes is happy and shows us what they found. Apparently, there was an auto parts store on the east side of the city that hadn't been hit. When they went inside the place was a treasure trove of parts. Luckily, Smith knows cars and was able to grab what he thought they may need for the trucks and bikes in the near future.

"We couldn't grab everything, it would be too much," Smith says. Then he smiles and adds, "But I got a lot."

"Well, if you all were on the east side of the city. Did you hear the gunfire from the west earlier today?" I ask.

All of their team shakes their head. Hayes looks concerned. If there was gunfire on the west side and Ragsdill's team wasn't back yet, we may have a problem. Hayes sends everyone back to the transport with the exception of Matt, Smith and Reid. They keep Evee and send the rest of us back with the truck. They are going to start heading west slowly to see if they come across the group. Oakley is to get Matt's bike and then catch up.

"I'll get my bike and then catch up with you," Matt decides.

"No. I need your ability to see spore movement with me. Oakley hasn't discovered her ability if she has one. So she is just an Unseen. No offense Oakley. I don't have an ability either," Hayes starts.

"Well, if we are splitting up I should probably tell you about my discovery today," Reid says this as he's rubbing the back of his neck with his right hand. He's almost like a kid trying to tell his parents something that he did wrong.

Hayes turns in her seat. Waiting for him to continue. He looks at Matt and then Josh before he tells the others what happened to him today. The telling doesn't take long. There really isn't much to tell. But the questions that come after, seem to go on forever. Eventually, Hayes calls a stop to it all.

"OK, enough. I know we're curious. I know this is something new. But we have a missing team. We can't waste too much time before we go looking for them. So let's break it up. Reid thank you for the information. We will have to process what it means later. Everyone knows their role. Let's go."

With that, everyone drops their questions and we head on back to the transports. Oakley keeps asking questions about Reid trying to get more information from me and Josh. We don't have much else to tell her. Reid would have to tell her more if he even knew anything else at this point. We aren't in lab settings anymore to test these abilities out. They are having to learn on the fly. When we get back to the transport area, I jump down and start to look for Mom. It takes me a minute to remember that she's gone. When that sinks in, I hang my head and find the mess tent to grab a bite to eat, even though I just lost my appetite.

About the time I find the mess tent, I hear Matt's bike take off with Oakley at the helm. She's running that thing for all it's worth to catch up to the squad. Once I finish eating I find the soldiers that stayed with the transports and ask them to unload the truck. As they start off, I head off to find SGM Silver and tell him the news. I hate being the bearer of bad news. But that seems like all we've had lately.

I find Silver in one of the transports. He is talking to the scientists about the chemical production. From what I can hear, they are behind on production and running out of a certain chemical that they need. Well crap, more bad news. In reality, everything that they are doing is a guesstimate anyway. Would we rather over or underestimate? I don't know, I'm about as good at chemistry as I am at math.

School wasn't my strong suit. I never even graduated.

I stand around for a minute before Silver notices me. He then cuts the conversation with the scientist and tells him to just "Do your best". I know that isn't what he means, but it's said better that way. As Silver turns to me he points out of the truck. We step beside the truck and I tell him what's happening. He looks agitated but resolved. Almost like he figured that something like this was bound to happen. *And people call me a pessimist.*

Silver grabs a random soldier and tells him to gather up all of the others who aren't on watch and meet him at the truck. As we head back I can tell that Silver is thinking about the worst-case scenarios and how to handle this best. The stress of this trip has added more grey to his hair and you can see the stress lines on his face. It seems to have gotten worse since Testerman died. He has even let his beard grow out. As we wait for the soldiers to arrive, Silver inspects the items that we brought back from our mission. He seems to approve of the find, but what did it cost us?

As the last of the soldiers arrive I watch Silver's drooping shoulders stiffen as he stands tall in front of them all. He looks at each of them and fills them in on the possible situation that is occurring. He asks the soldiers to wait but to be ready to move at a moment's notice.

"We aren't going to leave the transports unguarded, but we will be running at minimal staff. We need as many able-bodied soldiers to be part of this mission, if there is one, for it to be effective," he tells them. "I will wait for confirmation from the front group before putting any plan into place. But I will not leave my people behind. I know we signed on for the unknown and lost people along the way. We need to know what has happened before we make any plans. Now go get some rest, or relieve someone on watch. Either way, we need to be ready to move soon."

With that, the meeting broke up. As the soldiers make their way to wherever Silver asks me to go to the cooks and ask them to put some rations together for the soldiers. If we need to head into the city we cannot rely on the cooks here to feed us. I do as I'm asked. The dogs love the fact that we are going back to the food tent. The cooks can't stop giving both of them treats each time. After that task is done, the only thing left to do is wait.

Not my strong suit.

It seems like hours later, but probably only about an hour, I hear Matt's bike making its way to camp. I gather up the dogs and head to the front of the transports. I want to hear what they have to say. A few minutes later Oakley pulls up on the bike in front of several soldiers and Silver. She seems winded and frantic. Unexpectedly, Reid shows up with Evee and two people in the back and bed. As they roll past us and into camp, I look and see two of the rear guard soldiers. They look pretty banged up and bloody. I turn back to Oakley as she starts telling Silver what they found.

"We followed the path that Ragsdill's team laid out going to the west side of the city. It took a while because the path seemed to roll back on itself a couple of times. When we had spoken to Washington's team prior," Oakley pauses a second and looks at me. "they told us that the bridges were all barricaded. We found this to be true too. We think that is why the team backtracked. They had to go further south to get to the west."

"Why didn't they just come back and report?" Silver asks her.

"I'm not sure. The two soldiers we found were kind of out of it. They didn't say. I assume it's because Ragsdill is hard-headed and doesn't know when to quit. It's kind of what we like about him in reality," Oakley adds. Silver smiles, but it doesn't reach his eyes.

"Anyway by the time we found these two, they had been walking for a while. They were badly injured, but they should be stable soon. They lost a lot of blood from several gunshots each of them took. They did say that Ragsdill and that girl Susie were taken by the people of the city, along with the prison truck. They couldn't say how many there were, just that the barricades were up on the west side of the city too. They have barricaded themselves in pretty well. If we try to go in hard, it may not go well for us," Oakley then sits down on the ground hard. Ragsdill was part of her original squad, she can't like that this is happening to him.

I'm not a fan of Susie but she doesn't deserve to be captured for whatever reason. This isn't a Home of the Brave situation either. These people came at our team hard, wanting the truck or prisoners, or both. If our team had the time to retreat they would've. This was something else. It isn't just a group of people protecting themselves.

Silver asks a few more questions and Oakley answers what she can. "Where is the rest of your team?" Silver asks as he sits down next to Oakley, for some reason. He then puts his arm around her shoulder to comfort her. Odd, is there something I'm missing?

"They went deeper in to see what they could figure out. Now that they know how the city will respond, they can be more careful. They aren't as good as my team sir. We can get them out," Oakley says, but it seems to be more for her than anyone else.

Silver breaks up the meeting and tells the soldiers to be ready to move out in ten minutes. We have the bike, Evee and the truck, we can haul everyone together. As he says this I look around for Josh. I hadn't seen him since I asked him to have the soldiers unload the truck. Where could that boy have gone? If we're leaving soon he needs to be with me. I look around then wander off in search of the little bugger. This isn't the time for hide and seek. With the two dogs in tow, I look around the camp. It takes me a while, but I finally find him on the complete opposite side of the camp. He seems to be staring out into nothing as I approach. I was going to hang back, but Peanut has a different idea. She runs up to him and body-slams herself into his lap. No choice there.

Josh starts to absently pet her but doesn't move otherwise. "Hey, watcha doing?"

He shakes his head out of his revelry and looks back at me. He is still petting Peanut, "j\Just thinking. My mom went out and disappeared. Kind of like that team today. I never found out what happened to her."

"Yeah, you told me before. I bet this is very similar huh?" I say to him. I want to keep him talking so he can tell me where his head is.

"It scared me when we were told that they were missing. Did we find out anything?"

"You haven't heard?" I ask him confused. Forgetting that I came right from that to find him.I sit down next to him. "Sorry, yes we have information. They were in a firefight and two of them are hurt, the other two got captured."

Josh hangs his head, "That's what we heard when we were looking for the golf place, huh?" I nod. "Are they going to be ok?"

"They should be. At least the two here. They're hurt pretty bad, but the docs should get them set up ok." I move closer to him to sit down, Andromeda sidles up to his side. She can always tell when someone is hurting.

"Are we going to get our people back?" He asks expectantly.

"Yes."

"Well, let's go," he says as he pushes Peanut off his lap, gives Andromeda one last pet and stands up.

"What if they don't let us go?" I ask him, looking up at him as he stands over me. I'm looking to see his reaction.

"Like that's stopped us before," is all he says as he puts a hand out to help me up.

I laugh because I know he's right. I don't know why these people put up with some of the stuff we pull. *This really isn't the real military is it?* But we move back to the front of the transports. It looks like we are all loading up to meet the rest of my squad. Matt is on his bike, and Oakley is sitting in the passenger seat of Evee. Andromeda runs up and jumps into the back. Peanut's looking at everyone and shying away a bit. Matt gets off his bike and bends to pick her up. He walks over and hands her to a civilian that was hanging around. He speaks to her and Peanut for a second then passes Peanut to the woman. Peanut looks at him for a second then licks the girl's face and seems happy. That's good, she won't be any good with us today.

We quickly get everyone set and head out. It's a bit different not being the only soldier that isn't Unseen. We are taking the regular soldiers too. Since we aren't going against Deaders their skills will be needed. Matt starts up the bike and heads out to lead us to the squad. We are taking a lot of people into a dangerous situation to rescue two of us. Is this really worth it? I get the no person left behind, and we need all the soldiers we can get. But what happens if we lose three soldiers trying to save two? The numbers don't work. Plus you add to the fact that winter is coming, it's colder each and every day. We are running a tight schedule. Wasting days on this may hurt us later. I have to trust Silver's decision and hope he's right.

It doesn't take us long to reach Hayes and the rest. They are standing on the side of the road, their uniforms covered in mud up to their waists. *What have they been doing?* They don't look happy as we pull up. Silver approaches Hayes, they walk off to discuss what they found and come up with a plan. Smith and Reid join us, I can tell this isn't going to be easy.

"So, that bad huh?" I say as Reid approaches.

"Yeah, they have their compound locked down," Reid says.

"We only got close by walking down the bank of the river. It still wasn't good. They have the river fenced off too. I'm not sure how we get in there." Smith tells us. He kneels to rifle through his bag, probably looking for some dry pants.

My suspicion is confirmed when he brings the pants out and walks into the trees to change. A little while later the Sgt's come back and Hayes is shaking her head. Silver stands up tall again and clears his throat.

"Well, this isn't ideal. I think we need to show up at their gate and try to talk to these people. Hayes isn't so sure, so we are going to keep a small group back to make sure we aren't all in their sites."

Hayes steps up and tells everyone about what the team saw around the camp. It's a small camp but they have several layers of protection starting with the barricaded bridges. We can't get vehicles through there, but people can get through. It's not solid. The camp is then protected at the river by fencing, as Smith told us, and then more fencing made of solid metal around the small community. They have one big main gate, which is probably where they took the truck and our two soldiers through. This is where Silver will try to communicate with the kidnappers.

A small group will sneak up through the bridges and try to find a weakness in the defenses. This can't be a big unit because they will be seen. Silver also needs more people with him to show force. If we appear weak as they talk we'll have no leverage. The truck, bike and UTV will go with them. Hayes ends her talk and walks off. Matt and Oakley follow her to see if they will be on her team. Smith and Reid start getting ready and check their equipment. They seem ready to go. I look at Josh and try to see what he's thinking.

Access

Hayes comes back with Matt, he looks disappointed. He must not be part of the raid. He always seems to want to be on the front line. Hayes calls Oakley, Reid and me over. They speak for a bit, then Hayes tells Matt to get his bike and meet up with Silver. He listens but I can tell he isn't happy. Josh and I aren't sure what to expect as Hayes approaches us.

"Listen you two. I need to know that if you are given an order you will follow it. No questioning, no working around it," she says as she stares at both of us in turn. Both of us look at her and nod slowly. "No bullshit. This is way too important for your antics. If you don't listen you could get someone killed. More so today than any other time."

"We get it Sarge," I say. I'm wondering why she is being so serious right now. If she's sending us with Silver then we will just be a show of force. That doesn't seem to be that important. Oh crap, that means she's sending us with the raiding party. But who's leading us? Matt was just sent packing.

"Oakley, get your team together. I'm taking the UTV and picking up Silver. Hey! Turner. Grab that truck and pull it to the front. We have a ways to go to get around these barricades. We need to get on the road. We're losing daylight." With that, Hayes walks off and leaves us with Oakley.

"So as you can see it's just us on this. Reid, Smith you will be our rear guard. Josh will stay in front of you two while Washington and I lead us through the area. Andromeda has the hardest job. She has to let us know if she senses anyone before we can see them. Washington, can she do that?" Oakley turns to me questioning. I just nod and bend down to Andromeda.

I talk to Andromeda for a second and let her know what we're doing. She has to be on her best behavior too. Oakley watches this then resets the strap of her rifle on her shoulder and heads out. We all follow her lead. We had met with the squad on the east side of the river, out of the way of the kidnapper's area.

This means that we are going to have to work our way through the bridge barricades. I'm not sure if we should do this during the day, but Silver and Hayes don't want to waste too much time if we don't have to. They are probably hoping that the caravan at the front gate will attract all of the attention. I hope they're right.

We make our way easily to the first bridge. I figure that we're going to cross here, but Oakley keeps taking us North. I'm confused, but listen to what I'm told. We travel for a little longer until we come up on a train bridge. This bridge isn't blocked nearly as much as the others. This is where we'll cross. I look at this and have an unreasonable fear of getting part of the way across and having a train come. I know that trains aren't running but my dad made me watch *Stand by Me* when I was a kid. This scene always stuck with me. Not a good omen to think about this movie right now, since they were on the way to look at a dead body.

I send Andromeda off in front of us to keep an eye on everything. I follow closely behind her and everyone else falls in line behind me. Oakley says that the compound is still a bit north of us. We will travel across the bridge and then head up the river bank. The trip across is easy and we don't encounter any resistance. Andromeda seems easy and undisturbed. She knows her job so I just let her do it. Once we get off the bridge, Oakley takes the lead again but Andromeda stays by her side. I think she wants to lead. Smith was right, we have to stay right on the river bank to stay outside of the fence which is right there. We try to look for anything we can to get on the other side without having to cut it. Suddenly, I see Josh jogging up beside me and heading up to Oakley. It doesn't seem odd until I realize he is on the other side of the fence.

How did he get there?

As he gets Oakley's attention she stops and seems to wonder the same thing. "I can run up the fence line faster now that I'm on this side and find an opening for you guys," he says smiling ear to ear.

Oakley seems perturbed but allows him to do just that. He runs ahead and is quickly swallowed by the high grass on his side of the fence. We keep trudging along. I can hear Smith complaining about his dry pair of pants getting muddy and soaked again. I laugh a bit but then realize I hate being wet too. Ten minutes later we come across Josh, back on our side of the fence.

"I guess you found a way in for us," Oakley says to the smiling munchkin.

"Yes, right under that next bridge. They didn't connect the fence completely and we can get everyone through. Even those two big guys back there," Josh tells her while pointing at Smith and Reid. The boy seems to be enjoying this. We make our way to the break in the fence. As we enter the grassy area I can see that just ahead of us are a few buildings. Beside the buildings are the town streets. We should be able to make our way through the buildings and streets to the compound.

"Oakley, do you know how long it'll take to get to the compound?" I ask.

"Just a few minutes," Reid answers for her. "They built it close to the river.

As Reid takes the lead with his map, Oakley falls back with Smith and Josh. We take a few turns around the streets and then come up on a large metal fence. Whoever built this has some serious welding skills and some equipment to lift it. The metal is over ten feet tall and is solidly welded together. I'm guessing they built this before blocking the bridges. They've been working hard for the last two years. If they are this set, why did they need our people and truck? I guess it really doesn't matter. We need them all back and we are going to try our hardest to do it. Oakley has us split up and go down each side of the wall until the next turn to see if there are any weak points. I head west with Reid and Andromeda. Reid is intent on the job at hand and I mimic his intensity. This isn't a time to goof off. I can hear people moving around and working on the other side of the fence.

About the time we reach the corner, without finding any way in, we hear Silver yelling at the people inside. I can't make out what he's saying but the voices from the other side don't sound happy. After a minute or so of yelling back and forth a gun goes off. I'm not sure which side shot, but I'm guessing it wasn't us. So negotiations are off the table. That means what we're doing is that much more important. Reid taps me and points back to where we came from. We wait a minute for the others to come back. When I can't see them I start to panic. Just as I am getting ready to send Andromeda to look for them, I see them come back around the far corner. When they get closer I can see that Oakley seems relieved and Josh is smiling.

"Good news and bad news," Oakley says as she gets close enough to talk. "We found a way inside the fence. Some animal has dug a hole under it next to a building. They must not have been able to get the metal down far enough there. We tried digging a small hole in a couple of other places and kept hitting the fence." She takes a second to look at Reid and Smith.

"What is it?" Reid asks, worried about her pause.

"I am too big to fit, so you two really won't be able to go. We will have to send Josh and Washington by themselves," she finishes.

"Nope," is all Reid says.

"Well, actually yes. It will be a recon mission only. Since the negotiations didn't work we will wait the two hours until dark. If I know Silver and Hayes they will try again. When they do we will send these two in to find the others," Oakley explains. Well, orders I think.

"If they find them, they can't get them out," Reid counters.

"No, but while they're in there we will continue to widen the hole. Once it's big enough I'll go through and help," Reid isn't happy with what Oakley is telling him. He walks off a bit then turns back around.

"Why don't we widen the hole now?" he asks.

"We'll work on it, but we have to work slowly to not attract attention. We don't know what they are guarding. We'll widen our side now, then work on their side after dark," Oakley explains then walks off in the direction of the hole.

Reid is still clearly unhappy, but it's a plan. It's better than we had hoped when we came this way. We reach the hole and I look at it hesitantly. I'm not sure Andromeda can fit, let alone Josh or I. She proves me wrong though by shooting into the hole and onto the other side of the fence. I freak out for a second until she comes back. She shakes and throws dirt all over everyone. It breaks the tension a bit. We look at each other grab any tool we have in our bags and take turns digging out the hole.

The next two hours are tiring, dirty, grueling work. The river bank is not the sand and clay that I'm used to at home. It's all rock and hard dirt. It takes us two hours just to make the hole big enough for Josh to fit into. As the sun sets we send Andromeda through again. When she doesn't bark or growl, we send Josh after her. He needs to make the other side a bit bigger for me to fit. We continue on our side for another thirty minutes before Josh pokes his head through and tells me to join him. I take off my bag and send it through with him. I then get into the hole head first. I freak for a second but take a deep breath and squeeze myself through. As I get under the fence, my hips get hung up. It almost causes me to panic again, but a swift push from the other side lets me slide through quickly.

Once through I take a look at our surroundings. We come out of the hole with a large building directly in front of us. Good, there's cover. I whisper what I see to the others, just loud enough for them to hear me. They tap once letting me know they understand. I look at Josh and point to his hatchets.

"Lose them and stash them here. We can't walk around with weapons. If we're seen they may question it," I tell him.

"But what if they are all walking around with weapons? It may raise questions if we don't," Josh brings up.

He has a good point. So we ease around the building to see if we can see anyone walking around the streets. There aren't very many lights so the shadows are deep. Even though it isn't fully dark yet, we have a lot of places to hide. We ease our way around until we get a view of a group of people walking down the street. Josh and I hide quickly, with Andromeda following us. The people pass us and I see that every one of them is carrying some type of weapon. As they pass I look at Josh and he has a smug look on his face. The little jerk was right. After they pass we come out of hiding and look around. I'm not sure where to look for a prison. A shrill scream splits the night, coming from the back of the compound. I'm not sure if that was Susie or someone else but screams usually only come from prisoners.

We turn around and make our way to the back quickly. There are lights on in a small building that stands by itself. It seems like it used to be a house but it seems pretty old. The buildings that used to stand around it are nothing but ashes on the ground. The building in question has a watch standing out front with sight lines in every direction. We aren't getting close to it. To get in there,we will need a distraction to draw people's attention somewhere else.

I have an idea, so we run back to the hole and I push my way back onto the other side. The others are surprised to see me so quickly but understand when I tell them my plan. Reid checks his bag and hands me a few small cylinders then puts his bag back on and heads out with the others. If they create a distraction on the back side of the fence, while Silver and the others approach from the front, Josh and I may be able to get inside. I know the EMPs are for Deaders but I also know that they screw *me* up. If they aren't ready for it and don't know what to expect, it may give us the advantage we need. I take my grenades and squeeze back into the compound. As I get out from the other side I shake my head to clear the dirt. The amount of dirt in my hair is ridiculous but there isn't anything I can do about it now.

Recon

After I get as much of the dirt off of me as possible I scramble over to Josh and Andromeda. We need to find a place to lay low for a few hours. There is no point going after something like this when most people are awake. We are going to have to wait until an hour or two before dawn. After the others inform Silver of the plan, they are coming back to keep widening that hole. Afterward, everyone is going to relax until it's time to go.

While I was gone Josh had scoped out the area and found a small outbuilding that seemed to hold farm tools. There shouldn't be any reason for someone to be in there at night. I give him the thumbs up and follow him through the growing shadows. As we get into the shed and close the door I see one small problem with his plan. We can't see outside at all. The wooden shed is in pretty decent shape and doesn't have any holes in it to look through. Josh smiles and with a quick snap of his wrist and a few twists, he makes a small peephole with his hatchet. The noise was minimal and would be lost in the regular noise from the compound.

Andromeda seems to know that we are going to be here a while, so she curls up next to Josh and starts snoring in seconds. I look at Josh and see that he could use some rest too. I tell him that I'll take the first watch, then have him relieve me in a few hours. He agrees and lays down with the dog. It would be a cute sight if not for the two shiny hatchets protruding from his hand and belt. They are hard to see in the shed, but I know they're there. As he rests and falls into a quiet sleep I go through my plan a few more times.

Typically, I let the others make the plans. I need to make sure this one is as good as I think it is or someone may get hurt. I run over it and any contingencies until my head hurts. I keep a lookout often while trying to keep the screams that occur randomly from spooking me. Whoever is screaming is being tortured. The screams are of utter pain and terror. Why are these people doing this? What information is so important that you need to do this to another human being? These people were just passing through, they didn't make a threat to your people or property. I really hate people sometimes. The longer I sit here the angrier I get.

After a few hours, I wake Josh and tell him to stay put. I have to go for a walk. I tell him that I have to use the bathroom, but that's a lie. *Well, not totally a lie.* What I want to do is see if there are any roving guards or anything else that may interfere with the plan. He looks at me skeptically and then looks at Andromeda, wanting her to go with me. I tell him no, and I tell her to stay, she would stand out too much. I look out and see that the coast is clear. I open the door and shoot out quickly. As I cross the road I can see a guard standing outside the entrance to the building. It's not the same guard, so they have switched out at some point.

I slowly work my way around a few buildings. Narrowly avoiding a few people that come out of a few different buildings. It seems like people are heading home for the night. A lot of them are coupled off or toting kids in their arms. It would be wholesome if it wasn't for the small bit of torture happening in the rear of the compound. I wonder if any of these people know anything about it.

Eventually, I make it around to the other side of the building. It looks the same here, no extra entrances or exits. This site only has a few windows. I'm not sure what this building was used for before the Fall. Without thinking too much about it I try to get a better look at the rear of the building. I go back into the other buildings a bit then work my way to the fence. With the looming fence, I should be able to stay hidden in the shadows. This is a time when not being a blonde comes in handy.

That's a weird thought.

As I work my way back to the building I trip on a hole and fall into the fence, hard. There is a loud metal bang that seems to reverberate along the entire fence line. I jump up and run to the nearest building's shadow to make sure that no one is coming to check it out. I barely make it to cover before a flashlight sweeps across the area that I was just in. There's no way that's the guard from the building, I'm still a block over. They must have people stationed away from the building too. If I hadn't fallen, I may have stumbled right into him. This complicates things.

I wait for him to move past me, then work my way to where he was. I can see that they have an area set up between this building and the next for someone to sit while on watch. If they have these along the fence line, there may be more trouble than I expected. I check the time and see that the moon has already set. It's later than I thought, it must have taken me longer to get around here than I expected. I take note of this location and head back to the shed. Josh is probably worried. I make it back without any other problems. As I close the door behind me, Andromeda and Josh both accost me. One with words the other with whines.

Ok, I'm late, sorry.

I quickly tell Josh about the hidden watch area that I found. He asks if it's the only one. I shrug. I didn't check the other side. Josh nods and I settle down to get some rest. This night may be longer than I thought. As I do the little jerk dips out of the door and runs off. He is out of sight before I even get to the door. I sigh and realize that he lived on his own for a year without help. He is just trying to do what he thinks will help. It's frustrating, but at this point there isn't anything I can do about it but wait for him to get back. I lay back and try to at least relax a bit before we have to get started.

I guess I doze off, and the next thing I know Josh is opening the door and sneaking back inside. I jump up, scared out of my wits before I realize who it is. Once I calm down he tells me that there is one guard post on each side of the building. The guards don't seem to be military, just regular people. They are a bit sloppy according to him. I laugh and let him tell me the rest. According to Josh, we'll have to deal with four guards on the outside. Then there are at least two inside. He was able to look through a window quickly and saw two sitting at a break room table.

Guess you need a break from torturing people.

If we add two in the room with whoever is screaming, that makes 8 in total. I don't like the odds, so I sneak back out and find the hole. I climb through, much easier this time and find the squad relaxing in the shadows. I know they have guns pointed at me so I say my name quickly to let them know it's me. I approach them and sit down to explain my dilemma. Oakley listens and comes up with a quick answer. They go in with me and take the guards out as the commotion in the front starts. I agree that I would feel better with them taking the lead. They all nod in agreement and pick up their bags to get moving. It won't be long before Silver and the team get started.

When we make it back to the shed we all pile in. It's a tight fit with our gear, but we won't be here long. Oakley and Reid talk over the plan a few more times, making tweaks since they got a quick view of the layout. They ask Josh a few questions about what he saw and tweak the plan a bit more. The more they talk the more polished the plan gets. Josh has great intel and a knack for knowing what to look for. I only found a guard because I fell into the fence and made too much noise. Besides using the distraction the plan barely resembles mine. I guess it was a good thing I brought in the professionals.

I really shouldn't be left in charge of things like this.

Raid

Reid wakes me up when it's time for us to go. I slept lightly but was able to relax because of the others taking over the plan. Tonight is still going to be insane, but I feel better because the others have been through this before. I stretch and check on Andromeda, she's up and looking for Josh to give her a bit of the protein bar he's stuffing in his mouth. He ignores her but drops a bit, unknowingly giving her a bite. Oakley eases out of the door first and crosses the road to get set. Reid and Smith follow closely after. They are going to go around our little shed and approach from the far side. Josh and Oakley are going to the east side and take out that guard, Reid and Smith will take out the other. Once I know that they are good, I am to throw one of the EMPs to disable the front guard. We will all then charge in and take out anyone in our way. That;s the basic plan, but should be workable.

The thing we have to rely on is Silver and the rest of the soldiers drumming up enough noise to draw more to the front so we don't have to worry about more people coming to help. Just as everyone's getting set a loud bang reverberates along the fence. A few seconds later it happens again. Just as that settles down I hear Silver screaming through some type of PA system. He is telling the people of the compound to turn over our people. He's being quite obnoxious.

I love it.

I give my team the required time, then send Andromeda out to get the guard's attention. She just walks by, paying him no mind. The guard yells at her, apparently not recognizing her, or realizing that they don't have any dogs in the compound. As she passes I throw the EMP behind the guard, between him and the door. I duck behind a building corner and count the grenade down. There's a small flash of light as the guard yells out. I turn the corner in time to see him drop his gun and fall to the ground holding his head.

I call Andromeda as I shake off the small effects of the grenade that still reached me as far away as I was. I run up and grab the guard's gun as he tries to rise. Smith appears and hits him with the butt of his rifle. If he thought he had a headache before, it'll be a lot worse when he wakes up. Smith quickly grabs the guard and drags him around the corner of the building. The other two are already lining up at the door. As soon as Smith is behind them, they breach. Josh and I are to follow after they clear the first room.

"Clear!" comes the call from Oakley.

They continue through the rest of the first floor, while Josh and I secure the front door. There is another scream as I enter the house. It seems to be coming from below me. This place must have a basement. Oakley seems to come to the same conclusion but tells Reid and Smith to clear the first and second floors first. The break room is empty, those two are either gone or down in the torture room. It's late. Maybe we missed a few leaving. After they clear the first floor the three professionals line up and head upstairs. As soon as they get to the head of the stairs I see them stop and back up. I see Reid signal to the other two that there are three upstairs. He then mimics sleeping. So they must have beds upstairs.

Smith hands up a flash-bang grenade, then he and Oakley back up a few more steps. Reid mouths a warning. Then yells "Hey" and throws the grenade deep into the room. A few seconds later there is a muffled bang and a less muffled scream from the multiple throats in the room. They move fast and after a few quick bursts of fire from their rifles, everything goes quiet. The noise seems to have been heard from the basement. I hear heavy boots beating on the steps getting louder. I slide out of the way of the door as it bursts open. Josh is standing in the middle of the hall with his hatchets raised. The two men that ran upstairs stare at him for a second before Josh releases his favorite weapons. The first one hits the man on the right in his chest. The one on the left misses slightly and only clips the man's right arm. Josh is now unarmed and directly in the line of fire.

I slide to my left to clear my background and rip off one quick burst from my rifle into the body and head of the guy who was still standing. He twitches and falls to the ground quickly. As quick as he falls bile rises in my throat. I turn quickly and vomit all over the floor in the room behind me. I hear Josh move. I turn to see him pick up one of his hatchets and lodge it in the throat of the man who had a hatchet in his chest, finishing him off. Another round of vomit escapes my mouth.

Reid, Smith and Oakley turn the corner and take in the scene quickly. Reid and Smith turn the two bodies over and start to finish them off so they won't rise again. Oakley quickly stops them and tells them to just throw the bodies outside. If they rise, they may cause more confusion and fear, letting us go unnoticed. They don't seem happy about it but do as ordered. Oakley starts to check on me. I wave her off and point down the stairs. The hostages are more important than me right now. She nods and heads downstairs with Josh following. Andromeda sidles up to me to check. I pet her head, wipe my mouth and follow the other two down the stairs.

At the bottom of the stairs, we all spread out, and are joined quickly by Reid and Smith. The basement is dank and smells like mold. The lights are bare and barely light the area. Four different doors are lining the two sides of a short hallway. Our people must be in two of these rooms. Oakley quickly gestures for us to line up, one at each door. I stop her for a second and whisper to Andromeda. The dog quickly walks down the hallway, sniffing at each door. She isn't too familiar with Ragsdill's scent, but she knows Susie's well. As she reaches the far right door she sits, telling us that is where Susie is, or was at some point. Oakley nods and takes that door. Josh and I line up just outside the closer right door. Oakley doesn't want us to enter, but we are to take care of anyone coming out of that room.

Oakley counts down from three, at one they all barrel into their door. Our door stays closed as a few shots are fired. Reid comes back out quickly, shaking his head. It's empty. He then lines up at our door and counts down to himself. Shots had come from Smith's room, he comes out a few seconds later helping someone walk. I can quickly tell that it's Sgt. Ragsdill. He's beaten up pretty badly and is having trouble walking. Josh runs down to help him. Oakley comes out of her room empty-handed. Just as she does, the wall to my right shakes as a big body slams against the other side. Smith eases Ragsdill down and bulls his way into the room.

As soon as he does he turns around laughing. Reid follows him out holding his shoulder and the side of his face. Behind him is Susie. I look around the room and don't see anyone else. I look questioningly at Reid and he just nods. Susie is the one who slammed him into the wall when he entered. Andromeda had been wrong, but that's ok. She can be wrong now and then. Oakley and Smith help Ragsdill back up as Reid works his way slowly up the steps. Susie seems to be ok. She takes the rifle from Oakley to cover Reid and follows him up. Josh and I follow so the others can take their time.

As we reach the top of the stairs, nothing has changed. We can still hear Silver yelling at the compound, doing his part. We planned to go out of the back door so we weren't walking out into the main street. As Reid checks the door he sees that it's chained and padlocked. It'll take too much time to pick the lock or break the chain. He makes the quick decision to go out of the front anyway. As he gets back to the front door, Oakley and Smith reach the landing with Ragsdill. In the light of the first floor, I can see how much damage was done to him. I guess those were his screams that we heard.

Oakley sends a questioning look to Reid and he just shakes his head. She nods and waits as he opens the door a small crack. I peek over his shoulder and see that the two bodies had been found. Two soldiers are standing over them looking around. As one of the men gets ready to yell out for help, Reid fires his rifle and drops him quickly. Before the body even hits the ground our big man rushes out of the door, tucks his rifle behind him and tackles the other man to the ground. Josh runs out after him, hatchets raised to help where he can.

Reid has the man in a headlock before he can react. A few seconds later the man loses the fight and passes out. Reid lowers him to the ground and waves the rest of us on. We move quickly. Reid and Josh rush off to secure the hole to our freedom. I send Andromeda after them to check the way. I stay back with Susie to cover the other three. They are moving as fast as they can, but Ragsdill can barely move. After a few steps, Smith hands Oakley his rifle. He turns and throws the sergeant over his shoulder so we can move faster. Ragsdill doesn't seem to feel good about it but stays as quiet as he can while being jarred on Smith's shoulder. Susie drops back and runs rear security for us.

This is where things start to go wrong.

As she is watching down the main road, the two bodies behind her start to twitch. I think I see something, but with the lighting being so bad I'm not sure. Two seconds later, I'm completely sure. They both jump up and run directly towards Susie. I yell out, but not in time. The first Deader slams into her and drives her to the ground. The second Deader bypasses her and heads towards me. Oakley hears me yell, turns and witnesses Susie hitting the ground. She wheels back towards the fight as I run away from the second Deader.

Oakley isn't sure who to help and uncharacteristically screams into the night. As she does both Deaders stop dead in their tracks and look at her. I don't stop to see if the one following me changes course. I turn a corner and head to the hole. I pass Reid heading back to the fight as Smith helps Ragsdill push himself through the hole. I don't see Josh but he is probably on the other side pulling from his side. Smith looks at me and tilts his head. I hope he knows I can't read his mind like the others can. But I assume he is asking what the scream was.

"The two dead guys we threw into the street came alive and attacked Susie and me. She was taken down. Reid and Oakley are helping," I explain quickly.

Smith nods as Ragsdill finally disappears from the hole, Smith points at me and tells me that I'm next. I don't argue and basically dive into the hole. I'm not even through before I hear others trampling up behind us. As I clear, Susie is almost thrown through the hole, quickly followed by everyone else. Smith grabs a rock that had been close and tosses it into the hole after we're all clear. It should slow down anyone tailing us. I'm not sure how Susie got away but I'm glad she's good. She doesn't look any worse for wear, so the Deader must not have drained her.

I'm sure we'll hear the story eventually.

Right now we concentrate on getting back to the hole in the fence by the bridge. Reid breaks off to the front of the compound as the rest of us hit the riverbank. He is going to tell Silver that we're good and that he can break off. It would be better if we had a flare gun, but we don't. We have to trust that he'll be ok and make it back with Silver.

We try to keep Ragsdill from slipping into the river while also trying to keep a decent pace. It's not long before we give up and slow down to a pace that Smith can keep while helping the sergeant. Oakley stays back to make sure we're clear. A few minutes later we get back to the train bridge and start to cross. We get about halfway across when Oakley joins us letting us know that we don't have anyone following us. Amazingly, the plan worked and we got out with both of our people without taking any losses.

I will have to work through taking a life tonight, but now is not the time to think about it. There is still a distance to go before we are safe. Then we will need a good night (days?) sleep. Until then we will continue walking south until someone with a truck reaches us.

Hopefully, it doesn't take too long, Ragsdill is in bad shape.

Healing

We don't make it far before Ragsdill has to rest. Even with Smith and Reid carrying him, his injuries are too much for him to take. The men have stopped carrying him over their shoulders, afraid of breaking a rib, or worse that ribs are already broken. Oakley looks him over and tells everyone but Josh to stay here with him. She and Josh are going to catch up to the group and get something to transport him the rest of the way.

"It's too risky to continue on like this," she says.

As they take off jogging, Susie jumps up and joins them. I'm not sure why, but she just takes off without warning. I start to send Andromeda after her but Smith just shakes his head. Maybe she had to get away from this place and what they had done to Ragsdill. Maybe she just needed to move.

As we wait Reid tends to Ragsdill's wounds as I ask him questions. The first thing I find out is that his first name is, Trey, well it's actually Roland but he was the third so he has always been called Trey. I ask him questions about where he's from, and if he was ever married. Did he have any family with him when the Fall happened? You know really personal stuff. He answers most of it, and all of that was in the negative. Smith just looks at me after one of my questions and smiles. He know what I'm doing. I'm keeping his mind off of the pain, as much as I can anyway. The more personal the questions the more concentration it took.

"Ok, so now I want the real personal information," I tease.

"How much more personal can you get?" he asks, "do you want measurements or something? I'm a 33 waist. That's all you get."

"That's not it. I want to know..." I drag this out a bit then spring it on him after the tension has built, "What's your favorite football team?"

"Whoa, that's too far Washington?" Reid says sarcastically. " A man's favorite football team is not something to take lightly. He will take that to his grave."

"Hopefully, not too soon," Trey laughs, then winces. "But since you must know, it's..." now it was his turn to drag out the tension. "the Green Bay Packers. Go Pack!"

"Nope, Reid we tried but he died on the table. It's time to let him go. The world doesn't need another Packers fan. Even if there isn't any football being played." I get up and walk a few steps away. "I can't work like this. These conditions are hostile," I say over my shoulder.

"Stop! You're making me laugh. You must be a Bears fan, but you're killing me. I think my ribs are broken." Ragsdill says between laughs.

I turn back around and sit down to help Reid patch him up. He smiles and mouths thank you to me then lays back down. Reid just gave him something in the IV he'd started so I'm sure it is an opioid pain reliever. That means Trey is going to go night-night for a bit. I hope I was able to get his mind off the pain for just a little while. My pain on the other hand can't be cured with a shot. I mean people in the past had tried to cover the pain with drugs, but it always comes back when it's in your head.

I have to come to a resolution on how to live with the fact that I just killed a man. In cold blood. I know I had to, but I was also the one who came up with the basic plan. That plan is what put us in a situation for me to kill this man. A man that I know nothing about, a man that could've been a good man put into a bad situation. He was just trying to do his job, to protect his community. Here we come and blow things up and shoot them in their house. Sure they were keeping prisoners, that they kidnapped for no reason, but he might not have been part of that. He may not have known anything about it.

Alright, I need to think about something else. I walk away from the group a bit since my mind is starting to spiral. Fortunately, I see a truck heading our way. I call out a quick warning and hide in the shadows. As the truck passes me I see Josh hanging out of the back. I get up and walk back to everyone else. Oakley spins the truck around on the bank and backs up so Reid and Smith can load the sleeping sergeant into the bed. I watch Andromeda jump in the back with them, so I get in the shotgun seat.

"Silver and the team didn't encounter any resistance," Lyla tells me as we start the drive back to the transports. "Did Ragsdill tell you guys why he was tortured?"

"No, I was asking him questions, but I was trying to get him to stop thinking about it. He's in pretty bad shape. They worked him over pretty good," I tell her.

"I saw. As we were heading back, Susie told me a bit of what she could hear. I think it had to do with him being Unseen. That's why she wasn't tortured like him. I guess he wouldn't tell them why his eyes glowed so they decided to beat it out of him," Oakley looks at me for a second then back to the road, well if you could call it a road.

"Why did they take them to begin with?"

"She wasn't sure. Maybe for the truck. Maybe because they thought those four were an advanced scout unit. Who knows. People get paranoid when they are secluded for too long. I think these people fall into that category," she hypothesizes.

I turn serious for a second and look at Oakley while she's driving. She glances at me quickly then back at the road. "What?" she asks.

"Have you ever killed someone? Not a Deader but a living?"

She takes a second to answer. "Is this about that guy?" is all she asks. I nod. "You don't have to feel bad about that. You saved yourself and Josh. Possibly more of us too."

"I know!" I yell. Then feel bad for yelling.

"OK, yes I've killed a few living people. Before the Fall. I was a soldier even then. I know what you're feeling. You think it could've gone differently. But if it had and he had lived, who among us would be dead? We aren't at war with these people. But we are at war. War for our survival. Don't forget that when you wallow over this at night. And you will wallow. We all wallow over it each and every night," she says as her eyes get a distant look to them.

"Does it..." I begin.

"No," is all she says.

I let it drop and we continue the rest of the way in silence. It doesn't take us long to get back to the group. They had continued up the road, just in case there was any blowback from our raid. We catch and pass them easily. Oakley knows how far they want to travel this morning, so she takes us there. As we pull up to our new camping spot, Matt and Hayes greet us. I see a few others and Susie sitting around Evee and getting a fire started. It's dawn already but most of us have been up all night, so we are going to take a half-a-day rest before we travel any further. I'm quick to lay down with Andromeda. As I do Matt walks over and asks me how everything went.

"I'm sure you've heard," I say. I know he's trying to be nice, but I'm not feeling it right now.

"I have. But I wanted to make sure you're alright," he says as he sits down next to me and puts a hand on my shoulder. His other hand starts to pet Andromeda.

"I'm fine. Will be fine. Eventually. I think," I stammer.

Matt doesn't say anything. I know he has killed living people before too. Hell, he was killed by the living at one point.Hopefully, I never have to endure that. Maybe this is why his emotions are dulled. You have to be a bit dull to get through life like this. I never wanted to know this feeling. Now that I do, I would do anything to give it away and take it all back. I feel tears welling up in my eyes and roll over to try to sleep before I bawl in front of my brother and everyone. I feel Matt stand up a few seconds later to let me sleep. I'm still awake when the transports arrive. A few minutes later I feel Peanut snuggle up between me and Andromeda. Andromeda groans but makes room for her to lie down. After that, it all falls into oblivion.

I am suddenly back in the building. I'm aiming down the barrel of my gun but the man on the business end of it is pleading for his life. This image keeps repeating. One time he is a father, another time he has a sick wife at home. Another time he's trying to help the prisoners because they were being held illegally. On and on this goes with so many iterations that I lose track. I try to wake myself up but I can't. Each time it ends with me pulling the trigger anyway and his head exploding, the blood, brains and gore a lot more grotesque than in real life.

I'm crying in my dream now, probably in my sleep too. I can't take it. All of this is just too much. About the time I think my psyche is about to break I hear my father's voice. I'm not sure where it's coming from but I hear it all the same.

"You do what you have to do to survive, Punk. You can't let others move you from your intended path."

He says other things. Things I know I am just remembering hearing him say. He said things like this all of the time. Especially after the Fall. Hearing the words in his voice is comforting though. It's like he is telling them to me again.

I let this sink in and soothe me as I fall into a deeper dreamless sleep.

I while later, I'm shaken awake. I look up and it's Josh shaking me. I grab his hand and pull him into a hug. He resists at first then relents. At least he has me laughing. That isn't something I could've done earlier today. I get up and figure it is already well past noon. Everyone else is up and eating. I rub the sleep from my eyes and get up to grab a plate. As I turn I see Sgt. Ragsdill working his way gingerly to our fire.

"How are you feeling?" I ask as I pass him.

"Like crap that was beaten with a Mack truck," is all he replies. At least he is moving on his own.

I reach the food area, no tent today, and grab a small bit of food. I'm not that hungry and I'm sure Andromeda and Peanut have had enough already. As I turn, I run right into Susie. Some of my food spills off the plate and onto the ground. I stop and start to apologize, but she beats me to it.

"Sorry, I wasn't looking. You ok?" she asks as she bends to pick up the dropped food.

I hope she isn't going to put it back on my plate.

She doesn't, she walks to the edge of the area and throws it in the woods. Something will eat it later, probably Andromeda or Peanut. As she does I reply "I'm good. But I wasn't held hostage. Are you good?"

"Yes, they took everything out on Trey. I hope he'll heal soon. We need him to run the rear guard. I hear Hayes is going to take his place while he's down."

I just make a face and shrug. She continues without a prompt. "They only wanted the truck at first. Not sure why they took us to begin with. But then they saw his eyes glow, you know how the Unseen's eyes glow. They freaked out. You pretty much know the rest. By the way, I heard you planned to rescue us. I didn't know you liked me like that," she finished with a smile.

"I don't," I say with a mouthful as I walk away.

"Ok, Ava. I know it all now," she calls after me. I try not to but I do smile. I'm glad she's back with us. And back on the rear guard.

As I get back to the fire, it's being put out. I pout for a second then stuff the rest of my food in my face. We must be getting ready to move out. We need to gain more distance between us and the compound before nightfall. Hayes leaves Oakley in charge again and then leaves to join the rear guard. As she passes me she puts A hand on my shoulder. A weird sense of calm comes over me as it usually does when she's near me. I don't know what it is but it always seems to happen. She must have a calm aura, especially for a soldier.

We start to load up, and the dogs, Josh, Smith and Reid ride with me. Oakley is riding with Matt. He doesn't seem happy, I think he really likes being alone. We're heading back up front and staying as forward watch for the next few days. Since the rear guard lost its truck, they got ours. Hayes' order I think. It's fine we have enough room with Hayes running with them. As we get ready to hit the road, SGM Silver walks up. I turn off Evee and stand up. He walks directly to me.

"Washington, you're staying with the transports for s few days. I want you cleared. I heard you had to kill an enemy soldier while on the raid to recover our lost people. It can be hard to deal with something like that. I need you to check with Bella, she isn't a psychiatrist but she's the closest we have. Sgt Ragsdill and Susie are being relieved of active duty until further notice too," he informs me. Once he is done he turns to walk away.

I start to argue but Lyla grabs my arm and shakes her head. "You need to do this. I know you want to get back on the horse but take the time. It'll be good."

I consent but tell Andromeda to stay with Josh and Peanut. She can help protect them while I'm gone. Not only will I have to be stuck here worrying about the team, I have to do it with Trey and Susie around all of the time, then talk to a shrink on top of it all.

Maybe this is some kind of punishment.

Abilities

As I watch my squad drive away, I feel lost. Oakley ends up taking my place and driving Evee, so Matt's happier than before. I on the other hand am not. I figure I'd go find this Bella and get the head shrinking out of the way. Then maybe I can leave and catch up with the rest of the squad tomorrow. I mean, I get it but Susie was held hostage, Trey was held hostage and beaten within an inch of his life. They need time to heal from their trauma. Even if Susie wasn't tortured, I can't imagine what was going through her head, being a woman in that situation.

Then you have me, I killed an enemy combatant. That's my job, right? We are put in this situation over and over again. It just took a while before I had to actually pull the trigger. It'll take a while then I'll get over it and move on. Or I won't and I'll be scarred with emotional trauma for my, most likely tragically short, life. I find the medics and ask about Bella. They tell me that she is in with someone and that I am to get up with her at the next stop. I nod and go look for Susie to see where we are riding for this leg of the trip. At least I don't have to walk again.

I find her and she looks around like she's missing something. "Where's your shadow?" she asks.

"Oh, I sent her with the others. They need her more than me. She helps keep Peanut calm."

Susie continues to walk so I turn and follow her as we talk. "Why didn't you keep both of them with you?" she asks.

"Peanut likes Matt and Josh more than me. So she would be whiny without them. Plus I don't want to deal with anything right now," I say gloomily.

She just nods as we reach the transport. As we climb in I see Trey is there also. "Did you hear about the new Unseen abilities that the others discovered?" he says. He may be hopped up on pain medication but he is acting like a teenage girl trying to spill the tea.

Susie and I just shake our heads as we sit down next to him. A few others around us lean in to listen too. I don't think it'll be too hard, Trey is amped and will most likely be loud enough for the driver to hear him. I'm going to slow the whole conversation down and make it a little more stable, I guess is the right word. The way Trey told the story was the very long way around. I'll truncate it for you so it's easier to follow.

The first thing that he talked about was the old abilities that the Unseen had. I knew of most of them. Matt could see spores move in the air. It was limited by the time of day, as his ability only allowed him to see the spores glow in the dark. Trey was very proud of himself as he bragged that his ability was better than that because he could see the complete outline of any NLB animal. He found out that this included humans. Again though it was limited to a glow-in-the-dark ability. Smith is able to tell if any object currently holds an electrical charge. It comes in handy but isn't a very battle-needed ability. A few of the rear guard guys have started to see abilities manifest too.

One could affect the spores in a plant, it wasn't very useful yet, but maybe with time and practice. Another could move the spores like they were floating on the wind. He somehow controlled them like they were living entities. The third ability that came from the rear guard was probably the most useful, she could speak into another Unseen's mind. She couldn't hear them yet, but she could pass along commands at a very limited distance. It would come in handy if you couldn't talk for some reason.

As cool and interesting as all of these were, Trey got really excited about the next two. I have already covered Reid's ability. He can draw energy directly from a Deader. He hasn't tried to pull power from anything else that I know of, and I know Reid was trying to keep it a secret because he feels like it makes him a freak. He is the closest thing to a living Deader at this point. He's afraid that others will become scared of him like he'll drain them if he's hungry. Trey tries to talk about this more, but I stop him for Reid's sake. Other people are listening.

"OK, OK. As cool as that is. There is one cooler though. We now have an Unseen that can control the NLBs," he says.

I think about this for a second. Then back to the raid. "Oh, crap! You're talking about Oakley," I yell.

Trey just smiles and points at me then at his nose. *Yeah, he is feeling those meds.*

So he tells everyone, as we were all running for our lives and the Deader was chasing me, Oakley got angry and screamed at them to stop. I heard this and witnessed the Deaders stop for a split second before I ran. I wasn't taking that break lightly. Apparently, after that Oakley was able to concentrate on the two Deaders in her vicinity and tell them to go the other way. She pictured the front gate and what she thought it looked like in her mind and "told" them to find it. After a second of them thinking about it, they turned and ran towards the front of the compound.

Oakley is sure that they did this because she told them to. She told Trey that the concentration it took was huge. It was so much that she got an instant headache from it. It only lasted a minute, but it was intense when it hit. Does this mean that if Oakley ever turns into a Deader she would be considered an Alpha? Trey voted that she should lead her own squad now because of this. If they ever get into trouble she could control the Deaders. "Shoot," he says. "If her power continues to grow she may be able to control us before too long."

I'm not sure if this is what Oakley wants, but Trey thinks it is. About this time he started to get sleepy. He had talked for a solid two hours about these abilities and the meds were starting to wear him down. He quickly sat back and fell asleep in seconds. I look at Susie and laugh for a second then lean my head back to rest too. I don't fall asleep, I just think about these abilities. My first thought is that if they all have these abilities developing why is becoming Unseen a bad thing? They all say it has its drawbacks. Matt is the only one that has said anything about it and that's just an emotional detachment concern. Right now that sounds pretty good to me. I mean, I am overthinking all of this to stop myself from thinking about the boy, man, I killed.

One thing I did think about though was that all of the abilities are about controlling, seeing, or manipulating the spores. None of them have any abilities that affect living beings. If that's the case and our little adventure here works, what will it do to their minds? They all have a connection through the spores and to the massive amount of spores in our environment. If this connection is that strong and we succeed in killing the spores in the air, will it affect the Unseen? Is that why the chemical hurts them to be near it? I have thought about this before but talking about all of the new abilities just shows me the Unseen's strong connection to the spores and the creatures that are linked through them.

I think about this in silence until we stop for the day. I don't know how long we rode, I think I fell asleep a few times. All I accomplished was to wrap my head around a problem that I couldn't solve. It did keep my mind off of the recent deaths that have surrounded me though.

I get out of the transport and start to help everyone set up the camp. I could tell that the squad was here, Josh left me a few hatchet marks in a tree. There was a note under a rock at its base. He was just telling me that the dogs were good and that everyone missed me today. I smile and tuck the note in a pocket as a small-framed woman approaches me. I turn to greet her, she introduces herself as Bella the mental professional.

That's her words, not mine.

I shake her hand and she has me walk with her to talk a bit. She asked about the shooting and how it affected me. I was trying to be aloof at first, but then the words just came spilling out. I told her everything that I had done and thought over the last few days. I even talked about Mom's death and Matt's insistence that it didn't affect him the same. I think I overwhelmed her, she wasn't used to people opening up so quickly because at one point she stopped me and took a big breath. I'm not sure if she was telling me to breathe or if she needed it herself. I did the same anyway.

After an hour or so of this, she stopped me and tells me that I would be able to join the squad again in a few days if I kept being open like this. That made me happy, yet I still didn't want to be away for that long.

"If I'm this open and in touch with my feelings shouldn't I be ok to operate?" I ask her.

"Maybe. But being in touch with your emotions also shows me how raw all of yours are. You have had a lot happen in a short period of time," she tells me. I didn't even talk about Jordan.

"So is being this way good, or bad?' I ask as I start to feel anger welling up in me. I wanted to be in touch with her face about then.

"Neither and both, We'll talk again tomorrow. I have to go find Susie now. Get a good night's rest," is all she says before she turns and walks away. *I'll rest my hands on her throat.*

Ok maybe right now being in touch with this emotion is not good. I walk away and go back to helping set everything up. I need to calm down for a bit and working up a sweat should do just that.

Iowa

The next couple of days follow a similar pattern. I ride with Trey and Susie in the transport, talking about anything we can think of. None of it was as interesting or thought-provoking as the first day. It's good to see Trey healing though. He is walking better and is able to take a deep breath without almost passing out. It'll still be a few weeks before he's back in the field. After we stop for the day, Bella finds me and makes me talk to her for an hour. I'm not as open with her now, she kinda pissed me off and I don't really like her. I only talk to her so I can get back in the field with my squad.

Two days in Oakley brings Josh, Andromeda and Peanut back to see me. She also spends some time checking on Trey, so there was another reason for her trip, I'm sure. We all know that they are a thing now. I didn't know before this, but just watching Trey talk about her gives it away. Either way, I'm happy to see them all. Bella told me after today I should be good to join them, but she wants to talk to me in the morning. I tell this to Oakley and ask her to send Matt for me first thing so I can ride with them instead of in the transport. She agrees and then leaves with all of her passengers in tow. As she drives away, Andromeda whines and leans her head on top of the tailgate looking for me to follow.

I take a walk around the camp, and a bit outside, tonight to clear my head. As I do I come across an old road sign that says "The People of Iowa, Welcome you to Iowa. Fields of Opportunity." Opportunity huh, I bet it's just fields now. Fields of spore-infected plants and animals doesn't have the same ring though. I laugh at myself and the sign a bit as I return to the camp. I feel like sleeping early so I can be up early. If the doc is an early riser maybe I can get my last test out of the way and get out as soon as Matt shows up. It's probably not the best idea, but if it lets me sleep early I'll cling to it for now. I grab a quick bite on my way to find my bedroll and lay down by a fire. Sleep takes a bit to find me, but I am gone long before the moon rises.

I am woken up in the predawn light but the sound of an engine running hard in our direction. I pull my head out of grogginess of sleep and get up. I put on my vest and grab my rifle. The noise seems to be coming from what I would consider the front of us, but that doesn't mean that it's not hostile. As I get in front of the transports the vehicle is just coming into view. It takes me a second, but then I recognize Evee. I tell everyone to stand down and put my rifle behind my back. It's odd that they are coming in so quickly this early. I know I told them to pick me up early, but this is ridiculous.

As they come in I can see Matt is driving. The look on his face is serious. As soon as he can be heard he screams for a medic. Oh no! Who's hurt now? I follow the UTV as he passes me and heads to the medic area. He skids to a halt and runs around the back. Two medics meet him there and help him get the tailgate down. My heart stops when I see who is in the back. It's Andromeda and Peanut, both are covered in blood.

"What happened!" I scream as I run to the two dogs. I look over Andromeda to see the extent of her injuries. She is slashed open in several places. She looks at me but doesn't move. Peanut is in even worse shape, her eyes aren't even open. A few more people come out with flashlights to give them more light.

Matt comes up behind me and pulls me away so the medics can work on them. "They were attacked," he says. "They were just out in the field playing and looking for somewhere to pee. Suddenly, Peanut screamed and started whining. Andromeda went to her to protect her. They were both attacked by a wolf."

"A wolf? How did they get attacked by a wolf?" I start to cry harder. I know how strong a wolf is.

"We aren't sure. They weren't even that far from camp. No further than usual. When we heard them we all ran to them and the wolf ran off. It seems like it was alone," he explains further. He sits on the ground. *Is that emotion I sense?*

I barely hear him as he talks. I can see the medics working on both dogs. They're cleaning, stitching and wrapping wounds.

That's good, right? You wouldn't do all of that if the patient was a lost cause. Or are they doing it just to placate those watching? As I start to spiral one of the medics walks over.

"Hey Ava, I was just checking Andromeda and... what's the new dog's name?" she asks.

"Peanut," Matt replies because I can't. My heart is in my throat. I stare at the medic waiting for the bad news.

"Right, Peanut. Well, they are both going to be fine. Andromeda got the worst of it, which might be good because she's stronger than Peanut. The gouges aren't super deep and no vital parts were hurt. It'll take a bit for them to heal but they will heal and they'll be alright soon enough," the medic smiles as she pats my hand and walks away.

I turn to Matt, "They're going to be ok." I say with relief, tears still streaming down my face. "I should've been there. She should be with me."

"You did right. If Andromeda hadn't been there, we would've lost Peanut. There's no way she would have survived without Andromeda saving her. She was where she needed to be," he explains. It makes me feel a little better.

He smiles and nods. He was worried too. See there is some emotion. Finally. I plop to the ground as the world seems to spin on me. That was a very quick roller coaster ride. I'm not sure my heart can take that again. I haven't even had my coffee yet. Speaking of which, I should grab that. I put my hand up so Matt can help me up. He looks at me then my hand, laughs and pulls me to my feet. I nod in the direction of the food and coffee, he follows. As we pass the dogs we both stop and check on them again. One of the medics tells us that they gave them a small bit of pain reliever that will let them sleep for a bit. They will move them to a tent and let them rest. I nod, Matt and I continue.

As we get to the tent a few people ask what the commotion was. Matt tells them because I can't. Even thinking about it makes my anxiety flare back up. I can't even think about losing Andromeda like that. She should've been with me. But if she was

Peanut would be dead, that is a fact. In the end, I made the right decision and so did Andromeda, as usual. As we sip our bitter, no sugar, no cream coffee I look at our surroundings. In the light, it looks a lot better than it did at night. We're in the open countryside and you can see for miles all around, well if it wasn't for the small rolling hills you could.

As I'm taking in the sights, I see a dust trail coming from the same direction as Matt had just come. I look at Matt and then off in that direction. He sees it and shrugs. So he isn't sure why they are coming either. It'll be a couple of minutes before they make it here, so we finish our coffee and then head out to meet them. As we reach the front transport Oakley rides up on Matt's bike. She looks frazzled and unhappy.

That's not good.

"Get Silver, now!" she orders. "We have a serious problem."

"Is someone else hurt?" I ask her.

She looks at me for a second, then her face softens. "Not yet, but what the dogs just went through is going to be nothing compared to what's coming. That wolf was part of a pack. That pack is heading this way. It followed Matt as he came this way. I guess following the scent of blood."

"Is the rest of the squad ok?" Matt asks as he tenses to head to Evee.

"Yes, it seems that the smell of blood drew them more than we did. They just ignored us. They are heading back, it'll take a while on foot. But they aren't the ones in trouble. I passed the pack a while back, but they are coming fast. It won't be another twenty minutes before they are here," Oakley finishes this as Silver walks up.

"Before who is here?" he asks.

Oakley explains everything to him as they walk back to the center of camp. As soon as she starts talking Silver starts barking orders. We have to get the transports loaded and the soldiers ready.

Wolves are not easy to take on. Susie and Ragsdill come out in their gear with their rifles.

"Sgt Ragsdill, you are not ready for combat," SGM Silver announces.

"But a gun with a trained eye is better than no gun, even if I can't fight. I think if it comes to hand to fang, we lose anyway," Trey counters.

"Alright, but get up high, you can't run. You're still a broken toy soldier," Silver adds.

Ragsdill nods and looks for somewhere to get the high ground. He moves over to Oakley and touches her hand ever so slightly then moves on. I have to stifle a giggle, they aren't hiding it well any longer. After that he finds a way to climb on top of the transport cab, gingerly I might add. He then lays down and sets his rifle. He gets comfortable since it may be a while before the wolves get here. As he accomplishes this, the rest of us get the doctors and the few civilians that are left settled into the rear of the transports.

Oakley takes a second to make sure Trey is set then gets back on the bike to get the rear guard. They need to know what is happening. We could also use their help. Matt watches her zoom off on his bike with a sour face. He can be so childish sometimes. I like the fact that someone is making him share. He never did as a child.

Everything is set quickly, now we wait. I think about my dad as I wait for the pack of wolves to attack. He was an avid wolf lover. He knew they were dangerous, but each one was out for the pack. Very few wolves went through life alone, or if they did it was for a short period of time. He liked that about them. Right now I'm not sure if it's a good thing for us. About ten minutes into my rumination, Oakley comes back with the rear guard truck in tow. Hayes immediately jumps out and speaks to Silver.

After their conversation, Hayes orders one of the drivers to grab the rear transport and turn it around. He's then to back it up to the rear of the front transport. This way the backs are closed off. It should be safer. It's a good idea and we probably should have thought about it sooner. Once that's done we all sit and play the waiting game again. Wolves move fast and can travel great distances following their prey. This is why I'm surprised that it takes almost two hours before we see the first wolf on the horizon.

Ragsdill is the first to see it. His position on the top of the cab gives him a better line of sight. He concentrates on the first wolf he sees, then counts them off as they appear. "Two, three, five, six,...uh oh. Um. Guys? Something odd is happening."

"What is it Sgt Ragsdill?" Silver asks.

"I'm not sure, but I think that I can see a blue aura around the wolves. It's hard in this light and from this distance, but I definitely see a blue glow," he says shakily as he adjusts the scope to zoom in.

"Are you saying these animals are NLBs, Sergeant?" Silver asks in an agitated tone.

"Yes sir. That's what I see. Oakley, can you use your new Alpha power to stop these things? It would be cool if we could control them. No one would mess with us," he kids with her. At least, I think he was kidding.

For her part, Oakley just ignores him and gets set for the inevitable. This just got harder. We can't kill a Deader wolf as easily, plus we won't be able to scare them off. I start to think that I should join the other civilians in the truck, or get to the high ground like Ragsdill since I am a beacon these creatures can hone in on. As I think about this Ragsdill shouts out again.

"Ok, even weirder guys. Um. So now there are people with the wolves. There are NLB people walking among the wolves as they trek through the field towards us," he stammers out.

"What?" Matt yells. "Are you kidding me?"

"I wish dude," Ragsdill answers.

Silver climbs up to Ragsdill's position. He takes the scope from him and looks across the field. "Well, you missed something there Sergeant," Silver claims. Ragsdill looks confused and then looks to where the SGM is pointing.

"Oh yeah, I see them now. So we don't have wolves and humans," he pauses. Then adds, "We have humans, wolves and bears."

"Oh, my!" Matt chimes in. I can't help but laugh. It's a nervous laughter though. This is going to be ugly.

"What do we do?" I ask.

No one answers. A hush falls over everyone. People, wolves and bears. Someone finally breaks the silence and asks how many in total. Six wolves, two bears and five people. Thirteen in all, this might be our unlucky number. I remember back on what Matt told me once; the NLB animals can still see the Unseen. They use their other senses and treat them just like any prey or enemy. With the animals in play, no one is any safer than anyone else. I didn't think about this earlier, I wonder if anyone else had.

"Hey, you guys do remember that the animals will still attack you Unseen right?" I yell. Everyone stops and looks at me.

"Crap, that's right," Ragsdill says. "Remember the bobcat? It still attacked us. That will probably happen here too. No useful abilities today folks."

"Will the regular human NLBs attack us?" one of the rear guard asks. He looks scared as hell.

Who could blame him?

"Assume yes, hope no," Silver tells him.

The oddball force of nature has progressed towards us while we discuss the semantics of it all. I will tell you that this is the most scared I have ever been. I have fought men, deaders and even a dog in the past. But wolves and bears that don't feel pain, led by Deaders. I have no idea how we are all going to survive this. I can tell you that I don't think the people of Iowa are welcoming us. I tamp the fear down and do what I see the others doing. Mostly it seems like they are trying not to pee their pants.

I can attest, that's what I'm doing.

Attack

The slow march by the enemy only adds to our apprehension. When they are about 100 yards out they all stop and spread out. They have so much distance between them that you can barely see two of them together at any given time. This makes it hard to tell what they're all doing. My squad has not shown up yet, they are probably still a ways out. At this point, they may just get here in time to burn our bodies. These thoughts have been permeating my brain since these animals came into sight. I keep looking at some of the other soldiers. They are regular soldiers, like me, and are shaking in their boots. They have no idea how to fight this type of battle. The unseasoned Unseen are also pretty scared. They are so used to walking into scenarios like this almost untouchable, that being the prey is making them uneasy.

The few members of my squad are trying to set a better precedence. They look like they have everything in hand. I can see that Matt is nervous, but if you don't know him as well as I do, you won't pick up on it. Silver has been pacing and checking everything for the last thirty minutes. He's obviously nervous too. As the animals finally stop spreading out I see one of the human deaders raise his hand.

As he does, Oakley yells out, "Alpha!"

Ragsdill moves, takes aim and starts to pull the trigger. Before the gun goes off the Deader drops his hand, and lets out a short shrill scream. It then drops to the ground and disappears into the tall grass. As this happens there is so much else happening that I completely lose track of anything that isn't directly affecting me. At the scream, the wolves bound into our midst within seconds. Shots ring out followed quickly by living screams. I toss an EMP grenade to my left in the area of an attacking wolf. It goes off, the wolf whines and falls to the ground. Before I can approach, another wolf bounds in front of me, protecting its pack member. I raise my rifle and unload a clip into the front of it. I must not have hit the correct spot because the only thing that changes is that the wolf is now covered in blood.

A loud shot rings out and the wolf in front of me drops to the ground missing a large chunk of its head. Ragsdill is making his shots count. I spin to find the next attacker. As I turn I run directly into a large furry wall. It is a rotting, brown bear standing over six feet tall that is bearing down on me. *No pun intended.* I spin to my right and dodge under one of the transports. The bear is big, but a little slower and misses me with a swipe of his large paw. As I roll out from under the other side of the transport I'm attacked by a smaller grey wolf. I look up as the wolf is growling and drooling at my feet. I pull the trigger on my rifle and it only clicks. In the heat of battle, I have forgotten to swap out my magazine. *Rookie mistake.* I slowly try to back away from the wolf. It snarls and chomps at me as it slowly moves forward looking for the kill.

Just before the wolf pounces a soldier comes out of nowhere and tackles the wolf while stabbing it in the head and neck area with a very large knife. He must have hit something vital because the wolf stops moving. The eyes are still glowing and its jaw is still working, but it doesn't seem to be able to move anything below its neck. The soldier notices this, takes a breath then drives the knife home. The lights in the wolf's eyes go out, it's finally dead.

As I take a breath the soldier takes off looking for somewhere else to help. The camp is in complete and total disarray. I watch as Ragsdill falls from the top of the transport cab. A wolf had somehow gotten on top of the transport with him. Trey loses his rifle as he hits the ground and winces as he jars his broken ribs. Oakley must've seen it too. She takes a few shots at the wolf on the top of the cab. It ignores her and jumps to the ground at Trey's feet. Trey tries to move but the fall has reopened and inflamed several of his prior injuries. He seems to be struggling to breathe. As the wolf chomps down on his calf, Trey screams and so does Oakley. I quickly toss an EMP grenade to try and break the wolf's concentration. As it flies through the air a huge bear paw swings through and bats it away. The grenade flies into the field and goes off harmlessly. Wasted.

The wolf lets go of Trey's leg and grabs ahold of his neck. I'm close enough to hear a crunch as Trey goes limp. Oakley screams and empties her rifle's magazine into the offending wolf. I lose track of everything else that happens as the bear that batted my grenade, slams itself down onto all fours and charges at me. I wait until the very last second and jump to my right. I land on the ground hard and jar my shoulder. I quickly scramble to my feet and run to slide under the transport. This time I stay under it while I assess what I can do.

I look around and see utter chaos. Oakley is fighting with a wolf with tears in her eyes. Matt is using his bike to keep a wolf away from him as he dodges in taking potshots with a hatchet, trying to take the things head off. Two wolves are dead, and one bear seems to have lost use of two of its legs, but it is very dangerous if you get too close to it. The human Deaders have joined the fight now too. That is something that I can concentrate on. I scoot up to the front of the transports and reach past Trey's body to reach his rifle. He was using the only .50 cal that we currently have. It has enough power to take a human's head off cleanly at this range. I don't have to be a good shot, just a decent one.

I'm better than decent.

I quickly check the chamber and magazine. I have four shots left. Not much but I can do some damage if I can do it quickly. One of the humans is approaching Matt from behind while he's distracted by the wolf. Did Matt touch one of the Deaders? Or are they working off the instincts of the animals. If that's the case they can see the Unseen. They have lost that advantage. *No time to think about this now.* I aim and wait for my opening. Matt slides to my right to avoid the wolf. As he does I squeeze the trigger and watch the Deader's head explode. I can't take a shot at the wolf without risking hitting Matt and the bike, so I look for another target. There is another human stalking Susie at the edge of the fight. She has backed her way out so far that she is completely exposed. The Deader is moving slowly, waiting for its opening. I squeeze off another shot and end its hunting days.

I start to feel pretty good about things as I look for another target. I then feel a hand grasp my ankle and yank me out from below the transport. The human Deader that has me in his grasp is a small man. I have found that being a Deader and not feeling pain makes these creatures much stronger in death than they were in life. I reach for the .50 cal rifle, but it's out of my reach. I almost reach for my rifle attached to my pack, but then I realize that I still haven't swapped the magazine. The Deader is reaching for my hands and face. I'm able to kick him away, but I'm running out of time. I think quickly and pull my knife. It isn't big, but the blade is over 5 inches long. I get set and wait for it to lurch at my face again. As it does I jab the knife into the Deader's neck. The blade is long enough to go through its throat and out of the back of the neck. It's enough to separate the cerebellum and kill the Deader as it falls on top of me.

I push it off and spit blood out of my mouth. Unfortunately, it's the Deader's blood, not mine. *So gross!* I try to keep my stomach under me and get back in the fight. I look around and see several bodies on the ground. We are losing this battle. Just as I feel like we are never going to get away from these creatures, I hear the fabric of the transport's cover rip open. I look up and see a hand reach out with a glass beaker in its grasp. They toss the beaker and the liquid spills out onto the ground. I'm confused about what that accomplishes. Then suddenly there are ten other beakers being thrown around the camp. All of them breaking and spilling their liquid onto the ground. One lands near the bear that has lost the ability to move. I watch as it squirms and screams as it can't get away from the liquid.

I realize that the scientists are throwing the chemicals out in batches to keep the Deader animals away. The Unseen can't typically handle the smell or how it affects their spores. These Deader creatures should have a more visceral reaction.

"Get near the broken beakers!" a voice yells out from the transport.

All of the soldiers react quickly and follow the order given. The Deader creatures that are still moving keep their distance. One of our soldiers takes the opportunity to put a bullet in the neck of the disabled bear and put it out of its misery. It was writhing and foaming at the mouth. It seems like the chemical was slowly killing it. The sight was awful.

The human Deaders scream as the Alpha walks into the fray. He is obviously in pain but is working hard to ignore it. He seems to assess the situation and the loss of life on both sides of the battle. He then screams their shrill cry and falls back, all of the creatures that can, follow him. Within minutes they are back over the first hill and out of site. Everyone stays vigilant for a while, but it seems that they have been driven off.

Slowly, the soldiers start to venture out of the safe area to assess the losses that we have taken. The Unseen move out of the range of the chemical quickly and refuse to work their way back into the camp. There aren't many soldiers left that aren't Unseen. There seem to be only two of them left, plus me and Susie. Hayes, Matt and Oakley are off to one side. They are huddled together most likely consoling Oakley. At least they all made it today. The rear guard wasn't so lucky. Susie was the only one to survive from Ragsdill's team, including the team leader himself. Our armed forces took a major hit today, something that we will most likely never recover from. As we move around and pull the Deader bodies from our own people, the medics and mechanics come to help. I know the scientists came up with the beaker idea. I also know it most likely depleted our supply of the chemical that we so badly need. But it is the only thing that saved the rest of us. I'm thinking about this as I come around the far transport and find the body of SGM Silver on the ground.

OH NO! Not him too.

I drop to the ground and check for a pulse. I have one, but it's weak. I call for a medic and one responds quickly. Another comes to help and they pick him up into the transport so they can stabilize him. We spend the next few hours cleaning up the bodies and figuring out how many people we lost today. As we do I see Josh, Reid and Smith join the rest of my squad just outside of the chemical's reach. I wave and walk over to them to take a break. I get hugs from all three of them as I place my hand on Oakley's shoulder.

"We are going to follow up on the creature's retreat to make sure we aren't in danger any longer," Reid says. "Hayes tells us that you guys put a decent dent in their numbers."

"We took down both bears, three wolves and three humans. That's more than half of their numbers. But they did more damage to us than that," I tell them. "Silver was almost killed along with six of our soldiers total." I drop my eyes as I say that knowing that Trey was one of those.

"We would've all been killed if the science guys hadn't come up with that chemical trick," Matt says. He seems impressed and thankful for the genius that saved us all.

We all nod and get back to work. The Unseen members that aren't checking on the creatures are going to start building a mass pyre. We don't have the time or manpower to build individual ones. We are down to half of what we left Christiana with. A quarter of them are the scientists that we need for this to be worth anything. If we lose them, we might as well throw in the towel. With this loss of our soldiers, we might need to anyway. I can't see being able to make it the rest of the way with only 8 soldiers running security. The others seem to see this on my face, but it's Susie who comes over to talk.

"I know this is hard. I know we lost a lot of people in a very short amount of time. But we knew this was going to be hard. We knew we were going to take losses. We have to keep our chins up and continue on, or it is all for naught," She tells me as we pick up another body to carry to the pyre.

"Isn't it for naught though? We have lost so much," I say with a catch in my throat.

"No, not until we give up. We all knew what we were signing up for. All of us," she says. She takes a knee and catches her breath.

I hear an engine and watch Reid and Smith roll back into view. There doesn't seem to be any agitation in their movements, so the creatures must have moved on. After the fire burns down, we all huddle into the transports to get some sleep. Andromeda and Peanut seem to be healing ok. They are both sore but their spirits are high. The rest of my squad is staying out in the truck and Evee is outside of camp. They will run night security but are mostly trying to stay away from the chemicals. Josh had come in long enough to give a few pets to the dogs and make sure they were ok. As he headed out I told him to give Lyla my love and condolences again. He nodded and disappeared.

The ground was already being affected by the chemicals. I hate to see what we are going to wake up to in the morning. I decide that that is a tomorrow concern as I lay down and try to sleep. Andromeda and Peanut move closer to me but don't lean into me so they aren't pushing on their wounds. Hopefully, tomorrow will bring a brighter day and a better outlook.

Onward

In the morning I get out of the transport and see Silver walking gingerly around the camp. It seems he'll be fine. The plant life in this area, on the other hand, will not. Just like the spill that we had earlier, the ground is bare, down to the dirt everywhere the chemical touched. I guess since it was spread around further, it has done even more damage. Not only are the areas bare, but the grass in a huge circle around the transports is brown and crispy. I have never seen anything like it. The grass looks like it has been dried out in a drought for several weeks.

I look for the squad and see that they have been forced to move even further out from the transports than they were last night. I walk out to them and bring enough food for all of them. I ask about the change.

"All night we had to keep moving out. The spores were affected even further than the grass shows. I'm sure by the end of today the grass you're standing on will be dead too. It almost seems like the ground has been poisoned by the chemical," Matt tells me.

"If this is how it affects the plants and you guys. What's going to happen when we release this into the air?" I ask concerned. I look at each of them but no one seems to want to answer me.

Hayes finally does, "Hopefully, in its aerosol form it won't affect everything so badly." is all she says. She doesn't sound confident.

Susie's words from yesterday come back to me. *We all knew what we were signing up for. All of us.*

We eat the rest of our breakfast in silence. All of us are lost in our own thoughts. Eventually, we all get up and get back to work. We don't have the people for forward, rear and transport security. Hayes asks me to send Silver her way so they can talk about what we are going to do moving forward.

Silver planned to stay a few days and recover. He needs the time and so did many others. Hayes talked him out of it though. We were too exposed and the growing area affected by the chemical was making it harder for the Unseen to help with security. Silver relents and we are on our way within a few hours. With everyone able to ride the trip seems easy enough.

The squad breaks up into two teams. Oakley takes Evee with Reid and Josh for front security. Matt has his bike so he rides ahead to check the roads. Hayes and Smith use the truck along with Susie to run a close rear guard. No use being too far behind now, there aren't many of us left to protect. I stay with the transports along with one other regular soldier. We are all that is left. It's tough to see the large group of 60 people reduced by almost half during the trip. There has been a lot of loss lately and it is taking a toll on the people that are left.

The next day we wake up to a solid frost on the ground. It's been cold, but this seems like the beginning of winter. Luckily, the day warms up a bit and it's comfortable enough to be outside. Andromeda and Peanut heal better than Silver. They are up and about playing easily. It's good to see someone recovering from that nightmare of a day. The day passes mostly in silence. People are only talking to each other when something has to be said. I don't think there is really anything anyone wants to talk about.

The scientists are working hard to recreate the chemical that was used to save us during the battle with the wolves and bears. They say that they should have enough by the time we reach the missile silo. As potent as that stuff seems to be, I'm not sure how much we really need to launch. Too much may kill all the plant life on the planet. *Wouldn't that be something?* You try to save the world from one plague only to cause an apocalypse of our own doing.

The days pass in the same routine as they had before. We stop earlier each day to give the scientists time to do their thing. They can't make the chemical when we stop for the night, since we don't have enough light for them to work by. If they get the mixture wrong, it could be devastating.

I talk to Reid one night and he says that Matt is taking off in the morning to scope out the missile silo. We are close enough that we should make it within two days. The end is near, as they say. This is great news. Especially since we made it faster than we thought. Some of that is probably due to the loss of life and the fact that we didn't have people walking for the last two weeks. The trucks may be slow on the broken roads, but they are still faster than a slow walker. We wanted to be in the silo by November. It's only the middle of October. I lost track of the days exactly a while back, but we can't be too far past the 15th. When we reach the silo, we can take a break. The scientists can do their thing and we can all get the much-needed rest we deserve. Reid is skeptical. I'm trying to be optimistic for once. I mean what can it hurt to think that we will actually get a win in all of this?

The bad part of knowing that we can reach our destination in two days, is waiting those two days. Of course, the first thing that goes wrong is the rear transport fails to start the next morning. The mechanic takes half the day to get the thing to fire up and get moving. That costs us half a day, but we can make it up by driving deeper into the evening. We're still good. Silver seems just as ready to get to the silo as I am, so he pushes the transports further.

The next morning Matt returns from his foray to the silo. He says that it's only a day's ride out, but his face seems to be saying something else. He won't talk about it, he just takes Silver and Hayes aside. I can't hear what they are saying but their body language says that it's not good.

Was the place taken over?

When Silver and Hayes come back they get the group ready and we roll out like everything is fine. There aren't any battle plans or meetings with the soldiers that are left, so it must not be anything that's a threat to us. That's good. I don't think that we can take another battle of any sort right now. We just need to get to the silo and deal with whatever comes from there. The day moves slowly. The waiting to get there is on everyone's nerves. We all saw Matt return, we know what it means and how long he said it should take to get there. Nerves are racked and we just want the day and the trip to be over. It's been a little over a week since we

took the losses in the battle with the Deaders. A little over a week
to sit and think about all that this trip has taken from us. It's about
time that we had something good to look forward to.

No matter what the problem is at the silo. We can take the
time in a safe environment to figure it out. I think we all need to get
away from each other a bit and stretch our legs. The transport
seems to be growing smaller each and every day. With the end in
sight, it only seems to be making it worse.

Silo

As the sun starts to set, we start to see signs for the Minute Man National Historic Site. Apparently, there is a visitor center. That doesn't bode well for a working silo. As we see the signs a buzz starts to go through the people. If this is a museum, there is no way that the missiles work. There won't be any way to arm and launch missiles dumbed down for a museum piece. All of this was for nothing. As the whispers and buzz start to get louder Silver stands up and tries to hush the crowd.

"There was more than one launch site here. Yes, they turned one into a museum. That doesn't mean that the other silos were decommissioned. We have to check out the site. We only need one missile to be able to launch the chemical that we need into the atmosphere," he tries to sound confident to calm the crowd. He isn't very convincing.

A little while later we pull up to the silo's visitor center. A few of the people, including our last mechanic, get out and storm off into the building. They need to get away and deal with the utter disappointment that we have just been dealt. Everyone gets out and walks around the area. There is a visitor center, plaques and broken-down cars. A few of the scientists and doctors break down into tears, not just the women either. Everyone put their lives on the line and lost friends and family along the way for this to end at a museum.

Matt takes off on his bike to search the surrounding area. It's getting dark so I'm not sure what he's going to find. The rest of us get to work. We unload the supplies out of the transport and put them inside the building. There is a lower level, so we will be safe from the weather. We're going to have to stay here until we figure out a new plan. Matt comes back later in the night and lays down next to me and the dogs. He doesn't say anything, but I can tell he's just as agitated as the rest of us.

In the morning, no one seems to be taking the news any better than they had the night before. The squad is tasked with looking around the area for anything that would be the control station for the missiles.

"Just because this museum is here, it doesn't mean that nothing still works," Silver tells us, but he doesn't even believe it himself.

I grab Evee and ride with Josh and Oakley. We take off up the main highway looking for anything that may be a military base. Maybe we're just off a tiny bit. Maybe the real base is around. After a day of looking, we don't find anything. The place is barren. On day two we try again. We go a little further out and actually find something called Delta -01 launch control facility. We look at the sign and our hearts jump a bit. This may be exactly what we're looking for. As we pull up to the area it is fenced off and covered in barbed wire. That's a promising site. You wouldn't put barbed wire around a facility for the public, would you? As we pull up to the gate we get out and run a security check. Oakley thinks that the facility is shut down as it looks completely abandoned. As we look a little more, Josh gets to work and breaks the locks on the fence with Evee. We pull the gate aside and proceed to check the facility.

Once inside you can tell that this is an old base, but it has been kept in pretty decent shape. Well, except for the two years worth of dust on everything. We take our time but our hopes soar a bit. There are old computer terminals, that still seem to be in working condition. There are ladders down into areas that we haven't explored and rooms that were meant to house the missile techs. There are bedrooms, sitting rooms and even a small kitchen. People were meant to live here while serving their country.

Neither Oakley nor I know much about the computers and things involved so we leave the building, load up and head back to the visitor center to inform Hayes and Silver of our find. When we return Silver decides to check it out for himself. He seems hopeful and others around seem a little less dour. This may be what we were looking for. A few hours later Smith and Reid return telling us about another facility that they found. They didn't go in but it had plexiglass coverings over what appeared to be missiles in the silos. We sit on this news until Silver and Hayes return.

The news isn't what we want. The Delta-01 facility used to be a missile control, but everything is dummy-boarded. This means that it doesn't currently, nor will it ever work for launching a missile. The positive side is that the facility can be used to house all of us until we make our next move. A few people are unhappy with the move, but a real couch and bed do sound pretty nice, even if we'll all have to share. Silver and Hayes talk to Reid and Smith then follow them out to the other facility. It sounds a little bit different, but they expect the same results.

As they leave, the rest of us pack up. Once that's done we show the transports the way to Delta-01. The entire time we're driving back all I can think about is the fact that we left a dank basement with generators to move into a missile silo with no generators, that we know of, a few thousand miles away. The more things change the more they stay the same, my dad used to say. Once we get to the station, we unload again and close the gate against any unwanted visitors. I'm sure there are wolves out here too.

A couple of hours later the rest of the team comes back with similar news to this station. It is similar in layout and people could move there to spread out, but the missile isn't operational, nor can it be placed in operation. The whole area has been turned into a museum about defunc'd missile silos and what our nation had during the Cold War. Nothing is operational. There is no way to launch a missile from this facility. This news sinks into everyone and a large sigh of resignation settles over us all. Two days later we figure out how to ration our food to survive for a while without having to scavenge. We are in a national park. There are no towns near us, so we will have to hunt or fish for food. Winter is coming so we have to tighten down on our rations if we are going to make it through.

We were better off in Delaware.

Later that night, two people ambushed Reid while he was on guard duty. They opened the fence and stole the truck. They made off with a small bit of our rations, but not enough to hurt us too badly. The biggest loss was the truck. When Reid was found tied up, he told us that they had apologized to him, but they couldn't stay with our group just to slowly starve to death in an old bunker. The reason they came on this trip was to avoid that fate. None of us could blame them, but it was still a bad omen that people would resort to this type of violence and mutiny this early in the stay.

Each day, we would venture out with the bike and Evee. Sometimes we would go far enough that we would have to camp outside for the night. The loops got further and further out, with nothing more of note to be found. When we aren't on search rotations we are placed on fishing and hunting duties. We keep busy. Winter slowly moves in as we edge into November. A few people have taken to messing with the electronics in the place and hooking them to the transport batteries, using the engines as a sort of short-term generator. One got an old military radio working and would work through the frequencies during the day, trying to see if anyone else was still living.

This place is desolate. You could feel completely alone and lost out here. It's an eerie feeling, to say the least. Reid has started walking the closed-off parts of the bunker to see if he could find anything of note. The rest of us just stayed bored or invented new games to play to keep our minds from rotting. The days roll together and we just do the tasks that are assigned to us each day. We have been reduced from having a purpose to save all of humanity, to barely surviving and not living.

The desperation got to a few of the scientists and doctors. We would find them hanging, or bleeding out in obscure areas of the facility. Each took precautions to stop their undead body from wandering the halls and killing any of us who were still here. It's thoughtful, but creepy at the same time. One medic left the facility and just walked away. We found his Deader body three days later walking along our fence line. Smith had to take him out so no one would be killed. We arrived here with around 36 people. In the month or so that we've been here we are down to 23. we have 10 soldiers, Hayes, Reid, Smith, Oakley, Matt, Susie, Josh, Atkins, White and myself. Then there is Silver, 3 cooks and civilians, 4 doctors and medics and 5 scientists left. The people that have left have made it easier on the food reserves, but if we do have to leave I'm not sure what we'll do.

Besides being in the dark all of the time, the accommodations aren't too bad. We have split between the two launch stations and have been living pretty comfortably. Mentally though, I'm not sure how much more of this we can take. Snow is always on the ground now and it's making it hard to hunt or fish for food. Someone has to come up with a plan before we all take our own lives. There is only so much the human mind can take.

I lived in a bunker with just Andromeda for a year, yet this is driving me insane.

I'm not sure if it's the close quarters, not being able to go outside very often or the loss of purpose that has me spiraling. Sometimes I think it's all three. Matt and the others are struggling too. I can see it more each day. If we don't get a plan in place there won't be much reason to keep a journal any longer. The world will end around us and we probably won't even care.

Hope

Somewhere around the middle of November ,Atkins finally got a signal on his radio. He had been through every frequency a million times over, but he said that something in the atmosphere must have changed the way the signal bounced. Either way, it was a very stern voice telling people how to handle the power shutdown. If this is what they were talking about it had to have been on loop for over two years. As it looped again, I got bored with it and walked away. At least it could've been some good music to come through. I haven't heard anything on the radio in forever.

I leave to take the dogs outside for a bit so they can run. We try to keep the inside of our fence line clear of snow as it falls, almost daily now. The dogs love the cold weather and when I throw a ball for them to fetch. Each day I play with these two and try to remind myself to take joy in the little pleasures that life can still bring us. They were hurt and almost killed, but they still come out each day and play with the same ball, in the same yard like it is the newest and greatest thing ever. I try to emulate that feeling, but it only goes skin deep. In my heart, I still know that we failed. That we took a trip I didn't believe in only to lose so many people along the way to mindless killing or sickness. There is very little in this world that could bring me true joy any longer.

Later, I return to the room to see if anything has changed. As I approach,Reid suddenly bursts out of the room and runs down the hallway. I haven't seen anyone move that fast in a while. I wonder what's happening. I peek my head back into the room with the radio. As I do Reid comes barreling back up behind me, barely slows to move me out of the way and rushes into the room past me. Something on the broadcast must've piqued their interest. Maybe they are playing a game with the computer somehow. *Would you like to play a game?* No nuclear war, please. However if it could point us to a working missile, we would appreciate it.

Reid had a large paper map laid out on the floor by the radio. The map is old but with no cities any longer, I guess it doesn't matter. I can hear someone talking on the radio, it doesn't sound like a recording. I ease my way further into the room and see that Silver has joined them. He is talking to someone. The radio reads out numbers and Reid seems to be tracking them on the map. After the long bit of numbers that I assume can only be latitude and longitude, Reid smacks the map and hoots.

"It's about 400 miles from here, SGM," he says. 400 miles to where?

Silver says something more to the radio and turns it off. As he turns around I can see the man's actually smiling. He starts talking to the others and I pick up a bit of what they're saying. They're talking about going somewhere. I'm confused so I clear my throat and ask them, "What are you talking about?"

"Our mission young Washington. Our mission is back on track," Silver tells me.

He explains that while they were listening to the recording, Atkins tried to talk over it to see if he could break through it. When the recording started to loop again he tried it again and again. Finally, someone on the other end heard him and came back to us. We told them who we were and about where we were. They informed us that they are in fact the United States Army. They asked for a series of authentication codes, which is when they retrieved him. He answered the queries and they gave us a set of coordinates to meet them. Reid found the place and it's about 400 miles north. It is in North Dakota.

If they are right then this US Army fellow could lead us to a place where we could launch the missile. The man wouldn't say anything more in the open air but his location and that he was US Army. There wasn't much to go on, but it was something. The only trouble was how to get through 400 miles of open road with everything covered in snow.

A little while later Silver calls a meeting with the 23 of us that are left. He explains what happened and what his plans are. The chemical is made and is being stored in airtight containers. These are being loaded onto one of the transports with enough supplies for two weeks. The other transport is going to be used to transport the people willing to go and be used as a backup in case the other fails. Silver has already talked to all of the soldiers and they are willing to go. Susie and I both signed on too. Of course, Josh said that he was going anywhere that Reid and I were going. If the two of us ever decide to go separate ways, I'm not sure where the kid would land on that.

After he fills everyone in, we break for dinner to give people time to discuss the venture and make their own decisions. I sit with my squad as we discuss how we are going to run security. The transports are heavy and can push their way through the snow pretty easily. Evee will have to lead the way to make sure the roads are safe and that we don't run off into a ditch. The bike will be loaded on the transport in case we need it, for now. It'll be too hard to keep it running in the snow and too hard on the person riding it. Even Matt agrees.

In our forays, we had found a lot of broken-down vehicles and we have a good stash of gas at this point. Diesel might be tight, but we will have to see if both transports make it far enough to matter. We'll have to hunt on our way to give us enough meat, but in two weeks we only need a few days of meat to stay healthy. We are still living on some of those rations we found in the couponer's house. Dinner is a light fare, as usual, because of the rationing, so it doesn't take long to eat. People disappear into other rooms in pairs and small groups to discuss their decisions. The night is tense and I don't sleep well because of it. Silver is expecting everyone's answers in the morning. I think I don't like this feeling because of what happened the last time people had to make a decision like this. Of course, this is different, we aren't leaving anyone behind who doesn't want to stay. I'm still nervous about it though. In the morning a few people have bags that they've packed and brought to breakfast. Others don't. This doesn't mean that they aren't joining us, but it is a strong indicator. After we all eat Silver gets up and says a few words.

"OK, so for those of you that are going with us. Please load anything you have in the transport to the left as you exit the doors. If you aren't coming with us please let me know but we would appreciate your help loading supplies so we can get on the road. There is no point delaying any further."

With that, everything breaks up and we get to work. The hardest part is getting Matt's bike loaded up after the chemicals. We have a board, but everything is slippery and wet. Luckily, today is above freezing so it isn't too bad being outside. After the supply truck is loaded we get the people loaded up as the trucks warm up a bit. With the ten of us left I figure the party is going to be pretty small.

I'm right. Along with Silver, we only get 2 scientists and 2 medics to go with us. I get Evee started and loaded up. The dogs are comfortable with some blankets in the bed to make the ride a bit more comfortable. They love the cold, but all day is a bit much. Josh and I bundle up too and wait for Oakley to join us. Hayes, Matt, and Reid will swap out with us later but will ride with the transport for now. Susie is driving one of the transports, apparently she had a CDL before the Fall. Reid is driving the other transport. I hope one of the medics or Silver can drive a truck too, if not it'll be a hard 400 miles for Reid.

I think about this and send Josh to go ride with him. It'll be warmer and Reid needs a copilot I tell him. He hesitates then smiles and runs back to Reid. As we get ready to pull out, Silver loads up in the front of the transport, I see White and Atkins standing at the front door of the building. I look at Oakley and she just nods.

"They decided to stay behind too. It's just our squad now, or at least part of it," she has become less melancholy over the past weeks but when she thinks about Trey she gets a bit down. I think it's more the question of what it could've been over what it actually was.

So lucky number 13. That number again. Well, it was Taylor Swift's favorite number so maybe it'll work for us too. She was pretty famous before the Fall. We pull out of the parking lot as the two soldiers that stayed behind lock it up after us. I wish them all good luck and hope everything works out OK for them. Maybe if things go right we can come back here for a bit before we head on anywhere else. At least we could tell them that it's done and that we did accomplish our goal.

If we get that far.

I lead the transports out onto the main road as Oakley directs me where to go. We have a general idea of where we need to be but we need to plot our course to get there. I'm not used to driving Evee on snow and forgot to put her in four-wheel drive. As I pull onto the road, the rear wheels slip and I slide her sideways into a ditch. After I check to make sure Oakley and the dogs are ok, I look back and see Susie laughing in the truck. So a new trek and a new way to embarrass myself as we start the first leg of it.

Great!

North

After we get Evee back on the road, I put it in 4x4 and try it again. This time works better and we head off. The day goes pretty smoothly and we put a few miles behind us. The later start, plus shorter days, has us stopping earlier than we probably would've liked. With roads not being plowed and us not being completely sure where to go, it was better to be safe than sorry. We park the transports and use shovels to clear space around them for us to set a fire. With this weather, we saved the camping equipment and decided to sleep in the transports.

Andromeda and Peanut run off to play in the snow as we make dinner. Matt and Smith walk off into the fields to set a few traps if there is anything around. It's almost like the trek north I had with Jordan. I shake my head and snap out of it. I can't lose focus right now. I need to think positive thoughts. Hayes tells us about the long watch rotations because we can't have Reid and Susie standing watch and then driving all day. There aren't too many of us left.

The night goes well and we do it all again the next day. We have to take a few detours to find the right roads. Some of them have been wiped out, others were blocked completely by debris or cars. Three separate times we left the transports waiting at an intersection to drive up a ways to check the road before they followed. If they got too far down and we got stuck, they had a hard time turning around. All of this slowed our progress but Oakley still thought that we would make it in under two weeks. Our luck holds until day three.

The morning of the following day started normal and went well until about midday. As we are driving down a particularly bumpy and broken road the front transport suddenly veers off the road to the right side. Oakley stops me and we walk back to see what the issue is. Susie is cussing up a storm as she gets down and checks the truck.

"The damn thing just veered right. There wasn't anything I could do to stop it. Did the road give?" she rants as we all walk to the side of the truck.

As we get there we find that the road hasn't given. The truck's axle or wheel did. The tire is sitting about five feet away from the transport, firmly attached to the rim. Something seriously broke under this truck. There was no repairing this on the road, or without heavy machinery. Silver comes up to check on why we stopped and surveys the damage. He shakes his head and just nods to us, basically telling us that it's done and we need to unload the truck.

As we get everything unloaded and reloaded into the back transport, we struggle with what to do with Matt's bike. We can't haul it now, we need the space for people. Matt could ride it and wants to but we don't have the gear to keep him from getting too cold out in the open like that. In the end, Hayes and Silver leave it up to him but if they feel it is being detrimental they will have him ditch it along the road. Matt agrees but I can tell that is not going to happen if he has anything to say about it. He takes some old clothing and makes himself a scarf with it and then wraps more around the top of his head. This should keep most of the cold off of his face. He has gloves and a good jacket from the prison. He won't let anything like cold weather stop him.

The trek gets harder and harder the further north we go. The roads had to have been bad before the Fall, but now they are utter trash. They had no shoulder so they are now completely overgrown to where I can't see the road in front of me. About a week into everything we got a hard freeze overnight. It gets so cold that we don't even set an outside watch. We just wake someone up so they can listen to the wind and wake people up if something feels off. When we wake up in the morning, everything is frosted and rock hard. The truck is frozen and won't start. When it's this cold, we should probably leave it running all night but Silver isn't sure that we have enough gas for that. We lose the day sitting by a fire that we struggle to keep warm enough for everyone.

It takes another day before the transport starts and we get back on the road. Diesel engines are nice, but they don't like the cold. We get another day of travel in before we get hit with a huge snowstorm. I'm talking a complete whiteout. Winds are howling and blowing snow all around. We can't keep our bearings so we stop and hunker down until it blows past. This is the weather that Testerman was talking about, this is why we left when we did for South Dakota. Little did he know that we would still have to trek through it to finish his task.

The storm blows itself out that night, but it dumps so much snow that Evee can't break the road. I get up a little momentum then she'll bottom out on a drift. We try for the morning but don't get more than a couple of miles. It's exhausting and not sustainable for the day. We stop and huddle up in the transport for another cold and miserable night. Day after day we run into similar issues with the cold and the snow. Eventually, we had to abandon Matt's bike, due to the lack of fuel reserves and the necessity of the vehicle.

Little by little we make our way north. It's nowhere near the pace that Silver was expecting. In all, it takes us almost three weeks to reach the coordinates given to us by the US Army soldier. When we get to the coordinates we stop and survey the area. We are in the middle of a field, with nothing around. We all stop and sit stunned by the situation. We gave up everything and fought to get here, for it to be nothing but a hoax!

"Silver! You said this was legit. You said you knew that it was the US Army that you spoke to. But here we are and there is nothing around. They freaking lied to us!" Susie screams at Silver. A lot of us were thinking about it, but she was the only one to say it.

Silver doesn't respond he just takes a look around and walks away from her. He doesn't know what to do. We don't have enough food supplies to make a trip back to the silos in South Dakota. He knows this. Hayes has everyone set up camp as usual and makes a meal. Watches are set and we sit and wait to see what Silver decides to do. An hour later Silver returns and sits down beside Reid and Smith. He seems lost and broken. He doesn't say anything to anyone. He eats and then gets in the transport to sleep. Camp is silent, again. We have tried and tried to complete this task, but nothing seems to be working out for us. We all go to sleep and give up on setting watches. At this point, I don't think any of us care if we are attacked. It may be a faster death than starvation or freezing to death in this cold.

We are all woken up the following morning by a girlish scream. I scan the transport and see Susie, Hayes, Oakley and the female medic all snug in their blankets. Josh is even awakened as he slowly peals himself from under Peanut. A few soldiers jump up and out of the transport. I follow them slowly and see Reid being held at gunpoint. There are ten men in Army fatigues surrounding the transports backed by others in military-looking Humvees.

"I just got up to pee and these guys grabbed me," Reid tells us. So he was the one who screamed. I'll have to remember to tease him about that later.

"We are looking for SGM Silver. Is he here among you?" a little guy says as he saunters up to the front of his people.

Silver gets up and walks to the back of the transport. "I'm here," he states. He squints his eyes as he tries to see the people in the snow beyond the transport. He slowly eases himself to the ground and then brings himself up to his full height. "Who is it that is asking? How do you know my name?"

"It's Major Deleki, Sergeant Major," you talked to one of my men on the radio.

"Major Deleki? Do you mean Capt. Steve Deleki?" Silver asks with some newfound joy in his voice. It seems like he knows this man, or at least knew him.

"I got promoted after the Fall, but yeah it's me. I came myself to see if it was really you, Drew. How did you make it all the way here?" the Major asks.

"That's a very long story. My question is where is here? There isn't anything here." Silver waves his arms as he spins in a circle. "You brought us to nowhere."

"Yes and no. Yes, this is nowhere. We had to make sure you were who you said you were and that you weren't under duress. We sent you here so we could keep an eye on you and make sure. We have a base that's close but hidden. We'll take you there. We can be there by tonight. You kept us waiting for a while. We thought you'd be here a week ago, we almost gave up," the major jokes.

"Well, that's a long story too. Can I ride with you and we'll talk about it?"

"Sure. I'm right here. Tell your people to follow us. We'll clear the path. Are you hungry it is about breakfast time. We have a few MREs," the major offers.

We all take him up on the offer and dig into our meal quickly. After that's done we get turned and follow the caravan of Humvees into the distance. We have no idea where we're headed, but these guys looked fed and happy so it has to be better than here. It takes the whole day to reach our stopping point. As we do the major asks all of us to gather around him so he can fill us in on some etiquette while we are on site.

"First off welcome to the last standing base of the United States Military. You are the first ones welcomed here since the Fall of our society. We have some very high-level people that live on this base and you will treat them as such. Most of you are not military or weren't before. You will learn the military code and follow it accordingly." he starts.

"Where is this base?" Josh asks over top of the major. Looking around he's right. There is a fence and a small building but nothing more.

"This base is a bunker. The building over there will take us to the entrance of the bunker. It is well guarded by trained soldiers at all times. If you do not feel you can follow the rules that will be provided to you, I suggest you leave now and head back to where you're from." as he talks I can tell that he is used to issuing orders to soldiers and not speaking to civilians. "Is everyone ok with that?"

"I guess we have to be," Susie says. "It's either that or freeze while starving to death."

"She's not wrong," Silver adds.

I'm surprised by him speaking up to an Army officer. I guess he's lost some military bearing himself.

The major nods and then points to us. The soldiers with him, walk through and take all of our weapons. We look at Silver and he nods telling us to comply. As was said before we don't really have a choice. Once all the weapons are taken. One soldier gets into Evee and another into the transport then drives them into the base. After they go through, we are led, at gunpoint, into the underground base.

What have we gotten ourselves into?

Control

Once inside, it's a true cluster. We are separated by gender, and made to shower and change before we can go any further. Now, I'm not complaining too badly because my clothes were rank. A nice hot shower would have been heaven, but they were lukewarm at best. After that, we were all placed back together again and told to sit on a couple of benches while we were briefed.

"Did you ladies have hot water? We couldn't turn ours down and it almost melted my skin off," Smith leans over to me and whispers.

"I wish, mine was warm," I tell him.

"I wonder why they were so different," he says. Then looks forward like he's paying attention before the major starts speaking again.

I'm not going to go over all of the rules that he names, because it was a very long, very boring speech. Suffice it to say it seems to be worse than elementary school and we may not be able to talk at lunch. I did catch a few interesting things that he said though.

1. There seem to be some very high-ranking officials in this bunker. Apparently, this was a bug-out shelter for the top brass in Washington D.C. He made mention of the President of the United States. Multiple members of Congress and the Senate. A few generals and other high-ranking military members.

2. We would be kept separate from these areas and confined to the spaces that our badges allowed. We would not be able to move freely around the entire bunker.

3. Meetings would be held with certain members of our groups within the next few hours or days to figure out what would be done with us all.

4. Until the interviews were over we were all going to be confined to our quarters.

5. The only reason we were even allowed into this area was because SGM Silver was a friend of the major's and he vouched for us all.

6. No one in this bunker had seen anything outside of this area since the blackout. No one higher than the major had even been outside of these walls at that time either. These people would be making the decisions regarding the use of the chemicals and any missiles that are under government control.

So no fun, no walking around and the government is going to tell us when and where we can do anything. Well, dang. I thought we got out of this. I guess people like these were so used to control, that when they lost it all they had to create something so they felt useful. I bet they still hold meetings to talk about world affairs. *So, what do you think we should do about China, Todd?* Stupid!

After our lecture, we were separated into groups and placed into rooms that would be our quarters. Oakley, Susie and I were put in a room together. Since we had the dogs and there were only six females, we got a little extra room. The guys had to room with four people each. The dogs liked their accommodations and they both jumped on a bed each as soon as we entered. I guess they were claiming their spots, one would have to share though. I decided to share with Andromeda and lay down next to her. Peanut got instantly jealous, got up and laid down with us. Pretty much what I figured would happen.

The days moved slowly and we were confined to our rooms for almost a week. We were only allowed out to eat together and shower on a schedule. I talked to the others during our meals. Only the scientists, Silver and Hayes had been taken in for an interview. Silver had been moved into another area with the other military leaders. He was supposedly talking about the plan and how the chemical was made to destroy the spores. No one had seen him in three days and the only thing we had heard about him was from the major. He talked with the scientists personally, and I was told and asked a lot about the chemical compound, its intended use and its potency.

After the week was up we were allowed to use our little section of the bunker as we saw fit and bunk with whomever we wanted. No one moved their rooms. There wasn't much use, we were all used to having a lot more people crammed together. Having our beds and a daily shower was nice. It was nice to be able to talk to everyone whenever we wanted to though. Being stuck with just Oakley and Susie for a week pushed my boundaries of girl time. Oakley is cool but quiet. Susie is neither of those things.

Initially, all of the conversations were about the timetable and when we could launch the missile. Then it was about the fact that there was still a functioning U.S. government and how great that would be when the chemical worked and our society could start to rebuild. There were a few of us that grumbled about the last part a bit. It would be good to start over and clear out the waste that used to inhabit D.C.

As the day's drug on the conversations moved to question if we would ever be allowed to launch the missile and if there were really any missiles to launch. Then complain about how the government is always full of red tape and people talking and making decisions on things they know nothing about. I mean if these people hadn't even been outside since the blackout, they never saw the Fall. They haven't seen a Deader or fought a raider. They have been protected here like they were protected in life before. How are they going to make the right choice? By this time a lot more people were on board with the idea of starting fresh.

As the weeks drag on, we start to question if Silver's even alive. We haven't seen him since we were confined to quarters. The couple of scientists that are with us get pulled out to talk to different people every once and a while. It seems like they keep telling the same thing to different people. Almost like these people need to be convinced of the threat in the world. They also ask about the science behind the chemical and the plan. The scientists tell us that they can recite the whole thing almost verbatim by now, the questions are so similar each time. Nothing new seems to be coming from any of it.

Josh and I were allowed to take the dogs on a walk each day around the interior of the compound to keep them in shape. Otherwise, we were given times when we could use the bunker's gym to stay in shape. I didn't feel much like working out, but I figured it would be in my best interest. One scientist and doctor decided to work out with us, otherwise it was just the squad and Susie. Josh worked out like a little beast. He didn't like being cooped up like this.

By the time we had been here a month, people were asking if we could leave and head back to the silos in South Dakota. They would ask our "keepers" to just give us two Humvees and some supplies. Each time we were told no. Once we were here, apparently we had to stay here. The tension got thicker and thicker as we wore into the second month. It should be a new year by now. Thanksgiving and Christmas passed without so much as a "Happy Holiday". Not like there was much celebrating to do. We came all this way to leave the decision in the hands of bureaucrats, how distasteful.

But how could we have known?

January turned into February before we got a visit from Silver. He had a new shiny uniform and had been promoted to Warrant Officer. This made him able to be in the meetings with POTUS and the others. He apologized for being gone for so long, but he was in meetings every day to try to get the others to approve our plan. The President said that the vote had to be unanimous or he wouldn't let it happen. Silver had to take the time he wasn't in the meeting to schmooze with the others and try to win them over to our idea. It wasn't easy, he said, since none of them had seen an NLB or been outside.

By this time he had all but two of the Congress members on his side. He told stories of what we went through just to get from Delaware to here. Silver had taken some of the pages of my journal and showed them to the members to convince them that he wasn't making all of this up.

I wondered where my journal had gone.

The last two were very tenured, he told us. Meaning that they were as old as dirt. They probably helped Mary birth Jesus. They refused to listen to an upstart Sergeant Major who let his platoon fall into such disregard during this war. Their words, not Silver's. Silver wasn't sure what more he could do. He asks each of us if we had any suggestions.

"Let them outside to breathe the spores in deeply," Matt suggests. "It'll probably kill them with spore sickness in a few days."

"That's not an option, Washington," Silver says without *much* hesitation.

"Let an NLB in here and show them what we're dealing with," Oakley suggests. Again met with disdain from Silver.

"Wait," I said while still thinking. "Have they seen any of the Unseen? Do they know what you guys are and what you can do? Has any of this been explained? It would almost be like having a Deader, sorry NLB, in here without actually putting lives at risk."

Silver looks at me and I'm sure he was going to shut the idea down. "Washington? Matt, I mean. Why aren't you as smart as your sister?" Silver says as he smiles.

Matt doesn't laugh, then he gives and smiles. "I am, I just don't talk as much. My brain actually filters things before they come out of my mouth. Sir!" the last part was added as a slight, I think.

I stick my tongue out at Matt as Silver pulls Hayes aside and talks with her. Apparently, they get a game plan together and think that it may work. Silver leaves and Hayes fills us in. She tells us that Silver is going to bring up the idea to the members who are on his side. If they do it right, they could scare the last two members into voting our way. It's a long shot, but what about this whole thing hasn't been?

The next day all of the scientists are asked to leave with the guard for questioning. They are gone until well after lunch. When they return they seem like they've been put to work. They say that they had been answering questions and looking at schematics the entire time they were gone. I asked if they talked to the two members that were voting against the plan.

"No, it seems like the plan is moving forward though. Maybe they changed their minds? All I know is that I'm hungry and tired and I wish Testerman was here to deal with all of this," she grabs some food that we had out for them, leaves the room and I don't see her again.

So the plan is going to go through, as long as they like what the scientists went over today. That's good.

It shouldn't take them much longer to make that decision.

Silver comes back later that evening and said that the plan was in the final stages of approval. The plans that the scientists gave the rocket scientists on staff seem to be workable according to the geeks. *My words, not his.* All they have to do is design an aerosol system and attach it to the rocket. Then we can launch. Everyone was happy and thought that maybe we should send someone back to the silos to tell them the good news.

Silver had thought about that too, or Hayes had told him to, and he had asked. The request was denied. The people here could lead other groups back to the secret bunker and put everyone here at risk they said. I shake my head and left the rest of the discussion to everyone else. We were going ahead with the plan, that's all I was worried about. I grab Josh and the dogs, then take them for a walk around the fence line.

As we're walking, Andromeda comes alert and was growling at something in the distance. I couldn't see what it was with the snow, but she senses something. I looked at Josh and he nods his head towards the door. Yeah, good idea. Let's head back inside. As we did I inform the guard on watch of what Andromeda had sensed. He nods but seems to blow me off. Oh well, he was warned.

With everything going on I decided that the rest of the night would be a good time to catch up on my journal entries. I spent the rest of the night snuggled in my bed with Andromeda, Peanut and Josh. Josh didn't read my journals, he just liked being with the three of us when he could. It was a good night all in all.

Well

Later that night, I was woken up by alarms blaring throughout the bunker. Soldiers were running everywhere. At first, I reached around, trying to find my gear and my gun. When I couldn't find it, I remembered that it was all taken from me. I thought about getting up to see what everything was about, then decided against it. If they didn't want me to be a soldier, they could figure it out on their own. I was a little tired of being here, to be honest. I just wanted the plan to go through and to leave these people and their idea of control. I have no idea how things got done before the Fall.

It's a while before the alarms stop blaring and I could fall back asleep. Just as I do, I'm disturbed again. This time Oakley and Hayes are being beckoned to help with injuries and casualties. *What?* That has my attention. I get up, dress quickly. I follow them out into the main part of the bunker, a place we were rarely allowed to go. As we step into the area, it's in complete chaos. Soldiers are bleeding on everything. It looks like a major battle happened while I slept. As I try to help one soldier tie a tourniquet on his arm to stem the bleeding, I'm grabbed from behind and thrown towards the door.

"Who let this child out here?" it's a guy who had a lot of pretty jewelry on his jacket. Some high-up general or something. "Child! Remove yourself and let the adults work."

Now, I should've just said screw it and went back to my room. It wasn't any skin off my back if this place loses soldiers. But if you've been around this long, you know that isn't what happened. "CHILD! Are you kidding me? I have been out in the world for the last two years! On my own for most of it! You have hidden yourself here like a scared child afraid of the dark. You and your little band of misfit toys have hidden your heads in the sand. Now that something happens and you can't control it you lash out at a younger person calling them a child. I know more about first aid and how to keep these soldiers alive than you do. Even before the Fall, I'm sure you got your soldiers killed from an office. You don't know what it's like. Did you pick up a rifle and help these men out? No! I didn't think so," about this time I had the general back on his heels a bit. He wasn't ready for me to fire off at him. I'm sure everyone here was a good little soldier so they got their pets each night as the President read them a book to go night-night. I should've stopped and walked away, or continued to help the soldier.

But, I was mad. I was mad at being called a child, at being treated like nothing we say or do has any meaning, at this prick for just existing in a place like this while the world fell apart and went to complete shit. I was mad that my mother, my father, and my friend all had to die fighting for something in this world, while this high-feluting bag of air thought of himself as important. I was mad that we treated him like he was important for the last few months. Allowing them all to tell us how to live, how to breathe and when to eat. I was done with it all and I let it out.

I'm not going to go into everything I said to the general. In fact, I was so mad that I don't actually remember it all myself very clearly. *Have you ever been that mad?* Let's suffice to say that I'm glad I didn't have to kiss my mother with this mouth anymore. And that I was literally picked up and carried back to my room. I was thrown on a bed, not even mine and the door was locked behind me. I throw myself at the door for a good ten minutes before I give up and laid back down. As the anger slowly abates, my eyes get heavy and I fall asleep in a puddle of tears.

I wake up to Hayes and Oakley coming back into the room, most likely, hours later. They were clean from showers, but they looked exhausted. When they see that I'm awake they both shake their heads in a pity type of way, lay down and go to sleep. Well, that's not good. I guess there will be repercussions in the morning. I'm so worried about it that I lay back down and fall instantly back to sleep. What will be will be, as they say.

As breakfast time comes I am approached by a few people, but most of them ignore me or stay a distance away. It's like something I said would leap onto them and they would be just as guilty. I take it all in stride and eat while talking to Matt and Josh. A few minutes later, Silver comes in and grabs my arm, hard. He lifts me easily and walks me out of the room like my dad used to do in the grocery store when I threw a tantrum. I guess it's similar. When we get to the hallway he lets go of my arm and turns to me. His look is stern, but then the facade melts away, he smiles and hugs me.

"I've always hated that guy. The things you said were so spot on that you don't even know," he said. Then he stood back up and became stern again, just not as stern. "You can't do that though. We are here because they allow it. They can make us leave at any time. What you said isn't wrong, but the weather isn't warm enough yet for us to survive without their help. Plus, we need to launch the missiles. I hope you got it all out of your system. I went to bat for you, and so did the major. The general calmed down, but you embarrassed him. He won't let that go easily. Just keep your head down for a bit. Maybe read a book in your room for a week or so." with that he laughed a bit and turned around to get some breakfast. "Oh, and tell everyone I yelled at you and was very stern," he made a face that was funnier than stern, but I got the point.

I laugh and tell him I would. I let him go before I follow. I figure I'd ham it up a bit to break the tension. When I came in the door I drag my right leg and hold my eye with my left hand. With my right hand, I hold my ribs as I cry, "medic." I call as I enter.

Silver turns towards me, as does everyone else. As he sees my act, he laughs and shakes his head. He then looks at me and mouths the word "Stop". I laugh at him, stick out my tongue and drop the act. Everyone in the room starts laughing and just like that, it all gets back to normal.

The days are good like that for a bit. Everyone has ideas about what happened that night. Some say it was a horde of Deaders, others say it was a group like the wolves and bears that attacked. Hayes and Oakley shut those rumors down by saying that the soldiers had bullet wounds and weren't drained. It didn't stop the rumor mill though. Eventually, they just stopped trying to stop the rumors. At one point I think they had a competition going on who could get others to pass around the most unbelievable rumor yet. I have no idea if anyone is winning, but the tales are getting larger. I do know that Josh and I are not allowed to take the dogs for walks on the surface anymore. We are confined to below ground. The dogs miss their walks, but they are coping just fine.

Weeks go by. We are stuck in this hole as the world should be breaking into spring. We've heard rumors from Silver that the geeks are close to making the rockets work. How is this taking so long? I thought Testerman had this all worked out. I say this to Matt and he laughs.

"Testerman knew the chemical side. He was hoping someone else could figure out the delivery system. He just knew we had to leave. Figured we'd make it up on the way I guess," he tells me. Typical.

As March is coming to an end, we are notified that the missiles are completed. They are taking us to a different location. The new location is where the missile launch controls are. From there we can watch the missile launch and detonation. Excitement runs rampant through the room. We loaded up in the transport that we came in. We are going to follow a couple of Humvees to the other location. As we come out of the tunnel the sun burns my eyes. It has been a while since we have seen it. As my eyes clear I see the destruction left by the battle from a few weeks ago.

I can see why we weren't allowed to walk the fence any longer, there is no fence. There are large ruts, from something akin to a tank, in the ground. There had to have been a few explosions of some kind, according to the large craters. Oakley and Hayes were right, there was no way this was Deaders. If Deaders can drive tanks, we have already lost this war. We quickly leave the destruction behind and head to the new location. The day drags on. I thought the place was close, but I was wrong. Unless they are driving us in circles to confuse us as to where the place is.

I wouldn't put that past them.

Eventually, though, we show up to a plain-looking building with large windows in the front. We pull up and stop next to it. I look around the landscape and don't see anything that would mark this place as anything special. *Probably the whole idea, to be honest.* We get out as the military uses an old keypad to open the door. We walk inside and are told to stay in the "lobby" while the scientists and military personnel proceed to the launch control area. My favorite general passes by me with a stern look on his face. I didn't even know he was traveling with us.

As they disappeare behind a locked door, I look around to see who else was there with me. Matt, Oakley, Susie, Reid, Smith, Hayes, Josh and the dogs are the only ones here. I know that the scientists went with the group, but I thought that maybe there would be more with us. I look at everyone and they are all tense with anticipation. If everything goes well the launch will happen today. Then what? What will be our mission after that?

"What happens after this?" I ask out loud trying to gauge everyone else's thoughts. I'm answered by blank stares. "Anyone?" I try again.

"No idea," Matt says. The others all shake their heads and agree with him.

"Good talk," I say and turn towards the windows. "Does anyone know what day it is?"

"April 1st according to the calendar at the bunker," Hayes says.

I turn and look at her, then laugh. Others slowly join in as they recognize the significance of the date.

"Seriously, we are going to launch a missile that is supposed to change the world, on April Fool's Day? Are we sure this isn't the joke?" I ask incredulously.

Before anyone can answer an alarm goes off in the room. It isn't blaring but it lets you know it's there. We spin to look outside as a huge cloud of dust plumes in the distance.

"They're opening the silo," Hayes informs us. "Silver told me what to look for. I guess that answers your question Washington."

"That's a huge blast door," Reid announces.

As quick as he says that, a huge flame bursts from the opening. It's so bright we all have to shade our eyes. Smoke billows after it fills the sky. The noise is a lot louder than I thought it would be. It feels like the whole building is going to shake itself apart. The flames climb to the sky through the smoke. It's all so thick that we can't even see the missile that was launched. Typically these missiles were to be launched and would detonate as they impacted the ground. This one would need to be detonated at its peak to spread the chemical throughout the atmosphere. Supposedly, it would slowly spread across the planet and filter down through rain and wind. At least that's what the scientists told me. If the geeks didn't get this right we may be sorely disappointed.

We wait and watch the missile slowly climb into the sky. I'm not sure how long it takes, yet it feels like forever before we see a bright light signifying the detonation. A few seconds later the air rumbles as the sound makes its way to us. We continue to watch as the light and smoke dissipate in the sky. I'm not sure what we are waiting for, we won't see a change, but we still stand there willing something to happen.

"Did it work?", "Was that it?", "It blew up, but did it do it right?" All these questions and more were asked by everyone. We all stand there wondering if it worked. A few minutes pass before Josh breaks our paralysis.

"Pickle," he says. I turn to look at him and laugh, probably a little too hard.

The laughter is infectious and soon we are all leaning over or sitting on the floor trying to catch our breath. The dogs are getting their time in too. Leaning in for pets and licking people's faces if they get too close. The joke wasn't funny but the timing was on point. It took all of the tension we had been holding for so long, that we forgot that we were even holding onto it, and released it all at once. There was a weight that slid off my shoulders as we laughed. We had done what was asked of us. We had completed. The mission that Jordan had asked me to do with her.

Mom and Jordan should be here with us today. I think about this as I look around at the people surrounding me. This is my new family. Every one of them here has been there through thick and thin, even Matt has stood up and become a better person and a better brother because of it. He has had something to stand for, someone to stand for and he has become such a better person because of it. Others would have folded and given up if they had gone through the things that he had over the last couple of years. He took it and got stronger with each challenge he faced.

I didn't know any of the others before the Fall, or even before the Air Force base. But I have still seen each and every one of them grow. They took this mission on their shoulders and they were the ones that made it work. Without these people here, we wouldn't have this day. The world would've suffered even longer than it has. I start to cry a little as I look at all of them laughing and making fun of each other. All of them are acting like we didn't just do everything we could to save the world.

Matt looks over and sees my serious face and the tears running down my cheeks. He tilts his head a bit then walks over and hugs me. I'm stiff at first, then lean into it. "For Mom and Dad," he says. "And Jordan," I add.

He doesn't say anything more, he doesn't need to. The job is done. Matt can rest if he needs to, he has completed his job. I followed my destiny and saw it through. Maybe I can rest a bit too.

After

After the missile launch we all kind of flounder with what to do with ourselves. Our group of 60 had fallen to a measly 13. But even with this small number, we can't come to an agreement on what to do. The options are endless. Some want to return to the original silo and spread the word among our peers that the missile was launched and our mission had been a success. Others want to stay here, while others want to head back to Delaware now that the world should start to be a little safer from the undead.

The options changed daily. In the end, all it really did was keep us all rooted in place. Even though we all seem to want different things, the one thing that we do agree on is that we all want to stay together. We have gotten used to each other and feel safe as a unit. Even the scientists agree with this. We've all been through so much together it only seems right to see the next chapter together too.

Unfortunately, that isn't to be. A week after the missile launch a few of the squad members start complaining of a headache that won't go away. The people in the bunker have some decent medications but nothing seems to work. With the headaches come uncontrollable irritation. I get it I hate to be around people when I have a headache too, but theirs seem to come out of nowhere. The scientists do some checks on them and conclude that the spores are reacting to the chemical in the air. With this, it's affecting their hormones and chemicals in their brain. Everyone's hopeful that it'll all settle out after a while and they will get back to normal.

The team is able to adjust a bit and they seclude themselves when the headaches are the worst. This becomes the new normal for the following weeks. One day Smith comes out of his room and walks past everyone without any recognition on his face. He beelines to the doors that lead outside. The powers that be have reduced the restrictions on our time outside, but they still don't like us just walking outside whenever we want. One of the soldiers puts his hand out to stop Smith. Smith looks at the hand at his chest and something seems to break inside of him.

Smith growls at the soldier as he grabs his arm and wrenches it to the left until we hear a crack. The soldier screams as his partner pulls out a taser and shoots Smith in the chest with it. I can hear the taser clicking sending thousands of volts through the prongs stuck deep in Smith's chest. Smith ignores it, in reality, it seems to make him stronger. He pulls the prongs out and tosses them back at the soldier. Smith growls again and charges the man. The man looks at his partner's broken arm and turns quickly to move out of Smith's way. Smith sees the man retreat, turns back to the door and walks outside. Matt and I follow him. As he gets outside, Smith looks to the sky and screams. It's a visceral scream that curdles my blood. Matt tries to talk to him to see what's going on. Smith is either ignoring him or can't hear and understand him.

He's breathing heavily, to the point that he is starting to foam at the mouth. After a few minutes of this, he looks up to the sky one more time and falls to the ground in a heap. Matt and I run to him to see if he's ok. He's lying on the ground, his eyes are rolled back in his head as his body seizes. As Matt holds his head and tries to get him to snap out of it, I run back inside to grab a medic. I bust in through the door and run into a group of armed soldiers. I skid to a stop to figure out what they are doing. It quickly dawns on me that they are going after Smith.

"Medic! I need a medic! Smith has passed out and is seizing on the ground. Matt is helping him but we don't know what's wrong with him," I yell at them.

One man moves others out of the way. I look and see a medical bag on his shoulder. I think he was coming to help the man with the broken arm, but Smith's condition must seem worse. As he gets to me he spins me around and pushes me out of the door. He quickly joins Matt and assesses Smith's condition. I don't like the look on his face as he waves to people behind me. I guess others have come out to see too. They join him and at the medic's direction, they pick Smith up and carry him back into the building. After they take him inside, other members of the squad join us asking questions on what happened. We tell them what we know, as little as that is. Everyone seems confused since Smith was always so even keel. We are all worried as we return inside. We all kind of know that there isn't anything we can do, so we stay close to each other without talking.

A few hours later the same medic comes out and tells us that Smith is stable, but he seems to be in a coma. "As we were checking him, we checked his light response. Wasn't he one of your special soldiers? An Unseen, you call them?"

"Yes, almost all of us are," Hayes answers.

"Can I check your eyes please?" he asks as he pulls a small light out of his pocket.

Hayes nods and the medic flashes the light in and out of her eyes. "So your eyes have a normal response. Has the other man had any hits to the head, maybe when he fainted?" he looks at Matt as he asked this.

"No, he kind of folded into himself. Like his body couldn't hold himself up any longer. Why?"

"His eyes are reacting like he has a concussion. One eye reacts completely differently than the other. The other odd thing is that his eyes are no longer glowing blue at all, like yours are,' He says as he looks at Hayes.

Smith's eyes aren't glowing at all? "Are you sure?" I ask. The medic nods. Hayes grabs the man's arm and walks back into the hall with him. A few minutes later she comes back shaking her head.

"His eyes are off, but they look normal in color. I can't remember what color his irises' were before, but they are almost white now. Almost like a killed NLB," she tells us.

No one knows what to say. We all look at each other and then shuffle off to our beds for the rest of the night. Reid stays and goes to sit with Smith. They are close, like brothers, it seems right. Each day we all stop in and check on Smith. We each talk to him telling him about our day or whatever comes to mind. None of us stay when another comes to take their time with him. It's almost unspoken that each of us likes to be alone with him. Andromeda and Peanut even take their time with him. Either lying at his bedside or jumping on the bed and lying at his feet. The medics aren't really happy with the last, but they don't say anything.

The visits slow after a week. The longer it goes the less it seems that he will ever recover. We don't give up on him, but other things keep happening to pull us away. Whatever we did with that chemical, we are starting to see some of the effects. Maybe Smith's condition was the first real effect that we saw, we just didn't realize it at the time.

The first real signs that things were happening with the spores were happening outside. The uppers had allowed me and Josh to take the dogs outside on walks again. The fence hadn't been replaced, but the craters and ruts had been filled in. One day we went out and everything was normal. The grass was green and growing again as spring progressed. The next day we went out and everything was a sickly yellow. We came back in and told Silver about it. He passed it up the chain, who then sent a crew out to investigate.

This happened two days ago. When they return they tell us that they had driven out for half a day and had seen the same thing the entire time. Something was killing the grass in a very large area surrounding the bunker. This plus the Unseen's headaches and what happened to Smith was all connected. It had to be the chemical killing everything connected to the spores.

Gone

As the days progress the vegetation around us continues to die. We have also noticed that the Unseen have been affected in different ways too. Besides the headaches and the irritation, all of them have different symptoms.

-Hayes has symptoms of dementia. She keeps talking about leaving Christiana and heading to South Dakota before the winter sets in. We keep telling her that we have already done all of this. When we do she looks confused and then agrees with us. She walks away shaking her head.

-Oakley has developed a shake in both of her hands. It gets so bad at times that she can't hold a drink for herself. She hates it but she has to ask for help to accomplish basic tasks.

-Matt has issues with his memory. He does not have dementia like Hayes, but he will ask you the same thing multiple times in a row. He forgets where he is, not the bunker but what room he's in and why he's there. His short-term memory is almost nonexistent. Days seem to disappear slowly working backwards.

-Reid is in pain all of the time. Every one of his joints hurts, even though there is no inflammation or swelling. There are days he can't even get out of bed to go to the bathroom. They have confined him to quarters with a catheter until they can figure out what to do about his symptoms.

-Luckily, Josh's only symptoms have been a slight fever and swelling around the lymph nodes in his neck. It seems like his youthfulness is helping him keep other symptoms at bay.

Everyone is on edge waiting to see if their symptoms get better or worse. The scientists have confirmed that all of their symptoms stem from the death of the spores in their systems. With them being Unseen it is affecting them at a much higher level than everyone else. Susie and I haven't been dealing with any of the issues that the others have, but we haven't been 100% either.

"Would it help if we got away from the epicenter of the chemical explosion?" I ask one of the scientists. "I mean it seems to be worse here, right?"

"We don't know. We have nothing to measure what the rest of the world is like. It may be worse here, or it may be the same everywhere else. We just don't know." he replies. He looks defeated too. He has been trying to help everyone and they are working themselves to death doing it. I nod and walk away. They are doing what they can, but we just don't know what the chemical is doing to everything in the world. As the days go by, everything seems to worsen. The 'powers that be' seem to be ignoring everything happening in their bunker and have turned a blind eye to the struggles of the people living with them. I've had about enough of the so-called government and take Susie aside with a plan.

"We need to get out of here. Hayes, Oakley and Matt are all getting worse. It won't be long before they are as bad as Smith and Reid," I say to her.

What do you suggest? Take these medical patients out of here and do what? Where would we go?" she asks sarcastically.

"Back to the original silo. I don't know. Away from here." I tell her. I'm frustrated, I need help, not an argument.

"No. I'm done," she turns on her heel and walks away. Ok, I'm on my own.

Later that night Reid starts to scream from the pain he's enduring. We try to help, but nothing we do seems to relieve the pain for him. I hold his hand for a while and look into his eyes. Josh is with me when Reid asks us to kill him.

"Please, I can't take it anymore. I need to rest. I need to stop feeling pain. I know it's all in my head. I need it to be gone," he says as he cries into his pillow. The tears streak down his face.

It breaks my heart to see him this way. I tell him that I can't and I walk away. I look at Josh and he just hangs his head. I hear them talking as I leave the room. A couple of hours later there's a loud bang that rings through the bunker. A gunshot followed by another. I run into the hallway and see Josh standing at his door in his pajamas. He seems calm like he knew this would come. The realization hits me and I run to the room that they are housing Reid. Nothing. All of the monitors and equipment that had been on him were thrown around the room.

I run to Smith's room. As I get there a soldier grabs me and pushes me out of the room. I scream at him, but he holds tight. The door opens as another soldier leaves. As the door swings shut I see all I need to. Reid is in bed with Smith, and both of their faces are covered in blood. Each other's blood. Reid took a gun and took himself and Smith out of this world, away from their suffering. Their shift has ended. Their watch is through. They both brought joy to this world and we lost two bright lights in an already darkening world. They are done with their suffering, and moving on to their rewards beyond.

At least that's what I hope.

I approached Susie again the next day. Her stance hasn't changed, even with the deaths of Reid and Smith. I was on my own, or so I thought. Josh came to me later that day.

"I heard what you want to do. I agree with you. We need to leave, even if it's so the others don't die here, in this place," he says. His eyes are still red from crying. He was close to Reid and Smith. I also have a sneaking suspicion that Josh helped the ailing Reid get the gun and gave him the strength to not only get to Smith's room but into bed with him.

We agree and come up with a plan. We can't tell Hayes or Matt what we're doing. Well, we could tell Matt he'd just forget anyway. But it's better not to risk anyone else knowing. Josh quietly checks on the trucks and finds Evee hidden away among the Humvees. She's small, but big enough to carry everyone and a few supplies. Winter is over so we don't need cold weather gear, and the roads should be more passable. We decide to head back to the original silo for now to meet up with the others. From there we can decide what we need to do.

Over the next few days, we squirrel away supplies and food. Josh sneaks it down to Evee and gets her all packed up. A week later we are ready to go. Out of everyone, Lyla is going to be the hardest to save. The night before we are going to go I decide to tell her our plan.

"No," she says.

"No?" I ask her. I'm confused.

"I'm not going. My shakes are getting worse and there isn't any way for me to help you. I'll stay here and deal with what may come on my own," she explains. She is sitting in her bed, barely able to sit up on her own. Her shaking has moved from her hands to her arms and legs. "I hope that I won't be long in joining Trey, Chris and Will. This is not how I want to live, but I definitely can't live my life on the run like this. I would be a danger to everyone around me."

"We don't care. We can't lose you too, Lyla. We have lost so much already," I say through tears in my eyes. She places a shaking hand on my face and wipes away the tears. Her tremors are so bad that they shake my head as she rests her hand there. I take a breath and clear my head. "Is there any help you need? Do you want to join the others now?" I ask this knowing that she'll understand.

Lyla takes a few minutes and thinks it over. As she does I watch how bad her shaking has gotten. As I start to think about other things, she nods her head yes. Yes, she is ready to join the others. I look at her and make sure. I can see in her eyes that this is what she thinks will be best. "Not the way they went. I want to go quietly," she tells me. I nod and know what she wants.

I approached one of our doctors later that day and quietly asked them what we could do to help Lyla. I know they have an oath, but they can at least suggest. She nods and tells me that she can't help me. She wouldn't be able to. As she walks away though, she leaves a bottle of pills on the counter instead of putting them away. She had just been counting those pills out when I approached. After she leaves I check the bottle and see that they are sleeping pills. That, would allow her to go quietly. I pocket the bottle and find Josh so he can say his goodbyes.

Later that night the doctors rush to Lyla's room and find her deceased. I quietly throw the bottle in the trash far away from her room. Hopefully, they just think that the shaking and spore death finally took over. While they are all concentrating on Lyla, Josh and I grab Matt and Hayes work our way to the garage area and load up into Evee. Hayes is a bit resistive, but I tell her that Silver is asking us for a mission. It's a stealth mission and it is only the four of us. She relents and starts giving orders like she did in the past.

Josh and I smile and let her take the reins. Matt follows orders and loads up holding Peanut in his arms. Since his memory has gotten worse he has clung to her more. Maybe hoping she could help him hold on to more, even though he can't remember how she came to be with us. His love for her seems to transcend memory.   Minutes later we are out of the gate and speeding south, away from the control of the pseudo government. We got a lot accomplished here, but we lost a lot too. As we drive off I feel the weight of those people leaving me. I feel bad about not telling Silver about our plan, but he would've never gone with it and he might have put a stop to it. We needed it to be just our squad.

Susie made her own choice.

Lost

The days go by. We've been on the road for three days. Three days of driving through an area that used to be lush green, but was now filled with brown brittle grasses and wilting trees. Nothing seemed to be surviving the death of the spores. What good would it be to kill the spores to save humanity, yet kill the Earth in the process? Josh and I look at the damage that our group has caused, hoping that the damage is just vegetation shock. Like when you move a plant in your yard, it turns brown and then grows back fine. Maybe it's just shock from the spores dying so suddenly.

As the sun goes down we come to the Missouri River. When we passed this on the way north, it was almost frozen. If that's the case it must be fresh water. That's good because this trip is taking longer than we thought and there is nothing to supplement our supplies. As we come up to the river, I'm looking for a place to cross when Josh tells me to stop. I do, then look at him. He quickly jumps out of Evee and runs towards the river. Both dogs jump down to join him. Matt gets out with me and follows me to see what Josh is up to.

"Look," he says pointing to the water.

"It's water, it flows. What else are we looking at?" I ask him a little annoyed. He is a smart kid but sometimes his lack of words is frustrating. Other times it's the massive amount of words that he uses that annoys me. I wish he'd find a happy middle.

"The plants, dummy." he points out.

I look closer and see that he's right. The plants are bright green and thriving in the water. Along the edge the plants are green, but a sickly-looking green. Is the water allowing the plants to survive?

"Fish!" Word Boy yells. Again he's right.

This is the first food source that we've found to supplement our supplies. I turn back to Evee and look for something to make into a net. If we walk the river with a net between us, we can catch a few of the fish to cook later. We take thirty minutes to make a makeshift net and catch five nice-sized fish of some sort. I'm not that familiar with them, but I'm sure they'll taste just fine. We take another half an hour to clean the fish to store them for later. We can't wait too long to cook them, we don't have any ice, but they'll keep until we get to the silo.

As we get back on the road, Hayes asks us who we are. She has been doing this lately. When she does Matt usually leans in and tells her his name. This seems to calm her for a while. Matt seems to be leveling out a bit. He remembers things at times but seems confused a lot too. He still thinks that we need to start our mission to South Dakota. It's almost like everything that has happened since then has disappeared. I guess it's better than the others. Josh still seems fine with all of the dying spores. I keep a close eye on him just in case something starts to show itself.

A couple of hours later we approach the original silo. I'm hoping that the others are still there and haven't moved on for some reason. Josh and I exchange glances as we approach. The building has taken damage. The front windows are blown out and the wall has started to crumble. I see ruts and craters in the ground around the area. It seems that this place was attacked by the same people that attacked the bunker. We quickly park outside and run inside. We check the doors, everything is unlocked. As we get down the first set of steps, Josh and I split up. Matt follows along with me, looking a bit confused. As we reach the first living room area, I skid to a stop and suck in my breath.

All of the people that stayed here were tied up along the wall to one side. They had apparently been shot, execution style. It must have been before the spore's death because some of them had tried to move and pull away from the others after they were killed.

"Well at least we know the Deaders are dead now," Matt says.

He's right, but I wish there was a better way to have found out. I turn around and head back to find Josh. He doesn't need to find this too. It takes a while, but I finally find him around the kitchen area. He sees some of the food that's out has spoiled.

"They're dead. Aren't they?" he asks. I just nod and look at the floor. He sighs and then starts going through the cabinets.

"What are you doing?" I ask him.

"Getting what we can for food. We can't stay here, they don't need it," he tells me.

He's right, but it's still pretty cold. I don't say anything but Matt and I start to help him carry everything back to Evee. We take a little while to get everything together. When we get back to the surface Hayes is gone. Andromeda and Peanut are in the back of the UTV, but SGT Hayes is nowhere to be found. I send Josh back into the bunker to walk through and see if she came after us. Matt goes off looking around the other side of the building while I start Evee up and drive out from the building a bit. We couldn't have been inside the silo for that long, she couldn't have gotten far. I drive around for thirty minutes and don't find any trace of her.

I return to the silo to find that neither Josh nor Matt had found anything either. I know that she has to be actively hiding from us. She doesn't know who we are and is scared of being in an unfamiliar area. Josh or I should've stayed with her. Maybe that would've helped. We decide to stay here tonight and see if she approaches us throughout the night. If not I'm not sure what we can do. I hate the idea of her out there by herself, but if she is actively hiding from us, we won't find her.

We end up staying at the silo for two days waiting on Hayes. She never returns and our walks and drives around the perimeter haven't shown any signs of her. At the end of the second day, we decide that for us to survive we have to leave her to her own devices. Her dementia has gotten bad and even if she's with us it'll be a battle to keep her with us every day. I feel like I'm giving up on her, but I'm not sure what to do.

I decide to ask Matt his opinion, "Matt, what should we do with Hayes? She's run off. We can't find her."

"That Sergeant?" he asks.

"Yes," I tell him.

"If she's gone the others won't be near us either. We can disappear and head back home without them interfering. We can go find Mom. Where did you leave her?"

I look at him and sigh. He's getting worse too. He doesn't seem to remember his time with the squad at all. The death of the spores is slowly erasing his history. It's happening slowly but it's still happening.

"She's around Chicago," I tell him.

"Then that's where we're going," he says as he gets in the UTV.

I look at Josh and he shrugs as he loads the dogs up into Evee. "As good a place as any. We did leave that suburban near there will all of those supplies. We could make it a while with those."

"If we make it that far," I say, mostly to myself.

I'm lost. I have two people and two dogs depending on me. Josh is a huge help, but how long will he hold on? How long before the death of the spores affects him too? How long before it affects people like me? We all have spores in our systems. What if what I'm seeing in the Unseen is going to happen to all of us, just slower? Did we just complete a mission that is going to kill all life on Earth?

Did the loss of blue spores doom our world completely?

Author's note

Loss of Blue is a work of fiction, as should be perfectly clear from the subject matter. Many of the events occur in real places. While I have visited many of these places, I have not seen them all. No matter how much they resemble the real thing, please know that I have taken the liberty to change them to what bests suits the course of my story though. I hope that readers will not be too upset with my creative tweaks to reality in places that are dear to them